Praise for *The Lost Sol*

'Lailvaux's talents are clear to see in his exceptional world building. The book gets better the more you read on and it even has a twist that a lot of the more famous authors would be jealous of achieving'
Paul Dunn, United Kingdom

'Gripping plot. I stayed up all night to read this because I couldn't put it down. There were some emotional moments so have tissues nearby if you think you will need them'
Jennifer Blondo, United States

'*The Lost Sol* is a great tale that takes many unexpected turns and twists. You will just devour the chapters nonstop until you finally uncover the fate of the lives entwined with Colony C'
Nathan Kamphuis, Australia

'A story that elegantly weaves the classic narrative beats of science fiction with a humanised group of characters. The reader is given a rich sense of the world to explore and the pulse accelerates to an urgency that keeps the reader's fingers flicking the pages onwards'
Díarmuid Mag Ríabhaígh, Republic of Ireland

'The plot is different and engaging and what an ending! I would recommend this book to anyone, you won't be disappointed'
Debra Gray, United States

THE LOST SOL

RYAN LAILVAUX

ISBN: 978-0-244-45719-8

Cover Art by Rory Lailvaux

For my parents

ABOUT THE AUTHOR

Ryan Lailvaux was born in South Africa in 1985 and now lives in the United Kingdom. He grew up with a love for reading, especially anything that involved dinosaurs or science fiction. After achieving a first-class honours bachelor's degree and a master's degree, he pursued a career in information technology.

In his spare time, Ryan enjoys watching documentaries, playing video games and visiting new countries. He is also a political activist. His first serious creative project was writing about his experiences backpacking.

The Lost Sol is his debut novel.

Astronomy compels the soul to look upward and leads us from this world to another.

Plato

LEO

ONE

Leo couldn't determine the passage of time during his interrogation. He scanned the walls for a clock, but he couldn't locate one. The room had no windows to help establish the hour of day. He knew he had been in there for longer than intended, as his questioner paced, his face flushed a crimson hue. The air smelt stale, spoiled with perspiration.

During these breaks, Leo examined his unfamiliar clothing. A charcoal black jumpsuit covered his full body, except for his hands and head. White lines ran down the limbs and torso and outlined his trim yet muscular body. The fabric hugged him and felt soft against his skin. It kept his body cool when the temperature of the room climbed a few degrees. There was padding that supported the soles of Leo's feet and ankles. The number 1702 was printed in luminous text across the front of the suit.

He sat at a lone metal desk in the centre with two identical metal chairs, built in with teal cushions. The grey walls had no pictures. The grey desk had no ornaments. An electronic pad lay on the surface, with indecipherable scribbles of Leo's responses. A smooth chrome monitor sat to one side, accompanied by a matching keyboard and mouse. The light above magnified the harshness of the objects. Leo slid his padded feet across the laminated flooring to keep himself occupied.

The questioner sat down with a new resolve, scrolled through the disorder of notes on his pad, trying to find an answer. He was a heavy-set man, over six feet tall, streaks of grey ran through his thinning hair. His cheeks were flushed on his oval face. A chin peeked out of his neck fat. This contrasted with his beefy arms that broke out of his uniform. The arms had lost their definition but showed signs that he was once a sculpted Hercules, who had been sent back to the realm of mortal men after a period of inactivity.

"What you're saying, doesn't make sense," said the heavy-set man.

Leo stared into space.

"I need your cooperation on this. If we work together, we can find out what happened, and why you're here."

"Fine," said Leo.

His maroon shirt resembled that of a police officer but symbolised a stronger sense of authority. A dark navy book appeared from the man's shirt pocket. On the other side of his chest was a gold badge with some numbers across it.

"Your passport says your name is Leo, born in good ol' California."

The passport was too pristine to be Leo's real passport.

"Yes, that's correct," Leo said.

"Are you sure?"

"Yes, I think I know my own name."

"Let me tell you why that bothers me. I also have here a copy of the flight manifest. Your name is not on it. No one born in San Francisco is listed on it. Could you please explain why that is?"

"I don't know any other way to explain it," Leo said, as he planned a new way to phrase the answer. "I wake up and I'm in this pod. I don't know how I ended up in there. It opens and there are pods all around me. People start getting out of them, stretching and yawning. Then these doors open. It was so bright, it hurt my eyes. Next thing I know, everyone is walking towards the light. I wait until I'm the last one left and I follow them."

The man cut him off. "You've already told me how you arrived here, to this room. What I want to know is why you were on that ship."

"I don't remember."

The cheeks of the man turned a darker shade of red. "Yes, it's a known problem for those sleeping in the pods to lose recent memories. However, most arrivals know of signing up to the program. The training events. Attending seminars. You're saying you don't remember doing any of those things?"

"That's right."

"How can you not remember something so important?" the man's voice resonated through the room.

They sat still for a few moments. The breathing of the man had become irregular as he stared across the table. Leo kept his expression cool. He refused to offer the satisfaction of being intimidated.

"Let me approach this from another angle," the man said as lay down a holopad. "What's your IQ?"

"About 120."

"Do you have any renowned achievements?"

"No."

"Any special talents? Valuable skills? A professional trade?"

"Not yet."

"So, you're good at nothing? Is that what you're saying?"

"Not at all," Leo started. "I've set the homerun record at my college. They say it'll never be broken."

"Baseball? That is your special talent?" The man said with a sigh. "You sound like a very unremarkable person to me."

Leo clenched his fist. "What did you say?"

"Get out of here. I have no idea what I'm going to do with you."

Leo remained still, in his unfamiliar suit. The questioner made less sense the more he spoke. He tried his best to dig through the layers of fresh memories at the forefront of his mind, but they were hidden behind a fog. There was a list which he checked in his head to establish reality. His name was Leo. He was from San Francisco. He had graduated from college. His favourite meal was pizza. None of these facts explained how he arrived at this place.

"Are you deaf? Get out of here," shouted the man. "Take a seat in the waiting room outside."

Leo rose from his seat, keeping eye contact with the man across from him. The man reached for his phone as Leo stormed off to the exit. The door opened and slid closed behind him as he stepped out. The air tasted fresh. Leo took a deep breath and closed his eyes to steady his nerves. He exhaled and opened his eyes and examined the area. It reminded him of a hospital waiting room, with rows of red plastic chairs, spotless floors and informative posters. An unoccupied curved reception desk faced him, laden with monitors and a bell that shined like a forbidden treasure in a cave.

"Are you in trouble?"

His ears followed the sound. Against the wall, a lone girl sat slouched, with her feet rested on the top line of the chairs in front of her. She wore a charcoal black jumpsuit, identical to his bar the luminous '1701' printed across her chest. Unkempt blonde hair ran down her shoulders; against the black material it appeared golden. Her pale, grey eyes studied him intently with no portrayal of emotion. A mirror image to Leo's dark brown hair and naturally tanned skin.

"Sorry, what?" Leo said as he sat two seats down from her.

"Are you in trouble?" she repeated. "I heard shouting."

Her head tilted towards the side. From this distance, Leo saw that she wore no makeup. One of her ears became exposed, and it protruded somewhat from her head. The rest of her features were as if stolen from a chipmunk: a small nose and animal eyes. She had no expression, but one dimple had been etched into her cheek.

"Oh, that," Leo replied. "It was a dispute regarding my life achievements."

"Were you lying about them?" she asked.

"No, but I wish I had now. He called me unremarkable."

"I see." The girl reflected on his answer. "There are worse things to be than unremarkable."

Leo didn't say anything, and they sat in silence. Her comment lingered in the air like unfinished business. He cursed himself. Too much time had passed for an appropriate remark to be made, and the conversation had died the most awkward of deaths. The girl returned her gaze forward and rubbed her wrist.

He slumped back in his chair. Time to plan an escape, he thought to himself. Leo scanned the waiting room to find the exits. There were two doors; one which housed the heavy-set man with his rage, and one metallic sliding door from which he first entered earlier. A swipe pad next to the second door acted as the lock. No joy there. Tiny windows made a border at the top of the walls. Nothing could be used as a ramp to get that high, so the plot of escape ended as quickly as it had been conceived.

Leo turned his attention to his temporary companion. She had become fixated with a mark on her arm.

"Are you also in trouble?"

"No," she said without missing a beat. "There must be some mistake with my application." She looked at Leo and changed the subject. "Do you have a tattoo?"

"That is a personal question," Leo smirked. "I usually need a few drinks in me before I reveal that kind of information."

The girl rolled her eyes and dropped her feet to the floor. She stood up and moved to the empty seat next to Leo. "I meant do you have a tattoo like this one?" She pulled the sleeve up her left arm. Below her wrist was a barcode. The tattoo didn't appear fresh, as the pale skin around the dark ink of the barcode remained unblemished. Like tar poured in lines across a field of newly fallen snow. Beneath the barcode, the numbers 1701 were engraved.

Instinctively, Leo pulled back the sleeve of his left arm. A barcode tattoo materialised in front of his eyes. The lines were of varying thickness, and the number at the bottom read 1702. The same number as his jumpsuit.

Leo shot to his feet. His heart pounded hard, and a prickling sensation of his nerve endings ran up his back. There was a water fountain at the end of the chairs. He dashed to it and pressed the metallic button. Water streamed out into his cupped hand. It felt cool when splashed against his face. He breathed in as much air as possible and exhaled it slowly.

Nothing made sense. The questions from the heavy-set man, the tattoo, the girl with the matching jumpsuit. Leo tried to connect the dots, but this confused him even more. They were puzzle pieces from different playing sets that he had to somehow force together. The pieces would not fit.

The strangest of the pieces was the tattoo. All the possible explanations behind it ravelled before his mind. It had to have been weeks or even months since he received the tattoo. Someone must have given it to him when he was unconscious. Or perhaps he was conscious and didn't remember it. Leo explored the maze of his mind before memories stuck. He could remember his childhood growing up in California, his family, his friends. Random memories, unorganised in a brain thawed from a deep hibernation.

Leo pounded on the water fountain in frustration. The metallic booms echoed in its hollow chamber.

The girl had resumed her position in the chair and rested her feet on the chair in front. Her fingers tapped on the armrest at a steady tempo. Leo realised how erratic he had been. Time for some damage control, as this girl could be his only companion in this strange place. He sat back down in the same chair and composed himself.

"Sorry about that," Leo said. "It's this place."

"Don't worry about it," the girl said. "To be honest with you, it's not what I was expecting. There are expectations I have for being here, but I can't access them. I'm running merely on intuition now. Perhaps it was the pod that made my brain feel out of sorts. I'm doing my best not to freak out."

"You seem very relaxed to me."

"Honestly? I was about to have a panic attack before you came out. There have been a few techniques I've been working on to control them. One that works best is a game I play. A game from a story my dad told me when I was old enough to understand."

"Could you tell me the story while we wait?"

The girl sat up in her seat again, her posture formal and elegant. She ran her fingers through her hair, moving it behind her protruding ear. She studied him for the first time, as if he were an old acquaintance whose name had long been forgotten.

"You sure you want to hear it? It's rather boring," she said.

"Please. I don't have anywhere else to be."

"Well, the first thing to know is that my dad served as an officer in the army in his younger days," she started. "I was only two when they deployed him on his third tour. When he left, they sent him on this classified mission. Something happened, and he was taken prisoner. They didn't tell us anything. We didn't even know where in the world he was. Missing in action, they said. Five years had passed, and we thought he was dead. Then one morning he showed up as if nothing had happened. Anyway, the story he tells me is about the time he was in captivity." She rubbed her face before she proceeded. "They kept him in a tiny room, smaller than a walk-in closet. There was only a barred window that he couldn't fit his head through. He could only see desert from it. The room was made of stone and it was freezing, especially at night. They only provided him with a thin blanket. He was given a meal in the morning and one in the evening. Both were cold and mostly inedible. The rats finished the scraps he didn't eat. He wasn't allowed to leave the room to shower or relieve himself. They gave him a bucket instead."

"After weeks of solitary confinement, his fear faded, and hopelessness replaced it. Each day was the same. Food. Wait. Food. Rats. Sleep. He was losing his mind. He told me he invented a game to save himself from madness. He would relive a day from his past. He started at the age of fourteen, the first age which he had a reasonable grasp on his day to day routine. He would relive a day from his childhood in his mind. Instead of food, wait, food, rats, sleep, the days would become more meaningful. Breakfast. School bus. Physics. Lunch. PE. English. Football practice. Homework. Dinner. TV. Sleep. He experienced all the motions again, even the mundane ones."

"He conditioned his mind to do that for five years. When I feel hopeless, I escape into my mind and relive a day from my childhood. Not even a pleasant one, just any day to keep my mind off the current situation."

"That's incredible," Leo said. "Was he ever the same when he returned back home?"

"It took a long time. My dad said when I signed up to sports it was as though he was reborn. He had someone to coach and push." The girl paused for a few moments before she spoke again. Leo remained silent.

"It's a shame this place didn't exist when he was alive. He loved adventures." It was the first time the girl had smiled. Her cheeks rose to reveal a slight overbite. The dimple became amplified, and her eyes softened. It generated a warmness to melt away the mood of her dad's cold cell.

They sat in a comfortable silence. Leo reflected on the words of the story, the inflictions of her speech. He stored the girl's voice away somewhere safe.

A digital bleep came from the entrance. The metallic doors peeled back with a whizz of mechanical clogs to reveal a man in uniform, the same one as the heavy-set man, the maroon shirt with dark pockets and buttons. The badge shone from the light overhead. The trousers were black and fell over polished shoes. The uniform fitted the man's body well compared to his partner. He was broad-shouldered and stood tall enough that he could reach up and touch the doorway above him. His brown floppy hair complimented a face that could easily have been used in a toothpaste advertisement.

"Please come with me," the man said louder than necessary as he pointed at Leo.

Leo lifted himself from the seat and made his way across the waiting room. The soles of his jumpsuit slid across the floor effortlessly. When he reached the door, the man gave him a nod. The face had a shadow of stubble as if the man hadn't shaved in a few days, this might've been intentional. Even though his lips were motionless, his face had a natural smile. It was a kind face. Slight lines formed at the corner of the eyes indicated he was probably in his mid-thirties.

"Could you follow me?"

The man ushered him through the opening. Leo glanced over his shoulder at the girl. Her mind was already elsewhere, potentially lost in a day of her childhood. The girl's charcoal black jumpsuit stood out in the icy emptiness of the room. Would their paths cross again? He didn't even know her name.

The man marched Leo across offices that looked more like an airport border control area rather than a police station. The immigration booths were empty. There were two exit signs at the end of the room. They headed to the one on the right, which had a sign above.

Welcome to Colony C.

The man moved his wrist towards an inconspicuous sensor, and a familiar digital bleep echoed down the corridors. After a moment the doors parted, and Leo stepped outside for the first time.

The night sky displayed the cosmos in its glory. Stars that Leo never knew existed shone brightly as if they had exploded into life. The tints of purple and navy mixed in the cosmic sea of galaxies. In the distance, a blood glow seeped through the skyline of buildings. The air felt cool and unnatural, as if it had been generated artificially in a supermarket on a hot summer's day. A field of tarmac ran from his feet to a range of vehicles that resembled golf buggies, warmed by a soft luminescent lamppost.

One of the buggies pulled up to the entrance, with no driver. The man walked around the vehicle and entered in on the far side. He leant over and opened the door in front of Leo and signalled for him to get in. Leo banged the door behind him. A touch screen appeared at the centre of the car. The man punched in a code, and a user interface materialised with different options. He selected the maps option, and another code entered. The vehicle roared into action and followed the road ahead. They were about three miles away from the town of skyscrapers. A path of amber lighting led the path.

"Your arrival sure surprised most of us here," said the man. He had a heavy Southern drawl that accented his words. "We only prepared for so many new arrivals. I've been running around getting a place ready for you." He put his hands behind his head and leaned back as if he was about to take a nap.

"I have a lot of questions," Leo said.

"I bet. You must be as confused as a critter chasing its own tail. It's normal though. All the arrivals experience some sort of memory loss. Even I suffered from it when I arrived here a couple of years ago. First things first, name's Tony. I'm the deputy around here. You met my partner earlier, he's the sheriff. Don't let him scare you, his bark is worse than his bite."

"I wasn't scared."

"Of course not, you look like a tough cookie. But it's good to know how things work around here. Usually, we get informed when a new batch of arrivals are heading on over. We get everyone a home set up, devices, schedules. You name it, it's ready for them. Like the first day of kindergarten. Not like mine. Mine wasn't great. I had to bring in my own toys. Anyway, you weren't on the flight manifest, so we were freaking out. Sheriff thinks y'all are stowaways. I said no way. There must be a mix up. I say, the more the merrier at the colony."

"Sorry, can I stop you?" Leo interrupted. "You mentioned the word colony. What do you mean?"

"I don't follow."

"What is this place? Where are we?"

"Boy, are you kidding me?" laughed Tony.

Amber road lights lit up red soil that spread into the infinite darkness. No sign of trees. The night sky was the clearest one he had seen, void of light pollution. Now he noticed the glassy film that caged him in. His eyes followed the horizon to the ground. A two-story wall made up the base.

Tony continued to speak, unaware of the colour that had drained from Leo's face. "We lost comms with Earth earlier this sol. No one can figure out why they stopped. We have the tech boys checking the relay. No apparent damage. Strange, huh? They are saying the problem must be on their side. Once we get the comms back up we can confirm that you're supposed to be here."

Tony glanced at Leo and started to laugh again. It surpassed the hum of the car's electric engine and boomed into the night. "You still don't have a clue, do you son? Welcome to Mars!"

The concept didn't register. Numbness spread through Leo's body like a chemical. He stared outside of the passenger window. Mars. The word wouldn't sink in.

* * * * *

The vehicle entered the town. Skyscrapers climbed higher than Leo could see. A variety of pastel colours swept past, each building with its own unique signature. Once the road curved, smaller buildings came into view. Each seemed to serve a different function for the population. In the darkness, it was difficult to make out which need each building accommodated to. Not one soul could be seen on the streets, as though the town had only four inhabitants.

"It's past midnight, so everyone will be in their apartments by now," Tony said, reading his mind. "We have a strict curfew."

The vehicle slowed to a halt in front of a lilac building. Leo followed Tony's lead and stepped outside. There was no distinct dip between the sidewalk and road, an unblemished concrete path spread in all directions. Black lines marked off the road where the autopilot buggies travelled. The black lines reminded him of the tattoos.

The building Tony walked towards matched many of the others in the town, standing around ten stories tall. The lilac paint acted as its identification. A sign above the entrance read T – Apartment Block.

The door didn't open.

"The barcode on your wrist," Tony said in a forced whisper, conscious of colonists who would be asleep. A whisper by Tony's standards was still a notch up from most people's standards. "Have you seen it?"

Leo revealed his barcode tattoo to Tony.

"Excellent. That proves you're a colonist," Tony said loudly, forgetting the pretence of his softer voice. "The barcode acts as your ID card. You scan it to enter buildings. Those you're allowed to enter of course. That includes public colonist venues at opening times, the cafeterias and public restrooms. You have been assigned to Block T, so it'll be the only residential block you can enter. When you make some friends, you can buzz their room numbers on the touchpad over there, so they can let you into the other blocks. Understand?"

Leo nodded.

"Great, give it a try."

Leo moved his wrist towards the sensor pad and the doors opened. This new world became stranger by the hour. They rode the elevator to the seventh floor. The doors peeled away with a ping. He followed Tony down a corridor to the end.

"This is your new home," Tony said as he walked inside an open passageway. A studio apartment with a living area, kitchen and raised bedroom at the back. Only a double bed and a lone couch populated the area. The walls had a red brick finish that reminded him of a friend's place back in New York. An empty bookcase blocked a portion of it. Stacks of boxes and building equipment lay to one side. Some spare tools lay near the bed. They must have assembled these recently and in a hurry.

"What do you think?"

"I'm not sure I can put it into words," said Leo. "It's quite something."

"Nothing is too good here at the colony. Try to get some sleep. There's food and water in the kitchen. I'll pick you up in the morning and we will organise your orientation."

"Thanks Tony."

For the first time since he woke up, Leo was alone. The colony slept, but he took his time to explore his new home. The kitchen had been stocked with readymade meals. The fridge contained two bottles of still water, nothing fresh. There were only a few utensils, glasses, plates, a kettle and a microwave. He tested the couch and bed; both were to his liking. An opening to the side revealed a bathroom, compact in size compared to the rest of the apartment.

A flush of fatigue washed over Leo. He struggled with his jumpsuit until he found the zipper at the back. The jumpsuit peeled off in the way a snake sheds its skin. He wore nothing underneath, and his skin felt fresh in the air conditioning of the apartment. The number 1702 stood out on the jumpsuit on the floor. A reminder he was stuck in this dream world.

The shower also operated by touchpad; he experimented with the settings until the pressure was firm enough that he could get lost in his thoughts. He stood there as the water engulfed him. The barcode tattoo. It didn't wash away, even when he scrubbed. Panic conscripted his lungs. What did the girl say? The one with the matching jumpsuit. When I feel hopeless, I escape into my mind and relive a day from my childhood. Not even a pleasant one, just any day to keep my mind off the current situation.

Leo tried to recall a day from his past. The fog still heavy in his mind. A bike. One he was given for his birthday. Up and down the streets of the neighbourhood he rode it. It was the best present he had ever received. It was red, with a lightning strike down the side. He rode his bike every day until the school term began. The campus was too far away to ride to, but whenever he felt down, he rode his bike. Maybe he could tell the girl the story when he saw her next.

There were a couple of towels on a rack near the shower. Leo grabbed one and dried himself. He walked across the apartment to the wardrobe near the bed. There were no clothes inside. The jumpsuit was in a ball in the middle of the floor. He picked it up and threw it on the back of the sofa.

The numbers.

The bed sheets felt like silk against his exposed flesh. To no surprise, there was a touch pad to the side. A moment later, he found the light controls and the apartment fell into darkness.

Alone on an alien planet. Millions of miles from home.

The numbers.

The thoughts were too much. The escape of slumber too attractive. Leo fell asleep in a lilac building on Mars.

ALEX

TWO

The machine rejected the ticket with an offensive screech. Alex examined the ticket to ensure that there was no damage and the date was correct. Everything appeared in order. He tried again. It spat it back out, the light on the turnstile flashed red.

Alex scanned the ticket office to find a conductor but there was no one around. This was awful service, even for a Sunday. He glanced at his watch to check how long until the next train departed. Four minutes. The train waited on the opposite platform and he was stuck behind the barriers with his valid ticket.

The ticket booth was deserted. The office was littered with used ticket stubs and train maps. Clipboards took up most of the front counter space and a half-finished bucket of fried chicken lay in the corner. A lone, stocky man leaned over a sudoku puzzle to the side, oblivious of the world around him.

Alex stood with the hope that he would grab his attention. The man continued with his puzzle, writing a number down in one of the squares. Three minutes to go. Alex tapped on the window.

The stocky man looked up. Puzzlement turned to annoyance. He pushed from the wall and slid across the counter, the swivel chair doing its best to support his weight. A bushy handlebar moustache covered his upper lip. He looked like a walrus.

"Excuse me sir, my ticket is not working," said Alex.

The walrus signalled to hand over the ticket. He studied it for a while before laying it down and typed something in his computer. From the machine, a brand-new ticket emerged. He handed it over and slid back to his unfinished puzzle.

Alex raced through the turnstile and sprinted towards the stairs, which burrowed underneath the track. The thump of footsteps resonated in the graffiti-covered subway link. He emerged on the other side, relieved that the train was still there. A mechanical groan cried from the train as it laboured into life. It moved into motion and disappeared down the track without him. It would be an hour until the next one.

It was a late Sunday afternoon and the station was empty apart from an elderly couple who were at one of the tiny tables outside a coffee shop. They sat in silence as they took turns nibbling on their sandwiches. A barista had started to stack vacant chairs. Clouds had covered the sky in a grey blanket, yet the air was humid. Alex removed his blazer and folded it over his arm. His heart continued to pound from the sprint. Underneath was an old polo shirt, where perspiration had started to form under his arms.

Alex edged towards the side of the platform. Pebbles scattered across the railway tracks, which had rusted from the years of use. Weeds sought refuge in the cracks, their arms stretched out for a sun which was absent. The horn of a train could be heard nearby. The vibration in the ground suggested it was a heavy locomotive. Alex recalled a French phrase a friend once used. L'appel du vide. Translated, it meant the call of the void, the sensation to engage in a life-ending action. It ran through his mind as he stared at the rusty beams.

It would be easy to step out. One step. Then the pain would stop.

Alex's concentration was broken by a muffled sound. His eyes scanned the area until they came across a young girl who was sat against a supportive iron pillar. Her head was buried in her arms which were nested around her legs, drawn into her body. Straight, mousey hair was all over the place. A collection of earrings and studs decorated one of her ears. Alex couldn't see her face, but guessed she was thirteen or fourteen. She sobbed quietly. The elderly couple didn't seem to notice, or just pretended that they couldn't hear her. Alex stood there awkwardly and waited for the train to come, even though he knew it was an hour away.

A freight roared by and the rush of train wheels momentarily blocked out the noises of the world. Alex stepped away from the track and headed into the coffee shop. The air conditioner had broken down and the heat of the summer's day had been trapped inside and held hostage. He leaned on the counter and stared at the options. There was no need to, because he always ordered the same thing.

"Could I get a regular hazelnut hot chocolate to go?"

"Of course, you can," said the barista. A hint of annoyance in his voice. It was obvious he wanted to close the shop for the day. Sweat ran down his forehead in the furnace conditions.

"Actually, could I have two of those?" said Alex.

Once the hot chocolates were made, he picked up the tray and headed back to the platform. The young girl was still in the same spot. Alex crouched down next to her.

"Hi, is everything OK?" asked Alex.

Her head lifted away in the other direction. "I'm fine. What do you want?" She sniffed and rubbed her nose.

"I ordered a hot chocolate, but the guy accidentally gave me two. I was wondering if you would like one?"

The young girl turned her head to look at Alex. Her red eyes and nose masked her youthfulness. She wore scuffed jeans and a t-shirt of a rock band he didn't recognise. There were colourful bands around one of her wrists, which contrasted with her nails, painted black. Her eyes darted down to the tray that contained the two cups, each with a white lid and cardboard sleeve. "Who drinks hot chocolate in the summer?"

"It's always my go-to-drink."

The young girl hesitated before she picked up a cup and took a sip. "Hazelnut. Good choice." She set the cup on the floor and wiped the chocolate from her face. "I had a fight with my dad. It's OK, my aunt is waiting for me in the city, I'm going to go stay with her," she volunteered.

"I'm sorry to hear that."

"Why are you sad?" the young girl asked.

"Do I look sad?"

"Yes."

Alex pondered the comment. "I also had a fight with my dad."

The young girl deemed this as acceptable and picked up her drink for another sip. "Thanks for the hot chocolate," she mumbled.

Alex returned to the platform edge to wait.

The train arrived fifteen minutes late. The carriage Alex entered had no other passengers and litter occupied many of the seats. He found a vacant table and sank down next to the window. The air conditioning blew at full blast and he welcomed the cool sensation that gripped his body. He looked towards the platform as they pulled away. The spot by the iron pillar was deserted. The young girl had caught an earlier train, her hardships taken away with her. Everyone suffers.

Sprawling urban scenery flew past his window, an amber sun setting over the rooftops. His day wasn't too different from the young girl. Any time spent with his family wasn't a pleasant affair. The therapist suggested that regular visits would help to rebuild the bridges. Alex would keep the final Sunday of each month free to see them. He would take the train to the rich suburb to spend the day at their house. He hated these visits, filled with silence and thorny dinner table conversations. They were pointless. Alex and his dad were broken souls, a relationship unsalvageable.

It was dark by the time Alex reached his house. It was modest in size but contained all his worldly possessions. A tiny kitchen was tucked into the corner, home to a breakfast table with a glass top and two plastic chairs that you might find in a garden. A worn, L shaped sofa with an oak coffee table took up most of the space. A basic television set sat opposite, surrounded by three bookcases. Cheaply assembled wooden bookcases. Each one contained its own theme. The first contained Alex's passions, books on quantum physics, advanced computing and artificial intelligence. The middle contained the collection of fiction novels, which he had collected over his lifetime, from the classics to temporary 21st century writers. He always had a book with him to read during lunch and the evenings. The final bookcase was full of graphic novels and comic books. Captain America featured frequently.

Alex's most prized possession was his powerful personal computer, which stood alone on a sturdy desk. Two widescreen monitors flashed into life when he hit the power button. A few cans of an energy drink lay to the side, crumpled after their purpose had ran to an end. This was where Alex spent most of his time. Either, with work he had brought home or new independent projects he slaved on until the early hours of the morning. A lone monitor remained lifeless on the floor near the door, its screen shattered.

The environment tasted stale, so Alex cranked open one of the windows. Crickets sang sorrowfully outside.

Alex grabbed one of the many ready-made meals that filled his freezer, poked some holes in the film and tossed it into the microwave. When it dinged finished, he brought it over to his desk and ate it straight from the tray. One less dish for a dishwasher run. One computer screen had the technology news feed on, lines of programming code filled the other. It was a ritual to catch up on the news and prepare himself for the week ahead at work. His job was the only reason for existing.

* * * * *

The next morning, Alex woke up stiff, a deep throbbing in his head. He couldn't remember how long he took to fall asleep. He tapped his phone, 6:55 AM. No time for breakfast. He jumped in the shower and gave his body a quick scrub. The weather report said it would be another overcast day with warm temperatures. His khaki trousers and a polo neck would suffice.

The office was a twenty-minute bike ride away from his building. One of the main reasons he had rented the place. Alex had never owned a car, he preferred to cycle to anywhere within distance. Public transport was good enough for other occasions.

He broke the silence when he entered the workplace armed with a latte. Dozens of empty desks lined up along the floor. Last year they had removed the side partitions to encourage teamwork. Alex had his earbuds ready to avoid unnecessary colleague interaction. Knick-knacks and nostalgic mementos covered most of the counters. Instead of photographs of his family or friends, Alex's desk was littered with used paper cups, some perhaps a few weeks old. Instead of achievements plastered on the back wall, it contained notes on the projects he worked on.

There was no one else in, so it was a perfect opportunity to get a head start on his morning tasks. With earbuds glued to his head, he stuck on Coldplay's Yellow album and arrived at work. He liked to brief himself on anything he had missed over the weekend. There was less news than usual.

A few of his colleagues had materialised, and the background noise began to raise a few decibels. Alex cranked up the volume on his computer and sipped the remaining frothy residue of the coffee. He cleared out the remainder of his mailbox and opened his latest project. He loved any project related to Colony C. His latest software would upgrade the security protocols on board the spacecraft that transported new colonists to Mars.

The project had Alex engrossed. Ten minutes into his lunch break the claws of hunger sunk into his stomach. He unplugged himself from the workstation and grabbed a book from his rucksack. The office was alive with analysts on their phones, managers barked orders and keyboards were pounded on. Alex noticed none of the architects were around today.

A table near the cafeteria windows was free. This was Alex's favourite spot to eat lunch. This was especially true on summer days where an abundance of light filtered through to create perfect reading conditions. He would get lost in his favourite works of fiction. The words created a world far away that drowned out the pointless drone of co-workers. Office gossip, legal implications with the colony, possible promotions. They were pointless activities that Alex didn't care for.

An intern shouted instructions from the entrance of the cafeteria. His voice cracked with nerves as he delivered instructions presumably given to him by one of his seniors. The directors were to hold an emergency meeting in the Phobos conference room, mandatory attendance for all staff. The intern turned red and disappeared. A mass exodus left the cafeteria, engaged in excited chatter. Alex remained seated and finished the last page of the chapter. He placed a bookmark and made his way to Phobos.

The conference room managed to fit in the employees who were on site. It felt sparse even though most of the staff were standing up. Alex found a place at the back and leaned against the wall. Whispers were exchanged on what this meeting could be. Pay rises? Downsizing? A new project? Rumours were being thrown around, but Alex declined to join the debate.

Fatima Amiri strode in, her personal assistant slamming the door behind them. Her business suit was from a big label and her hair was even bigger than that, probably crafted by the most expensive stylist in the city. She took the seat at the head of the stretched mahogany table and started to speak in the same beat.

"Right. Let me get straight to it," she spoke with a soft Middle Eastern accent. "I was on the phone with the team in Houston. There are problems. Major problems. Status reports we're getting from Colony C. It looks as though something has damaged their infrastructure. The team are still investigating what the cause was. We don't know what this means for the colonists."

Alex's chest tightened. His legs felt like the bones had been removed. He cursed himself that he didn't get here earlier so he could be in a seat. He took a deep breath, he knew what Fatima would say next.

"Our first guess it has something to do with the shuttle that arrived there last week."

Alex was the lead analyst on the last containment sent out. If it failed, it would be his neck on the line.

Fatima spat out the next words, "we've lost communications with the colony. We need two volunteers to travel to Colony C, a senior architect and an analyst. There's a small window of Earth and Mars being closer to each other in orbit. If we don't go now, it could be almost two years before we enter another suitable window."

The bathroom was empty when Alex burst in. He ran to the nearest sink and bent over the basin. A mess of thoughts ran through his head as he splashed cold water into his face. The taste of coffee stained his taste buds. Would the company blame him? Was the malfunction caused by the last shuttle or was it caused by some external factor on the planet? His mind raced so fast that he couldn't catch up with it. Everything he had sacrificed and worked towards hung by a thread.

"No way," Alex muttered to himself. "Sure, I've had the training but to travel across open space? No way."

Masked by the running water of the tap, someone else had entered the bathroom. The metallic mechanism fell into place as they locked the door behind them. "There you are!"

"Rae what are you doing in here? This is the men's restroom."

"You're a mess," she said.

The woman squared up to him. Her fiery red hair fell down the shoulder of her business jacket. She wore a blouse with miniature stars, the collar poked up below her dimpled chin. Alex stared back at her.

"We need to talk about this," Rae said.

"There's nothing to talk about."

"Then why are you hiding in here?"

"I'm not hiding!"

"You listen to me, Alex. This might not be our fault but there's a real possibility that it was. We unleashed something experimental on that colony. Do you want that on your conscience, on top of everything?" Rae ran her hands down her face and stared at the floor. The drip of the tap filled the silence. "The responsibility lies with us."

"If you care so much, why don't you go?" Alex regretted the words as soon as they left his mouth. A bump was visible underneath Rae's blouse. The law restricted pregnant women from travelling into space.

"You know why I can't. If it was possible, I would be the first to volunteer." Alex believed she would have. He leaned on the sink and closed his eyes. His mathematical mind analysed all the scenarios. Even if it wasn't their fault, he and Rae were the two most able analysts. Anyone else up there would make matters worse. A hand rested on his back. One that generated warmth he hadn't felt for a long time.

An impatient knock came from the door, Rae ignored it. She lowered her head close to his. "You have to do this," her voice was softer now. The days of when they were inseparable were long gone. They had joined the company together on the graduate scheme. Competition was fierce, with only two places a year and thousands of applicants. Alex had instantly liked Rae. She didn't suffer fools or idle chit chat. Instead, she would uninvitedly sit on his desk and ask his opinion on the moral implications of genetically grown edible meat. Of course, she would be blunt if you gave her an answer she didn't like.

Over the years they had grown apart with different priorities. But circumstances had thrown them together again. Alone in a men's restroom, contemplating a mission with unknown variables. She rubbed his back, a touch he missed. "We knew the risks. We knew something like this might happen."

* * * * *

Alex waited outside Fatima's office. The company spared no expense on the furnishings. Plush carpets and seats fitted with soft cushions. An elaborate corporate logo faced the elevators with the words DEIMOS INITIATIVE underneath. A sphere with two smaller circles that orbited around it on pale blue and pink trails. It represented Mars and its two moons, Phobos and Deimos. The gods of fear and terror thought Alex.

Fatima's personal assistant sat at a desk far too large for his job title. The assistant's phone rang, and he snatched it up before the first ring had died out.

"Ms Amiri will see you now."

The office made the conference room appear insignificant. Books lined up against one wall, the type that no one would read. Ones related to law, engineering and management. On the opposite side, various television monitors. The majority were turned off or had no feed. They possibly displayed readings from Colony C.

Fatima Amiri sat at her carved desk made from rosewood. She was distracted by the transparent tablet in her hand. "Thank you for coming to see me. Please take a seat." There was an air of elegance about her, exaggerated by her high cheek bones. Lines were etched at the corners of her eyes and streaks of grey shimmered in her jet-black hair.

"I'm surprised to see you here, Alex. You have a brilliant mind. In the management meetings I'm told that you're one of our best analysts." Alex remained quiet. "We've had some interest from a few of the younger analysts, but I believe they are more attracted to a free trip to space rather than having the interests of the Deimos Initiative at heart. Do you have the company's best interests at heart?"

"Yes ma'am. I want to be on the team," he lied.

"Of course, you do. You also understand that you'll be gone from home for almost a year? And the risks that come along with a trip like this?"

"Yes ma'am."

"I'll get to the point. I've already spoken to Sean and he is keen to go. Sean has already been to the Mars station, so it would be good to mix experience with youthful enthusiasm. You're enthusiastic about your future here, aren't you Alex?"

"Of course, ma'am."

"That is what I like to hear. Have the rest of the week off to get your affairs in order. My assistant has a pack for you to read. We're counting on you."

There was no way to turn back now.

LEO

THREE

The chirps of birds disrupted his world of dreams. The sound of the birds' cheeps increased in volume as light engulfed the once dark room. Leo shut his eyes tight and turned away from the window. It was impossible to distinguish body from sheets. They merged into one being, which didn't want to be disturbed. The birds fell silent. It must've been part of an alarm as the window blinds had also disappeared. He lay still for a long time. The realisation of where he was flooded to the forefront of his mind. Mars. He would need to find a way back home.

The room appeared different in the sunlight. Materials for the construction of the furniture were covered in a red dust. Fixtures hung on the walls with the intention of holding objects, but instead were mounted bare. It was an unfinished job, they didn't expect his arrival.

Leo gave himself a few more minutes before he emerged from the sanctuary of the bed. His body felt good, as though a masseuse had given him a thorough session to stretch out his muscle groups. He stepped up to the lone giant bay window. He gasped. The world below him buzzed with thousands of people. The seventh-floor vantage point gave him a view of most of the colony, which sprawled for miles in all directions.

Colonists darted on the ground between the pastel buildings, more vivid now that they basked in the low glow of Mars' sunshine. Electrical cars, identical to the one he had ridden in last night, darted down the main street paths. The dome stood clearly against the glow of the morning. A red stone wall ran along the base. He would need to visit it before he left. Could he go outside the dome and play on the amber dunes in the distance?

Across the street in a matching residential block, there were other people in the bay windows. Oblivious to the marvels of the biosphere and focused on morning routines. They were of adult age, mostly single occupants. The odd window had couples. One old woman stood still at a window, fixated on him. Leo smiled and gave a friendly wave. He realised he was naked.

He fell backwards and landed on the laminated floor. The black jumpsuit hung at the back of the sofa. He crawled towards it, away from the prying eyes of his neighbours. The jumpsuit was even more difficult to put on than it was to remove. Leo wrangled with it, legs forced back into the former home of the suit. All the energy he once had, had become invested in becoming fully clothed. A couple of heavy knocks came from the door.

"Rise and shine, cupcake."

It sounded like Tony. "Just a second." Leo hopped around before he slid into the clothing. The number 1702 has been creased. He zipped himself up before he hit a red button under the word RELEASE. The door slid back with a whoosh to reveal Tony, in his maroon uniform. His smile vanished when he saw Leo.

"Why in God's name are you still wearing that thing?"

"It's the only clothing I have," Leo said. "I was butt naked and there was this old lady staring at me. It was very distressing."

Tony marched across the apartment. "Didn't the guys leave you any clothes?" He inspected the wardrobe and some nearby boxes but couldn't find anything. "We need to get that sorted straight away. We can't have you walking around the place with that get-up on. They'll think you're one of those rangers from the Milky Way Cowboy movies. Those guys suck. First things first. Let's get some food in you. I bet you're starving."

They headed to the elevators. Tony swiped his wrist on the control and selected the second floor. The elevator hummed into life and descended downwards. Noise erupted when the doors opened. Rows of turquoise tables stretched across the open space of the floor, occupied by hundreds of colonists. Leo had expected them to be wearing a variation of spacer suits like he had seen in documentaries, but these people wore unique brands of clothing. Like the latest fashion trends but none from the outlets he was familiar with. Some of the outfits were even more eccentric than normal street attire.

Tony led Leo to the side where a line had formed. The members of the queue gave him strange looks before they faced forward. It reminded him of a food court from back home. Two bright bays were built into the wall. Each were operated by a couple of colonists with outfits which could only be described as silly. It was too early in the morning to deal with this much colour.

At the first counter, lists of drinks available flashed on screen. Pictures of the most popular cold and hot drinks. A woman in a rainbow top waited patiently as Leo studied the menu. "I'll have a coffee and powdered cream please."

"Of course, sir. That will be 150 credits."

"Credits?"

"Don't worry, I'll get this," said Tony. He flashed his wrist over a scanner and the screen flashed the word PAID.

"You have your own currency in this place?"

"Yes sir. After breakfast, I'm taking you to a place where you will get your orientation."

The next station served food and more lists displayed the available breakfast options. Leo scanned the menus. A lack of meat dishes disappointed him. One caught his eye. Fried mushrooms, vegetarian sausages, cherry tomatoes, scrambled eggs and toast.

"Could I have the deluxe breakfast please?" Leo asked and smiled at Tony.

"That is 700 credits altogether."

Tony sighed, "you can buy me breakfast next time, kid."

Once their orders were ready, they found a free spot at a table. A couple of men who sat nearby laughed amongst themselves when they saw the jumpsuit. Leo ignored them and sampled one of the tomatoes on his plate. It was the sweetest tomato he had ever tasted.

"This is fresh. Was this not frozen and transported here?"

Tony shook his head. "We grow most of the fruits and vegetables here on the colony. The Mars soil taste gives them a funky taste, but I like it. Don't get used to it though. You'll need to earn some credits to buy meals like that every sol."

"A job? I don't plan on staying here that long."

"It's your choice but don't say I didn't warn you about the basic ration meals." He reached into his pocket, pulled out a holophone and placed it in front of Leo. "Here take this."

"What is it?"

"It's your holophone. It contains a news feed of all the events happening around the colony and a map, which tracks your location. Use it if you need to find your way around. This place is a maze at times. Even I still use it from time to time. There's a network you can join where there are groups to find fellow colonists with similar interests. There are details of shops, venues and bars. What movie is playing at the cinema tonight."

"You have a cinema?"

"We have a cinema. An incredible collection of films from the classics of the 1950s, right up to the latest blockbuster on Earth. Any time they're showing an old Western, I'm there. You can also message any colonist by typing in their number."

For some reason Leo thought about messaging the girl he met last night. He knew her number, 1701. One less than his own. It would be weird to message her out of the blue, so he decided against it.

After breakfast, they took one of the electric cars to the other side of town. Construction noises rumbled through the air-conditioned air. It was cool, perhaps too cool for his jumpsuit. Tony described the sites along the way. Leo didn't pay attention as he studied the colonists that walked past in the street. They came across as regular people. Some walked in a hurry. Some sat idly by. Most were glued to their holophone. Over fifty million miles from Earth and people still only cared about their social media accounts.

"Where are we going?" Leo asked.

"You boy are going to meet your mentor. She is the best one, she owed me a favour so agreed to take you on." Tony's tone became serious. "Treat her with respect or you'll have trouble ya hear?"

The car headed closer to the dome boundary. A majestic apartment block on this side of the colony had been designed to resemble a hotel from Las Vegas. A metropolis of its own, capable of residing a small village. The car pulled around the arch driveway, the greenness of trees created an enclosure. Two bellhops, one short and one tall, half jogged to the car and opened the doors for Leo and Tony. "Who are you visiting this sol, sir?" the tall one asked.

"We're here to see the lovely Jade," said Tony.

The tall one nodded and ran back inside. The short one slipped into the car and switched the car to manual drive. The car sped off and disappeared behind the vegetation. Leo followed Tony through the revolving doors and stepped into a grand lobby. Unlike most rooms Leo had been in so far, where furniture was made from metal and plastic, here they were made from wood. The lounge suite, the staircase at the far end, the shelves on the wall. Even the concierge desk was carved from a rich red wood, with a marble slab positioned on top. The tall hop behind the desk hung up a phone and told them, "she is expecting you."

Jade's apartment was large enough to fit in Leo's lodgings a few times over. An oak staircase on the side led up to an overhanging balcony with a glass wall. A dining room set with beige covers. A television screen built into the wall like a fireplace, radiating warmth to the room. An ebony piano stood idle, keys so pristine that they might have never been touched. An entire wall consisted of two storey windows that displayed a canvas of the planet. Leo gawked at the Mars wasteland, barren dunes and mountains spreading to the infinite horizon.

"I hear you are a lost boy."

"Something like that," Leo said as he turned towards the voice. "Nice place."

"Thank you, I designed it myself. The Feng Shui is perfect." A woman rose from the snow-white sofa and walked towards him. She wore a navy kimono dress, with flowery designs, which fell effortlessly over her body. Her skin was a deep brown with a flawless complexion. Curls of dark hair fell out from a bandana wrapped around her head. The woman studied Leo with inquisitive dark eyes. "We need to do something about that outfit you are wearing." Her smile, warm and sincere.

Leo stared down at the charcoal black jumpsuit with the number 1702 printed on it. "The other colonists have been giving me a lot of strange looks. Like I'm a weirdo."

"You are not a weirdo. More like a bear cub who has lost his way in the wilderness."

It was impossible to guess Jade's age. Her appearance suggested she was only a few years older than Leo but there was an eloquence to her voice, which could only be accumulated through the passage of time. "Come join me on the couch." She gestured. Leo complied.

Jade typed a message on her holophone and threw it onto the sofa nearby. She tucked her legs underneath her and studied Leo's face. "Sorry, I was not expecting you. Mentors get notified weeks in advance before they get a new pupil. I would have had materials prepared for you to take away."

"No problem, I wasn't expecting to be here either." Leo said.

"Most peculiar. You do not remember anything before arriving?"

"It feels like I'm missing a memory. Something very important. Why can't I remember getting on to the spaceship?"

"There is a known problem with the sleeper pods. Sometimes the sleep paralysis will block out the memories from the previous six months for a traveller. Most new arrivals can only remember bits and pieces. Our people back on Earth are working on a solution but it is the safest way to travel through open space. However, you should still remember signing up to the Mars programme. You must sign up a year before being eligible of being selected."

"I've no recollection of that."

"I am sure there is a good reason behind this. Once the relay is back up we can talk to Earth and find out why you are here," said Jade. "How are you doing?"

"Honestly? Like my brain has been ripped in half. Every time I look outside, it takes a lot of strength not to start hyperventilating. On the other hand, it feels like I've hit the jackpot. It's beyond my wildest dreams."

"Please do not stress about it. You are most welcome here. Whilst we wait for more news, let us turn you into a dedicated citizen of Colony C."

"What do you mean?"

"Leo, there are a few rules you need to understand. There is a curfew at midnight. You must be back in your apartment before then for your own safety. The security services can only do so much. The apartment blocks have all the commodities you need. Canteen, bathing areas, first aid rooms. There are entertainment centres where you can spend your leisure time. This is like any society back on Earth, there are laws here and you need to abide by them."

Leo's head started to spin. He now lived in a society on Mars. Far from home and he couldn't remember how he arrived there. He started to pace around the apartment, his breaths quick and loud. Jade noticed the change in his attitude. She patted the seat next to her. Leo took a deep breath and sat back down.

"Think of this place as a gap year destination. You can have fun and give something back. The colonists contribute and work to make Colony C a better place. A place where humanity can live and prosper."

"You mean I need a job?"

"Yes, a job. Even I have a job," said Jade. "What were you doing on Earth?"

Leo thought back to his interrogation with the red-faced, heavy-set man. "I was in my final year of college. I had a part-time thing somewhere. It's hard to recall the details. I'm good with people, I know that."

Jade pondered what he said, scanning her brain for potential opportunities.

"What's your job?" asked Leo.

A buzz from the door made Jade leap up. "Speak of the devil."

Outside was the short bellhop with two stuffed carrier bags in each hand. "A delivery came for you," said the bellhop.

"Thank you so much," Jade said as she took the bags from him. She placed the bags on the sofa next to Leo. "To answer your question, I am the lead clothes designer. One of the best designers on this planet, you could argue. I had my assistant run some samples over for you to wear. You strike me as a medium."

"Are these for me?" Leo asked as he rummaged through the clothes. "There's some cool gear in here."

"It is time to make your mark on the colony, little cub. Make sure you stay out of trouble."

* * * * *

Leo walked past the concierge desk with the bags Jade had given him as a gift.

"Would you like me to order you a car sir?" asked the tall bellhop. There was a distain in his eyes when he noticed the black jumpsuit.

"No thanks," Leo said oblivious to the man's conceit. "I've been cramped up since I've been here. I'll stretch my legs."

Leo walked outside and headed down the long driveway away from the luxury apartment block. He worked his way through the maze of buildings, trying to retrace the route, which he and Tony had taken. There were less people around now, they were probably at their jobs like Jade had mentioned. Second day on an alien planet and Leo would have to be stuck in a job hunt.

None of the structures around him seemed familiar. Leo stopped at a small park to get his bearings. He could only describe it as a park, but it was made of black asphalt, assorted benches and a few potted plants. He started up his holophone. A Deimos Initiative logo spun on the screen while it loaded the system. The menu screen made him disorientated. Where was the map option? Jade was right. He was a lost cub in the wilderness.

There were two men at the corner of the park in the middle of a conversation. Perhaps one of them could help him with the holophone maps application. The man who spoke loudly wore a black tank top and black jeans. A handsome face, which was bored of the environment. His hair was short and sandy blonde. Baby blue eyes narrowed when they picked out Leo.

"What do you want, newbie?" said the blonde man.

"Newbie. Because I'm wearing this jumpsuit? Smart," Leo replied. Perhaps the other man would be of more assistance.

The other man was skinnier and had bushy brown hair. Slight stubble sprouted from his chin. His doe eyes were wet. "Blake, I know you have my Game Gizmo. I saw you playing with it the other sol."

"That was mine. You should take better care of your stuff, Norm. Now get your face out of here before I plant it into ground."

Norm was on the verge of tears. His face steeled up and stared Blake in the eyes. "No, that is my Game Gizmo. Give it back to me now!"

Blake raised his fist, it rested on Norm's chin, ready to strike. "Are you willing to get pulverised for it? You snotty nerd."

Leo dropped the bags and wedged himself between them. His face was close enough to Blake's that they almost touched. "You better back off, pal," Leo warned him.

Blake chuckled to himself, unintimidated. "Seems like geeks flock together on this planet." He walked backwards, his eyes targeted on Norm. "Next time you might not have your boyfriend with you. You won't be so lucky then." He formed a gun with his hand, pointed to Norm and mouthed the word 'bang' as he shot it back.

When Blake disappeared around the corner, Norm exhaled loudly. He had held his breath for the past few seconds. "Thanks for that," Norm said. "That guy is the biggest asshole in the colony."

"Don't mention it," Leo said. "Norm was it?"

"Please, call me Norman."

"Nice to meet you. The name's Leo. It's my second day here."

"Lucky for me you chose to walk this way, even if meant that you almost had the stuffing kicked out of you."

"Hey, I could've taken him. Is everyone on this planet so hostile?"

"No, most of the people are awesome like me. Was there something I could help you with?"

"Actually, yes. That'd be great," said Leo. "I'm trying to find my way back to T-Block, but I can't get the maps app to work on this."

Norman snatched the holophone from Leo's hand and scrolled through the menus. "The problem is that you have all the safety features and tooltips enabled. Those are for losers. Here, I switched those off for you and put the most used apps on your home page. Also, I made you a member of the colony gaming community. I'm the admin."

"Is it a popular community?"

"I don't want to brag but we do have over twenty members. Did you say you were heading to T-Block?"

"Yeah, do you know it?"

"Bro, that's where I live," said Norman.

* * * * *

The next morning, Leo sat alone at one of the turquoise tables. No one paid him any attention now that he was dressed in regular clothes. A black leather jacket, over a plain white tee with some blue jeans. He studied the contents of his tray. A bowl of soggy grey oats, possibly some type of porridge. An orange. A glass of water. The rations breakfast would not pass jail standards back on Earth, Leo thought.

Norman plopped down opposite him. "Hey neighbour, cool jacket." Norman wore the same forest green hoodie he had worn yesterday. Norman picked up a fork and dove into his breakfast dish. A meaty aroma filled Leo's nostrils.

"Is that…is that bacon?"

"Hell yeah, there was a shipment of it on the shuttle you arrived on. I haven't seen it on the menu for months."

Leo thought of home. Meat was a rare commodity; his family usually could only afford it for Christmas or special occasions. The aroma of bacon brought back nostalgic flashes of his youth, when his parents would fry him up some bacon the morning after his team won the championship.

"Was it expensive?" Leo asked.

"Yes. Top tier prices."

"I don't even have a credit to my name." Leo slumped on the table, his head barely missed the grey porridge. He snagged

43

a strip of bacon from Norman's plate. "I'm taking this. Protection fee."

"That's fine. Your shuttle did bring the shipment. Take another piece however, and I will stab you with my fork."

They sat in silence while they ate their respective breakfasts. "You should get a job. Then you can eat like a king, like me," Norman said as he shoved some scrambled eggs into his mouth.

"That's real helpful."

"Well, what are you doing to get one?"

"I'm waiting for..." Leo remembered his holophone. He forgot to switch it on this morning. He pulled it from his jacket pocket and hit the power button. It beeped into life. There was an unread message flashing on the screen.

TO: LEO 1702
FROM: JADE 37
GOOD MORNING LITTLE CUB. TERRIFIC NEWS, I HAVE FOUND A PLACE THAT IS SHORT STAFFED, AND THEY HAVE AGREED TO TAKE YOU ON. THE PAY IS MODEST, BUT IT WILL GET YOU STARTED. BAR WORK. YOU SAID YOU LIKED PEOPLE, RIGHT? GO TO THE CHAMBERS BAR IN SECTOR 5 AT 13:00. ASK FOR LOUISA. LET ME KNOW HOW IT GOES AND DON'T BE LATE. GOOD LUCK. JADE

"I'll be eating bacon in no time," declared Leo.

Leo arrived at The Chambers ten minutes after one o'clock. Located in the third entertainment district, it took him a while to navigate the labyrinth of stores, bars and hot spots. The sign

44

outside had a simple design, the name in red. His eyes adjusted when he walked in, dim overhead lights cast bare outlines to the interior. The venue was cramped, a bar to one side, made of midnight granite, accompanied by metal stools. Streaks of red lights ran underneath. A trio of booths faced the bar, the red leather shone under hanging lamps.

"Hello, is there anyone here?" Leo asked the empty room.

A clatter of bottles came from behind the bar. Up popped a tiny framed woman with raven black hair and a skin tanned by the lifestyle of a tropical islander. "You're late," she said.

"Are you Louisa?"

"That's me, come back here now," her British accent was thick.

Leo navigated down the bar and passed through the opening where the drawbridge was raised. Louisa squatted between stacks of crates of bottles that contained an amber liquid. Some of the crates towered over her.

"Right, we open in less than an hour and there's a lot to be done. This is the new shipment that arrived in the shuttle. You need to stack the small bottles in the fridges down here. Whatever doesn't fit, leave in the crates and take them back through that door, and put them in the larger fridges. Don't drop any, we must make these supplies last as the next shipment won't be for months. Once you're done, I'll show you how to set up the spirits."

Louisa squeezed past Leo, the top of her head came up to his shoulders. She took a seat on a stool that faced him, a holopad on the surface of the bar. She started to jot some notes on the tablet. Leo positioned himself in between the crates. The bottles were divided into rows of five. He held one in his hand.

The orange label read Lønstrup – Danish Beer. The fridges radiated an artificial light, which made the beer glow. He pushed a button at the top and the door slid back. He started to lie the beers down flat on the top shelf.

"Can you stand them up please?" Louisa interrupted from the front of the bar. "The customer needs to be able to see what they're buying."

"Of course, your majesty," Leo said under his breath.

Leo threw his leather jacket into one of the booths as his skin prickled with perspiration. He carried the crates, some empty, some full, through the swivel door and placed them in the concrete back room near the spare refrigerators.

"Leave those for now," said Louisa with a frown permanently stuck on her face. "I'll show you how to place the spirit bottles in the liquor dispenser rack." She had a bottle of vodka in her hand. Leo watched his new overlord closely as she stood on one of the empty crates to reach a depleted bottle. She removed it from its place and fixed the full bottle. "Take down the empty ones and replace it with the same brand. Leave the ones that still have drink in them. Make sure you don't drop any." Under Louisa's supervision, Leo replaced his first spirit bottle.

"Have you ever worked in a bar before?"

"No," Leo said.

"It shows. Yet, I'm glad you're here. It's been rubbish running this place by myself."

"Thanks for giving me a shot, I really need some of these credits. What happened to your last bartender?"

"He was poached by the construction team. I don't understand why someone chose hard labour over the joys of conversing with some of the most brilliant minds every sol. I will train you up to be a marvellous bartender."

"Don't sweat it. I already have the skills to pay the bills," Leo said as he flipped a bottle of Jack Daniels in his hand. The bottle slipped through his grasp and shattered on the floor, the golden-brown liquid rushed over his shoes like an unexpected tsunami.

"That was our only bottle of Jack Daniels!"

"I'm sorry," Leo said sheepishly.

"That's coming out of your wages."

The next night, Leo began his first shift. He excelled when he spoke to the colonists who were after a quenching beverage. The jokes were abundant, and he built a rapport with some of the regulars. Even Louisa was impressed, though she tried her best to hide it. She told him to come in the next day for the late shift.

"Could I have a JD and coke please?" one customer asked him half-way through his shift.

"Sorry, we're all out," Leo replied

The bar transformed into a packed venue the later the night stretched. The booths were taken, and the stools occupied most of the standing space. Was it a Friday night? Leo had lost track of the date. They referred to days as sols here, he would have to keep that in mind. Was Friday called Frisol? Weird. He rushed between orders and asked the colonists to scan their wrists on the scanner to pay for their drinks. They ordered concoctions he never knew existed and asked them how to make them. His shoes peeled slowly off the floor, still sticky from the spilt whiskey. He would need to get some new trainers from Jade.

In the far booth, furthest from the door, Louisa sat with a bunch of young men. They laughed at jokes that Leo couldn't make out over the gentle hum of his customers. Louisa cosied up next to a handsome man with a goatee who was twice her size. To support Leo in his first job, Norman was also there, sat at the same booth. He didn't say much and sipped his beer.

Leo almost spilt a gin and tonic when he saw her. A young woman stood at the entrance. She had ears that stuck out from her blonde hair and a single dimple on her cheek. An azure blouse highlighted the greyness of her eyes. It was the girl with the identical jumpsuit. Leo watched the girl as her head scanned the room, he was oblivious to a couple at the end of bar who waved for his attention. The girl's eyes settled on the far booth, she smiled and hurried over. Louisa noticed her as well and leaned across the handsome man to give her a hug. How the hell did she know Louisa? The girl told Norman to scoot over and she sat next to him at the edge of the booth. She shook his hand to introduce herself. Leo needed to know more about this enigmatic being, but he was stuck.

"Excuse me, could we have a couple of beers over here?"

"Sure," Leo said, unable to break his gaze from the booth.

Maybe she'll come over to order a drink? If not, Norman could spill the details after the place closed. He noticed Norman only spoke when someone talked to him first. It'd be a cool group to hang out with. If Louisa didn't shout at him.

The harshness of the main lights filled the room. Someone had flipped the main switch and the bar transformed from a secluded ambiance to a red eyed daydream. It was early in the night and the customers complained in confusion to speculate why it was about to close. A heavy-set man blocked out the entrance with his huge mass. He wore the maroon uniform.

"Leo! Where are you?" bellowed the man.

The room fell quiet, only the music setlist played in the background. "I'm right here." Leo felt all the eyes in the room bore into him. "What do you want?"

The numbers.

The man made a beeline to the bar hatch, "you're under arrest for the disappearance of Steven Nesbitt."

He grabbed Leo by the arm, his grip like a vice on his bicep. "Let's go to the station for a little chat."

The numbers.

Leo was pulled past the booths. Louisa jumped up from the booth and blocked their path. "Excuse me, where do you think you're taking him?" she protested.

"None of your business," he snapped and brushed her aside.

The girl with protruding ears watched Leo as the man dragged him out of the bar.

ALEX

FOUR

A lone rucksack leaned against the hallway table. It had been packed with a change of clothes, thermal underwear, socks, toiletries, several paperback books and a Game Gizmo with the latest RPG saved for downtime. Alex wasn't sure what would be the most appropriate items to take to space. He had made sure to call his dad the previous night to inform him of his plans. His response was nonchalant. He told him to stay safe and send a postcard when he arrived. He wasn't exactly travelling to Germany, but he didn't have the energy to explain the high risks of the journey.

A bonsai tree rested on the window sill, its branches curled upwards, drinking in the rich sunlight. Alex should've asked his neighbour to water it when he was away. Who knows how long that would be? A return trip could last almost a year. The bonsai would be dead by the time he returned.

The buzzer shrieked. It must be Sean, his travel companion. The door opened to find Rae, bathed in the late summer sunshine. "Hey, can I come in?"

"Sure," Alex said. "Of course."

"Thanks," Rae said as she closed the door behind her. "Sorry for showing up unannounced. I wanted to apologise about the other day, I didn't mean to get angry. You know I would go with you if I could."

"You don't need to apologise. This whole situation is a mess. I'm willing to accept that I'm one of the main reasons behind it."

"Alex."

"I'm sure it'll be easy to sort out. I will get to Mars, fix it, and be on the way home in no time."

"Alex. Don't speak."

Rae wrapped her arms around his waist and rested her head below his chin. Her perfume triggered memories from long ago. They had joined the Deimos Initiative as interns. First a rivalry to be the new young star of the company. Later, they gave into their feelings. A short romance ruined by ambitions. The baby bump made the embrace different to those days. The baby wasn't his.

"When is the little one due?" he asked.

"The doctor says Christmas Eve."

"Andrew is a good man."

"He is," she hesitated. "Do you ever think about parallel universes?" An odd question Alex thought.

"What do you mean?"

"An alternative universe. Do you think they exist? One where I lived here with you. Going to work together. Having a baby together over Christmas. Do you think there's a universe like that?"

"No doubt there is."

Rae squeezed him tighter. "Promise me you'll fix this. No matter what."

"I will."

"Promise me."

"I promise."

They stepped out into the humid morning. Rae carried the bonsai tree, as if it was her new born baby. Alex slung the rucksack over his shoulder and locked the door behind him. A sports car purred by the side of the road, the engine still on. Rae walked down the hill in the opposite direction of the car. She didn't look back.

A whirling noise came from the car and the roof folded back. A clean-shaven man with a chubby face beamed a smile behind his sunglasses. "All aboard!"

Alex shook the moment he had shared with Rae from his mind. He pointed to his rucksack. "Where should I put this?"

The front of the car popped open. "Stick it in there and let's blow this popsicle stand."

Alex threw his bag in, slammed the hood down and hopped into the passenger side. Sean wore a polo top and khaki shorts, which exposed two hairy, podgy legs. Ready for a vacation rather than a serious work expedition. He extended a pale hand, "Nice to finally meet you, Alex."

"We've met a few times actually," said Alex as he shook his hand.

"Is that right?" Sean said as he raced away from his parked position. "I always hear good words about you. So, it's good to finally put a face to a name."

Alex ignored him and checked out the interior. An old model but still in a flawless condition. Most people in California drove electric cars these days but Sean still clung to his gas guzzler. He wasn't afraid to pay that little extra to stand out from the crowd. The fossil fuel prices had an extortionate tax band to deter commuters from destroying what little remained of the ozone layer. In a decade, it would be illegal to drive this car on a public road.

They joined the highway and Sean put his foot down hard on the accelerator. They weaved in and out of traffic, overtaking whenever possible. Their flight wasn't until tomorrow; there was no need to rush as they would get to the launch site before nightfall.

The Los Angeles metropolis faded from the backdrop, the urban landscape transforming into shrubs and grass. After an hour, the light vegetation had become nothing but desert. Nothing could be seen from the sports car but wasteland. They had left civilisation behind.

"Are you hungry?" Sean asked.

"Sure," said Alex.

The Porsche pulled off at the next exit. There was a row of fast food joints, their tacky colours clashed with the organic plains. The car entered the fast-food drive thru. Emissions poured from the exhaust as they queued between two electric vehicles. Sean studied the menu as his stomach growled. "I think I'll get the seven-layer burrito. Maybe a quesadilla as well. What do you want Alex?"

"I'll have an iced tea." Who would want to eat Tex-Mex food when they would be launched into space the next day?

They sat parked with the sun on their faces and the air con at full blast. The desert heat rose off the tarmac that surrounded them. Alex sipped his iced tea. Sean shoved the burrito into his mouth, sauce dripped down the side of his face.

"What's your story? Why are you doing this?" asked Sean as he wiped sauce away from his chin.

"No special reason," Alex lied. He knew the reason. "I thought it would look good on my resume."

"You scared?"

"Not really, I did the training when I joined. What about you?"

"Hell no, I've been to the colony before and I've been to NISS twice. Once as a tourist. Sure, I'll miss my boys. I have three of them, you know? The youngest started school. It's crazy how fast they grow up. Stunning wife too. Her family always had it in for me, said I wasn't good enough for her. I sure showed them. She lives a comfortable life now. Alex, when you get older, you'll understand. Sometimes a couple need some time apart to breathe. When I get back, it'll be like the good ol' days. I'll sit at the head of the table, enjoy the food, listen to my boys' days. You need to look forward to things in life. You also need to make your own success."

Sean reflected on his own words as he finished his burrito.

The next four hours passed slowly. A film reel of desert rolled on forever as they were lost in their own thoughts. In the distance, structures flickered out of the haze. A monstrous form towered from the earth, pointed towards the sky. It dwarfed the buildings located in the distance. Windows on the ashen exterior glistened. A menacing metal structure dug its claws into it, the grip was tight before it would have to release her. The spaceship, which would take Alex into space.

The car rolled towards a checked barrier. An armed man appeared from the booth and asked for some identification. Sean snatched Alex's passport out of his hand and presented it to the guard with his own. The guard nodded and walked back to his booth to check the details. Alex stared out across the desert. A scorpion crawled across the cracked dirt, hunting for food. An orange and black towhee bird swooped down, snatched the scorpion in its talons, and flew away. After a couple of minutes, the guard came back to the car and passed the passports back, "thank you Mr Manning. Please follow the road to the left and then proceed to the VIP parking area. You gentlemen have a safe launch."

The barrier lifted, and Sean sped through. The speed limit was exceeded unnecessarily as it was only a short distance to the car park.

Alex spotted hangers nearby with lighter aircrafts. Runways ran towards the mountains. Hotels poked out from behind them, with swimming pools and tennis courts. Was this a space base or a resort?

The car screeched to a halt with empty bays on either side. Alex stepped out and stretched. His head pounded from hours of exposure to the elements. He rubbed his forehead with his fingers. A sunburn was inevitable. Sean tossed the rucksack to Alex's feet and gestured to follow him to a solitary bungalow.

Inside a signpost indicated to have identification and tickets ready for inspection. Desks were scattered across the open-plan floor and a couple of clerks sorted out mountains of paperwork. Freestanding fans swivelled back, and forth as sweat patches seeped through the workers shirts. The construction of the building must have been an afterthought. A man wearing a pristine pilot uniform strode across the floor, his hand extended, "Sean Manning I presume?"

"Yup, that's me. Who are you?"

"Captain James Worthington at your service." The man held his posture well. An expensive watch clung to his wrist. A mature face, with a cheeky glint in his eye. Blonde hair was marked with streaks of grey. "Leave your paperwork with the chaps here and they'll get you sorted."

"Are you the pilot for the launch tomorrow?" Alex asked.

"Oh no, dear boy," James laughed. "Flying that ship is child's play. I'll merely be a passenger like yourself. Alex, was it? I'm the pilot for the trip to the Mars station. Much riskier business. Fear not though, I've done the trip a couple of times before."

An old man interrupted from behind the desk, he informed them that their paperwork was in order.

"Splendid, I'll show them to their rooms," said James.

The three men walked across the tarmac. They gave the hangers a wide berth and proceeded to the hotel, which dominated the scenery. Sean preoccupied himself by taking a selfie with the launch ship. Alex matched James' stride.

"Sorry for being ignorant, it's my first time going up," said Alex.

"You're in for a treat. There's nothing like it." James said. "You shouldn't be afraid at all. Tomorrow, we'll take the passenger ship up to the NISS. There'll be about one hundred of us on the flight, including Mia, my co-pilot. You'll like her. Smashing woman. It'll take us a couple of days to assimilate on the NISS. The Deimos Initiative have rented us an LDS to travel to Mars. LDS stands for long-distance shuttle. Not cheap. Once we get into Mars' orbit, I'll take you and Sean down to the station in a three-person landing pod while Mia keeps an eye on the shuttle. You guys carry out your work on the colony and then we head home. Too easy, huh?"

"Too easy," Alex echoed.

* * * * *

Alex stepped out of the shower and wrapped a towel around himself. The hotel bathroom was tiny, but bright. He wiped the condensation away from the mirror and stared back at his reflection. His cheeks had sunk, a reflection of months of unhealthy eating habits. Sooty bags rested under his eyes. Last night had been worse than most and his thoughts had prevented him from the sweet escape of sleep.

The rest of the hotel room had adequate amenities, blanketed in the darkness. A comfortable bed, with a duvet your body would sink into. What would sleep be like under an artificial gravity? Alex threw back the blackout curtains and welcomed in the sunshine.

Launch day.

Activity was concentrated around the colossal rocket ship in the distance. Tiny figures in florescent jackets hurried around the ground. A conveyor belt loaded zipped plastic carriers into the lower compartment of the ship. Alex had handed over his possessions to be stored away until they boarded the NISS.

When would he be back on Earth? His thoughts switched between the sorrow of Rae and the apprehension of the scheduled flight. The missed opportunities. The terrible decisions. Was it worth it? The advancement of humanity over his own humanity. He wished he lived in the parallel universe she spoke of.

Rae will make a terrific mother, he told himself.

Laid out on the bed was a charcoal black jumpsuit. White lines ran down the sides. The jumpsuit was the standard to

57

wear on the NISS. He dropped his towel and squeezed his body into it. He stepped in front of the full-length mirror. The suit hugged his body tight. His ribs swelled through the fabric.

Did he look like the towhee bird or the scorpion?

The departure lounge looked like an airport terminal. A variety of people occupied the benches, others stood around idly. There were elderly couples who held hands, groups of friends who chatted nervously and solo travellers who were in the middle of warm-up stretches. They wore the same charcoal jumpsuits.

"Alex, over here."

Sean waved him over. He sat next to James on one of the cushioned benches. His eyes were closed, and he breathed loudly in a slumped-back position. A young, pale woman propped him up with her shoulder. Her hair struck him from across the crowded terminal, a bright turquoise.

"Nice to meet you Alex, I'm Mia."

"Ah, the other pilot," said Alex as he sat next to her. "Any tips for the launch?"

"You'll be fine. Don't over think it." She leaned in and whispered. "I'm going to try and swap with Sean to sit next to you. The two of them were up to the early hours drinking. Sean insisted on hearing all of James' war stories. One of them will puke, I bet you. They can enjoy each other's company until the gravity kicks in."

Alex smiled for the first time since he left Los Angeles.

"Take one of these before we get onto the ship," Mia handed him a tiny white pill covered in a clear plastic and tin foil. "It'll calm your gut."

An hour passed and not much happened. Employees of the space programme ran around, constantly on their walkie talkies. It reminded Alex of the summer before he started college, when he waited at the Charles de Gaulle airport in Paris. The flight was delayed by five hours and he spent the time pacing around the departure lounge. There was only so much time he could tolerate on the VR arcades.

A buzzer shrieked, "all passengers please prepare to board the X-129 flight to the New International Space Station." James woke from his slumber with a jolt. With a dazed expression, he stared at Alex. "Looking sharp, kid."

Alex savoured the heat of the asphalt and basked in the sunlight as the passengers boarded the buses that took them towards the space ship. Everyone who had ever been remarked how chilly the NISS could be. He wanted to appreciate this moment.

The spaceship towered above the ground like a white behemoth. A guardian of the desert. The gatekeeper between Earth and the heavens.

The mass of people in charcoal jumpsuits queued by the elevators. They could only fit twenty at a time before it shot up towards the boarding platform.

The four of them boarded the elevator and waited for the gates to close behind them. Mia had to help James keep his balance as the elevator hurtled into the sky. Another gate opened to reveal a walkway through open air to an opened hatch on the spaceship. "Walk slowly and in single file," said one of the space crew. "Please refrain from looking down." Alex was the last out of the elevator. The walkway wasn't as sturdy as he would have hoped for, and he grabbed onto the side rail. Wind blew violently past him, it blocked the thunderous hum of the rockets. Counter to the advice, Alex looked down.

Nothing blocked the two hundred feet drop to the launch pad. Alex gulped and squeezed the railing tighter, his knuckles white. Frozen to the spot.

Turquoise hair blew in the distance. It melted his fear. He concentrated on the colour and edged forward, one step at a time. The next thing he knew, his feet were on the red carpet of the space ship.

"Welcome aboard, sir."

Alex peered down below. The seats were at a horizontal angle. Passengers were attached to a safety harness before they climbed down their designated ladder, built into the aisle floors. No chance of food trolleys being able to be pushed down them later. He didn't look down this time as he descended the second ladder. He stopped at row twenty-three, where Sean had already settled in. His eyes were bleary. It wouldn't be a surprise if he were to drift off soon.

It was an awkward movement for Alex to lower himself on the chair. He lay down; the leather cushion took his weight and rocked back a little. He unbuckled the harness from the front of his jumpsuit. It rose back upwards to the front of the capsule, ready for the next passenger, like a snake retreating from danger. Immediately, he pulled the four-sashed seat belt across his body and fastened the clips. Just in case he forgot to do it before take-off.

The remainder of the passengers lay in their seats as Alex studied the safety card, which he found in the seat arm. None of the emergency landing procedures looked pleasant. Especially the ones when docking with the space station.

"Good morning passengers, this is your captain speaking. In a few moments, a safety video will appear on the main screens. Please give it your undivided attention, as it will outline the safety precautions to take when aboard the spacecraft. The weather conditions are perfect for take-off. We're waiting on confirmation from the flight tower before ignition. As you're aware, you will experience an intense amount of g-force as we break out of Earth's atmosphere. This is a normal feeling. However, if you need assistance in any way, please push the red button on your armrest and one of our fantastic space crew members will assist you, once we have cleared the thermosphere. We're due to arrive at the New International Space Station in approximately seventeen hours. So, lie back, enjoy and thank you for travelling with us." Sean had snored through the entire announcement. After the video had played and the space crew had carried out all the safety checks, the captain ordered them to return to their seats.

"Doors locked, loading platform clear. Ready for launch," the captain said over the speaker system. "Stand by, t-minus thirty seconds to lift-off."

Some of the passengers counted along with the countdown in a chant, broken with nervous laughter. Three. Two. One. A deafening boom rose through the capsule as the engines roared into life. A force pressed Alex into his chair as if heavy cinder blocks had been lowered on top of him. His ears popped as his organs felt they were imploding into themselves. He forced his head to check the window. Clouds scattered by the window, as the sky altered from a soft blue into a deep indigo.

Alex had left the only planet he had ever known.

LEO

FIVE

Leo's left arm had gone numb. His neck was tight, like he had been strangled by the robotic villains in his favourite anime. His head pounded without end. The mattress in the prison cell didn't compare to the soft bed back at his apartment. The cell was about the same size as the bathroom, it also included a toilet.

Another night of interrogation by the heavy-set man. He learned that the man's name was Malcolm. What a stupid name he thought. Malcolm spent his energy to pin a disappearance on him. The word murder was uttered a few times. Leo had never heard of the name Steven Nesbitt before, let alone met someone who matched the description. He couldn't wait to get off this planet.

There was someone on the opposite side of the steel bars. They had watched him for a while. Leo peered up to notice a woman with a flowing pink dress and curly black hair.

"I told you to stay out of trouble, little cub."

Leo sat up on the mattress and stretched his arms over his head. "It wasn't my fault. The people in this colony are crazy. Especially that Malcolm guy."

"He is not the most savoury of characters, I agree. You would do good to stay out of his way."

"But Jade! I did everything you told me to. I started my new job. I was the star barman. I was flipping bottles into the air. Everyone started cheering for me."

"Did that really happen?"

"Maybe. My clothes did look cool though. Thanks for those. Um, any chance I could get a new pair of shoes?"

Jade shook her head as she suppressed a smile. "What am I going to do with you?"

The door at the end of the corridor clicked open. Heavy footsteps echoed around the cell as a man in a maroon uniform materialised. He wore a cowboy hat and his boots were especially shiny today.

"You're lookin' mighty fine this sol, Jade. If I say so myself."

"Shut up, Tony. Let him out of that cell."

"Of course, m' lady." Tony shuffled a set of key cards he kept in his breast pocket. He found the correct one and swiped it on the gate's reader. The door swung back. Leo jumped out of bed, his bare feet slapped down on the cold floor. He gathered his leather jacket and sticky shoes before he exited the cell.

"Seems like your alibis check out boy," Tony said. "You're free to go."

"Thanks," said Leo sarcastically. "Did you find this Steven guy?"

"Not yet. As you know, his neighbours heard a ruckus coming from his apartment. By the time Malcolm and I arrived, we found the place in a mess. Broken furniture, pictures smashed. Seemed like a struggle to me. It happened at Jade's block, roughly around the time I dropped you there so Malcolm pinned you as the number one suspect."

"No one see him leave the grounds?" asked Jade.

"That's the thing. No one saw him after the report was called in. Steven has a temper, something might've set him off and he trashed his own apartment. The colony is a pretty massive place, he could be sulking anywhere."

"Let me know if you find him," Jade said. "Come on Leo, I will arrange some new shoes for you, and buy you lunch."

"Could I have the super-deluxe lunch?" Leo's eyes widened.

* * * * *

Leo sighed and closed his eyes as he spread his body out over the soft duvet. He glanced around the room. They had removed the equipment in the corner and assembled the final pieces of furniture. The apartment now had a dining table with chairs, a television screen and a desk. Jade had also helped to fill out his wardrobe with new clothes. The place started to feel like a home. A temporary home, he corrected himself. The thought passed away and he declared he would never leave this bed again until he caught up on sleep.

The holophone buzzed from across the room on the desk. It was the second time it had gone off since he dived onto the duvet. Who could bother him at a time like this? A few minutes later and the holophone vibrated again with fury. Leo cursed under his breath and staggered across to check what the emergency was. Three unread messages. He opened the latest one in the inbox.

TO: LEO 1702
FROM: LOUISA 923
WHERE THE HELL R U? IVE BEEN TRYING TO REACH
U FOR AN HOUR. GET UR ASS TO THE BAR NOW!!!
SOME OF US HAVE LIVES YOU KNOW.

"Leave me alone," Leo said as he tossed the holophone onto the bed.

Louisa and the handsome man with the goatee waited inside The Chambers bar as Leo ran up to them. "I'm here," he said as he bent over and breathed in.

"It's about time," Louisa said. "We've been waiting ages."

"Sorry about that," Leo panted. "I had to get my hair just right, choose the right clothes. So that when I wore them I would think, yes, these clothes would make me excel as a bartender. Oh. I also spent the night in jail."

"Quit the sass. Is that sorted out now?"

"Yes, thanks for your concern."

"Good, I'm glad. It'll be quiet until later, nothing you can't handle by yourself. We're going to go out of the dome for a spacewalk."

"What's a spacewalk?" Leo asked.

"Basically, we get into these astronaut suits. They are pressurised and have the oxygen tanks on the back. We are tethered to inside of a loading shed that opens into the Mars wilderness and we can go walk out in the weak gravity. We can bound out in space and hold hands. He can be romantic when he tries." She punched her companion on the shoulder and he nodded in agreement.

"Well, make sure you don't jump too high," Leo said. "I would hate to hear that you floated off." Leo pictured Louisa floating helplessly through the galaxy and it made him smile.

"Behave yourself." Louisa grabbed her companion's hand and pulled him towards the exit of the bar, his towering frame stumbled after her. Leo mock saluted her as they disappeared.

Leo lazed around the bar. He inspected the booths and tested the stools. Golden beams ran along the bottom of the counter where clients could rest their feet. Glass shelves held an assortment of liquor bottles, brands he didn't recognise. The downlights made them glow like forbidden drinks in a warlock's castle. An idle silver telephone with a manual dial rested at the end, something out of the 20th century.

The bar counter was grubby. This wouldn't do. Leo grabbed a bucket from the concrete room and filled it with water and soap in the maintenance sink. He placed it on one of the stools and threw a sponge into it. The bubbles crumbled around it.

"What are you doing, buddy?" Norman poked his head around the corner.

"Working," Leo said as he slapped the wet sponge on the counter and started to scrub. The water ring stains put up a fight. "Don't ask about last night. That sheriff Malcolm has it in for me."

"Hard times, eh?" Norman strolled across the room and dove under the hatch. He raised himself slowly with a martini glass in hand. "Evening good sir, do you care for a beverage?"

Leo moved the bucket down a few stools and continued to run the sponge across the marble surface. Colonists walked by the entrance idly but didn't enter.

Norman dropped back down and reappeared, with a pineapple displayed in his palm. "You strike me as connoisseur of piña coladas. Do you like piña coladas?"

"What?"

"Piña coladas! Do you know the song about piña coladas?"

"Oh yeah, I love that song."

"Did you know it's about a man who wants to have an affair because he and his wife have drifted apart? He places an ad in a newspaper and the woman who replies to it is his wife. It turns out they shared the same interests all along, but they never realised."

"You're a strange one, Norman. Put it away, Louisa would be angry if she knew you were messing around with that. It must be expensive."

Norman complied and put the pineapple away. He leaned on the bar deep in thought as Leo started to rub it dry with a towel. "You know what the weirdest part of that song is? That someone would have to place an advertisement in the paper to get laid. A newspaper advertisement. People were crazy back then. Hold on, I would like to announce to the good readers of this fine tabloid that the only quality greater than my loneliness is my desperation. Would you like to go on a date with me?"

They both laughed. "How do you get dates then?" Leo demanded.

"Simple. One swipe on the holophone, and I'm the stud of the colony." Norman swished his skinny arm into the air in a melodramatic fashion.

Leo dropped the sponge in the bucket and stored it away in the back room. When he returned, Norman was sprawled out in one of the booths. There were still no customers, so Leo joined him. "Hey, you know last night? You were speaking to a girl."

"Yes of course, I spoke to many," replied Norman.

"No, in this booth. The one with ears that stick out."

Norman's expression hardened. He stared hard at Leo. "Do you like her? Is it even more serious than that?" He paused. "Do you love her?"

"No, it's not like that. I don't even know her. She arrived on the same shuttle as me. I didn't get a chance to talk to her. She might know something I don't. What did you guys talk about?"

"I told her a joke. She laughed. Fun was had by all."

"What was the joke?"

"You had to be there to understand it."

Leo jokingly gripped him by his collar. "Well, can you at least introduce me?" he demanded as he rocked Norman back and forth.

"Dude, I don't know what block she lives in. Or what her number is. If we had her colony number, we could send her a message."

"Her number is 1701."

"Wow, you're obsessed."

"No, not obsessed," Leo said slowly. He chose his next words carefully. "I know its 1701 because I remember seeing it on her jumpsuit. It was one down from mine." He showed Norman his barcode tattoo of 1702.

"Man, I believe you," Norman laughed. "Listen, I have an idea. The last sol of each month there's a party that the young colonists go to. That's only in a few sols' time. They even extend the curfew by two hours, so we can get wasted and have a good time. I bet you, she'll be there."

69

"We should go then."

"Of course, we will. You will be the dandy of the ball."

"Um, I forgot to ask. What's her name?"

"Amber? Abigail? I don't know. Something weird."

"You've been a huge help, like always."

* * * * *

A shoebox waited for Leo outside of his apartment door. He opened the box in anticipation, and it contained a new pair of navy suede shoes. "Thank you, Jade."

Leo showered, shaved and styled his hair. Basic toiletries had been stacked in the bathroom cupboard. He was thankful that he had remembered to close the curtains before he ran the shower to avoid nosey neighbours peeking in. He inspected his closet, which was now full of the garments Jade had given him. After much deliberation, he settled on a white short-sleeved top with blue stripes, khaki trousers and of course, the blue suede shoes. He felt like a million dollars.

In the lobby, Norman waited for him. It was the first time Leo had seen him without his hoodie. He wore a purple chequered shirt, blue jeans and black shoes. Each item seemed to be one size too big for him. "Ready to party, gangster?"

"Please, never say that again," Leo said.

The street lamps had started to flicker into life. Darkness seeped into the red sky, the sun setting over the wall of the dome. Stars fought to break through. A hushed stillness overcame the colony town. The roads were void of cars and the construction noises had ceased. Leo avoided the red dust, which blew across the sidewalk in soft wisps. He refused to get his second pair of shoes ruined.

The streets became dense with young colonists. They flocked to the party as a group of birds. Leo would have been impressed by their designer ensembles if they didn't wear them every day. Some wore only shorts or bikinis. A lot of abs were on display.

Leo caught the beat of music before he saw the venue. Steady trance music vibrated through the soles of his feet. They were outside the confines of the town now. A path tore across the Martian desert and ground lights gave the illusion of a runway. The scene emerged of palm trees lit up by neon colours. A sound system was arranged on a raised stage and a DJ in a silver jacket held his hand to his headphones. A chrome kiosk was staffed by two young people with neon face paint. The fixtures surrounded a centrepiece of a curved swimming pool, like ornaments on a banquet table. Violet and green strobe beams stroked against the sapphire ripples of the water.

Leo and Norman stood at the edge of the party and stared in, a forbidden land. Young colonists crowded the dance floor, moved to the beat. Others moved awkwardly. Some colonists chose to lounge in the pool, they threw their hands up at song crescendos. A girl pushed past them, she wore a top, which said, 'Martian girls have more fun'.

"This is not what I expected," Leo exclaimed.

"What do you mean?" Norman asked.

"This. I thought the colony would be a communal utopia, working on mad experiments and sowing the Martian fields."

"OK, calm down, Karl Marx."

"Do the colonists always behave like this?"

"You'd be surprised. This place gets very cliquey. Someone even wanted these parties to have an invite-only guest list."

Norman led Leo to the kiosk, and they grabbed two beers. They navigated through the bodies and found a comfortable vantage point at the edge of the pool. The sky had now darkened; the strobe lighting and pool lights outlined the figures of the colonists. Norman bopped his head to the music. Leo sipped on his beer. Then he saw her.

The girl stood alone at the edge of the pool, the toes of her bare feet curled over the concrete lip. A sheer black blouse floated over a dark top and shorts. Their eyes met across party goer infested waters. Her head titled to the side with a quizzical glare. Her brain worked out how she knew him. A flush of apprehension ran over him as her stare burrowed into his soul.

"Go say hi to her," Norman said. "I'll look after this." He snatched the bottle from Leo's grasp and gave him a friendly nudge.

Leo steered through the sea of bodies who had given into their primal urges and obeyed the music. He emerged at the other end, the girl right next to his side. She threw a glance in his direction.

"Hey, it's the unremarkable boy," she said.

"Hey, it's my partner in crime," he said.

The girl enjoyed the title bestowed upon her as her lips snuck back into a smirk. She turned to face him. Her blonde hair fell over one of her eyes, marked with shadowy eyeliner.

"Well, apparently you were off committing new crimes without me," she said and placed her hands on her hips. "Aren't you the one who was dragged off by Malcolm?"

"A misunderstanding. That guy has it in for me."

"Oh? I quite like him."

"Malcolm. You like Malcolm?" Leo gasped.

"Yeah. That night we arrived, I spoke to him for ages. Mostly, about football. You do realise he is Malcolm Driver? He played defensive linebacker for the Rams a few years ago."

"No wonder he's such a grouch. Wasn't he the one that cost them the championship?"

"That's the guy. Who do you support?"

"The greatest team in history. The 49ers."

"Ah, we can't be friends," she smiled. "I'm a Seahawks girl."

Someone nearby screamed with laughter as they fell into the pool. They observed the chaotic scene that unfolded. The DJ had changed, and the music switched to dance chart toppers. Young colonists moshed around. Two young men sat on their friends' shoulders in the pool, they wrestled to topple each other over. The melody of colours from the ripples danced across their bodies.

The volume of the music cranked up a couple of notches, so Leo leaned in to his new companion to speak. She ran fingers through stray blonde locks to move them behind her ear in anticipation. "What do you make of this place?" Leo enquired.

"It's hard to decide," she started as she tilted her head upwards. She was almost as tall as he was. Her arm pressed up against his as she spoke. The little heat of the day had disappeared, and her skin felt warm against his. "It's an amazing opportunity to be involved in this. History teachers will say to their classes, 'listen up kids, these were the first settlers on Mars'. That's us. The brave new pioneers of our generation. A fresh slate for humankind. No wars, no fighting the disasters of climate change, no poverty. Then when I look around, this party for instance, I question myself. Sure, the views are breath-taking. But how is this any different from being back on Earth? Did I make the right choice to come here?"

"So, do you remember? Choosing to come here?"

"Vaguely, I'm still putting the pieces together." She moved her fingers against her face as to remove some imaginary mark. "I remember learning about the colony. The type of life here. But nothing about boarding the shuttle or tying up the loose ends back home." She hesitated. "Do you want to go back home? To Earth."

"Of course, I do. I mean, I think so. Don't you?"

Her body moved away. She shook her head, but her eyes said otherwise. A swirl of sorrow twirled in the irises, mixed with the sapphire reflection of the water. Something caught her attention and she snapped out of her trance. Leo followed her gaze to see Louisa and her posse at the kiosk.

She changed the subject. "What's it like working for Queen Louisa?"

"The queen of Colony C? She has a certain way to her, but she's cool."

"She's lovely. I wouldn't want to get on her bad side though."

Leo laughed in agreement. "How do you know Louisa?"

"My mentor introduced me to her social circle," she said. "I better go say hi. I said I'd meet them here."

She started to move but fell back into her position. She slapped her forehead with the bottom of her palm. She revealed a grin so wide that Leo felt that he would fall into her lone dimple. "I'm so sorry. I was going to say goodbye and then your name, but I don't know what your name is. I thought I did."

"We never made it to the formal introduction part. I'm Leo."

"I'm Ariel," she winked as she shook his hand with a firm grip. The hand of an athlete, but a softness remained. "See you around, Leo."

Leo watched her disappear into the crowd. He sighed and moved in the opposite direction in search of his friend. The party was in full swing, with hundreds of bodies at the venue. They chatted, danced, kissed, drank and the occasional one would jump in the pool. After a couple of minutes, he found Norman slumped against one of the palm trees with two beers in hand.

"Bro!"

"Hey Norman, are you enjoying yourself?"

"Totally, I'm having the best time," he handed Leo one of the bottles.

"Is this one mine?"

"Yes. Well, no. It's yours. But not your original one. I drunk that when I was waiting for you. I got you another one to make up for it. Free beer, man!" Norman was already drunk. "So, that girl. Did she answer your questions?"

"Not really."

"Did you guys make out?"

"No!"

"Hey, I don't judge what two consenting adults do in their spare time."

"What have you been up to since I last saw you?" Leo hoped to get off the subject of Ariel and the questions he didn't ask her.

"So, I drunk some beer, no wait. Check this out. I went to the DJ and said, 'hey man, play the song about piña coladas' and he said 'no'. Can you believe that? What a jerk. Never mind, eh? Let's get wasted."

Leo was happy to join Norman for a night of drinking. He desperately needed an escape from the situation. He was no closer to the truth of how he had made it to Mars. He had spoken with the mysterious girl in the identical jumpsuit. Her answers didn't shed any new light. Or did he not ask the right questions? He knew nothing about her either. Except that her dad was in the army and she supported the Seattle Seahawks. Maybe she was from Seattle? Leo had never been to Seattle.

A sadness gripped Leo's chest. There were too many people around him, they closed in. He gasped for some air, but his lungs were not satisfied. Could the engineers here ensure that the oxygen wouldn't escape from the dome? It was like breathing underwater from a scuba cylinder. There was oxygen, but it didn't feel natural. He fought off the dizziness long enough to find a bench. He dropped onto it, his head spun.

Norman tapped him on the shoulder and sat next to him. "Are you OK?"

"Yeah. This place is a bit overwhelming."

"I understand. My first month here, I freaked out every sol." Norman's head darted up as he spotted something in the distance. "Speaking of freaks, Blake is here."

The man who had bullied Norman was near the kiosk. Louisa and her friends surrounded Blake. He wore some swimming trunks and nothing else. The girls who encircled him played with their hair and laughed as he spoke. He beamed a smile of pearly white teeth back at them. Ariel stood next to him, his hand moved down her back and rested on her hip.

"I might've forgotten to mention that her mentor is Blake," Norman said with a slur to his words.

"He's her mentor?"

"Yup. It's a bit unethical. A mentor messing around with his pupil. An abuse of power if you ask me. Then again, I can't say anything. My mentor was a seventy-year-old woman."

Leo slumped down. The night hadn't turned out the way he wanted it to. He felt more lost than he ever did since he found himself in the arrival terminal of the colony.

A young woman hurried past him. She was pursued by a man with an urgency in his step. Ariel and Blake had marched outside of the party perimeter, they began to shout at each other. It was loud enough for Leo to make out what they said above the music.

"Get back here. You're making a fool of yourself," Blake shouted.

"I'm not your slave. I don't have to do what you tell me," Ariel shot back at him.

Norman lowered his head to Leo's. "Do you think she needs our help?"

"It's not our place," said Leo.

Despite his comment, Leo watched them. They continued to shout at each other, their hands flew out in violent gestures. No one from the party had noticed them. Either oblivious or they pretended not to see. Blake put his hand on Ariel's waist and she slapped it away. Leo jumped up from the bench.

"Dude, you need to back off," Leo yelled as he approached Blake.

"Who the hell said that?" Blake demanded, a fury in his eyes burned.

Norman joined them and added. "Guys, can we just chill out?"

"I was right," snarled Blake. "You geeks do flock in packs. You two better move along or I'll floor you."

"I'll floor you. Who talks like that?" Leo mocked.

Norman took a swing at Blake. He missed by a mile. Blake repositioned his feet easily and his fist came up fast, meeting Norman's gut with a padded thump.

Norman crumpled up and fell sideways to the ground. Before Leo could put his thoughts in order, he rushed at Norman's attacker and tackled him to the ground. He had no plan after this. The two testosterone fuelled men wrestled in the red dirt. Leo managed to land some powerful punches to Blake's kidney before Blake struggled free of the tangle. He pinned Leo down, "you should've stayed on Earth." A lightning strike to Leo's vision. A mosaic of colours turned into a cruel black.

The thump of music vibrated through his bones. A searing pain tore inside his skull. Leo coughed as he propped himself up on the floor. There was no sign of Blake, Norman or Ariel. The party goers were still in manic dance mode. He staggered to the bench and sank back down, he steered his sensitive head to his hands. His once white and khaki clothes were now stained with red dust. Jade would kill him.

The sound was remote, Leo couldn't determine if it was real or not. A cry in the night.

78

The numbers.

He concentrated his mind to hear past the beat of bass. It was a scream. Was it his imagination thought Leo? He heard it again. He fought the pain and lumbered towards the DJ booth. "Stop the music," he pleaded. The DJ didn't notice him. He looked at the assortment of cables that ran to the speakers and without hesitation, pulled them out. The noise cut, and the atmosphere was sucked from the party. Young colonists booed and demanded the music to be put back on. A silence fell over them as a scream pierced the night sky.

No one stirred. The darkness gave no hint of movement. The air stood still. A further scream came from the shadows, closer now. Leo's blood curled.

A girl sprinted from the desert as she cried for help. Colonists rushed to her side to catch her before she collapsed over. "Please help her," she begged. Leo pushed his way to the front of the gathered crowd that circled her. It was the girl who he had seen earlier with the 'Martian girls have more fun' top. She cried hysterically.

"What happened?" the DJ asked.

"He took her, he took her," she repeated between sobs.

Louisa emerged from the group, placed a cardigan over the girl's shoulders, and squeezed her hand. "Slow down, tell us what happened."

"My girlfriend, Lily," she sniffed quietly. "We were out in the desert. This man. This man came behind us, pulled her away from me. She was screaming."

"You're safe now," Louisa reassured her. "Where did he take Lily?"

"I tried to pull her away from him, but he was too strong. I chased after them. But I lost them in the dark."

"What did he look like?"

"I didn't see his face. It was too dark. She was screaming so loud. Then she stopped."

The pain persisted in Leo's head. He peered out across the Martian desert. It remained silent.

ALEX

SIX

It had been over five hours since Sean had thrown up. It was fortunate that sick bags in the armrests were plentiful in supply. The space steward who came over once the artificial gravity kicked in was understanding of the situation and provided Sean with some water. The steward mentioned he had never been on a launch where no one was sick. "It's just one of those things."

Alex wished Mia had traded seats.

Passengers talked amongst themselves while the space crew bounded down the aisles in the weak gravity. They carried trays of snacks covered in plastic wrapping and water in hydration packs. The screen showed the flight route of the aircraft. A dotted path curved from Earth to an image of the New International Space Station.

The engine was a silent rumble now, as the spacecraft glided through the outer atmosphere on course to NISS. Placed on the wall, a double-bubbled sphere that allowed a view of the cosmic heavens. Alex unbuckled himself and leaned over his colleague, who now slept peacefully, to get close to the window. Earth had been reduced to a slant in the top right corner. A mass cloud system covered the exposed surface and a hue of blue lay beneath. It shone a brightness in an empty vastness.

Alex pictured what he was doing at this time last week. Hunched over a desk, waiting as code compiled. At a meeting. Redundant emails archived. Mundane tasks which felt like an eon ago since he last worked on them. Now he was on an adventure across the solar system. One that he didn't choose for himself.

"If you're from the Pacific Time zone, good evening," the captain declared over the sound system. "The shuttle is currently cruising 22,000 miles above sea level and the outside temperature is negative 454 Fahrenheit, or negative 270 Celsius for the Europeans aboard. So please dress warm." The passengers laughed charitably. "We've been in contact with the control tower at NISS, and we've been given the green light. In a few moments, we will manoeuvre the shuttle into position to prepare to dock. From the right-hand side of the capsule, NISS will shortly become visible. Sit back and relax, and if you need to use the facilities, please use them now."

"We're docking soon," Alex told Sean.

Sean's eyes blinked open. He squeezed the bridge of his nose and took a few gulps of air. "Remind me to never keep up with James. That guy drinks like a fish."

"We're docking soon," he repeated.

"Oh? Good. It's about time. Listen here Alex, I want to get one thing straight. This is not some all-expenses paid trip for you to brag about to your friends. This is work. A serious task." Sean took a long slurp from his hydration pack. "I need you to be my eyes and ears when we get up there. Take plenty of notes too. You might learn a thing or two from me."

While he spoke, Earth moved out of view and a bright flash briefly filled the capsule. The sun soared in and out of view before the darkness dominated. An object the size of a deck of cards floated stationary at the centre of the stars. Each minute that slipped by, the object grew. Metallic arms sprouted, each covered in reflective feathers. NISS took shape like a spirit. As the space shuttle floated closer, Alex noticed the arms were living quarters, with solar panels spread out across them. A dozen other shuttles and uniquely designed space crafts were attached across the station, like barnacles on a hull.

No sound could be heard from beyond the walls.

Bursts of smoke flew from the sides of the shuttle and the space station idled. The monstrous structures engulfed the windows. A hatch extended across the void, it reached for the spaceship. Movement could be seen past the decontamination bay. People waited for the two objects to come together.

A cumbersome metallic click rattled through the cabin and the safety harness lights turned off. The passengers cheered. The captain came on the airways, "Space crew, stand-by ready for boarding. Everybody, welcome to the NISS."

They allowed twenty passengers out at a time through the hatch and into the decontamination zone. Alex was in one of the last groups to bound in. Once inside the chamber, he grabbed onto the rubber handles, which dangled from the ceiling. The door to the space shuttle closed behind them and a vapour sprayed across him. His charcoal suit was damp from the liquid. Before the chill set in, the moisture was sucked out of the room, the fabric pulled from his skin until it was bone dry. He ran a hand through his hair, now fluffy and coarse.

The door to the space station slid open and the passengers poured out. A short, stocky woman with a fluorescent jacket and a touchpad stood at the entrance, she wore a matching charcoal jumpsuit underneath. "Please check in and pick up your key cards to your left, pick up your baggage on the right."

"Alex, grab our bags will ya? I'll fill in the forms and get our cards."

"No problem."

Alex walked over to the bag drop. There was a satisfaction to watch a conveyor of luggage running through space. From a window, he could see the items float around in a cylinder before they were sucked into a decontamination area. A sea of passengers had already formed around the drop, in anticipation for their bag to drop out next. A wild flurry of turquoise walked past him.

"I like the new look," said Alex.

"Not another word," Mia said, irritated as she tried to flatten her wild hair in vain. "There's no need for that decontamination room."

Once everyone had collected their bags, they joined the next tour that was about to start. James and Mia, as pilots, were exempt and walked off to find their quarters. The corridors of the NISS were a pristine white, with black padding between the gaps, which connected the compartments together. Screens flickered NISS information on the walls and lines of data showed the status of the life support systems. They were shown the mess quarters, entertainment area, work stations, the communications centre and the main attraction, the observation deck. Sean feigned interest, as he had done the tour before and simply went through the motions.

The pads of Alex's jumpsuit slid effortlessly across the glossy floor. The gravity was there but Alex no longer felt the weight of his limbs. He moved them oddly through the air to his amazement, without paying attention to the tour guide's memorised speech. A burly passenger with a shaved head collided heavily into Alex's skinny frame and it launched him across the passage into the opposite wall. If it wasn't for the soft gravity, Alex might've spent a considerable time in the medical bay that they had just visited.

"Watch where you're going," Sean shouted at the burly man as he yanked Alex to his feet.

"Get lost, mate," the shaved head man uttered as he bounded to the mess hall.

"What a jerk. You OK Alex?"

"Sure," Alex said as he rubbed his lower back. "Just testing out the gravity."

They were shown to their quarters. Despite its tiny size, everything had been designed to have a place. Walls shifted back to reveal storage space. Cubicles were hidden by closet doors that contained a compact toilet and shower. Neither looked that stable. A desk and stool could be pulled out to take up most of the floor space, and then pushed back in to complete the puzzle. A bunk bed was embedded into the wall, with a chrome ladder. At the far end, a one-seater sofa, which lay under a tiny circle window, with the wonders of the planet on the other side. Everything was white.

"I'll take the bottom bunk, OK?" Sean asked, but it was more of a statement than a question. "I'm going to take a nap before dinner, so go out and explore."

Alex made a beeline for the observation deck. He grew up with a fascination of space and to finally see Earth in its all glory, and not simply from vids or VR simulations, made him shiver with delight. To his dismay, everyone on the flight had the same idea. He couldn't even get past the queue at the entrance, let alone peak inside. He vowed he would return when the others had gone to sleep. Did people ever sleep in this place? He explored the other rooms, but they were of little interest. He played for an hour on the VR console in the entertainment area, but they were dated games from Earth. Eventually, he sat patiently in the mess hall and waited for the crew to join him.

The NISS staff had started to hand out the dinner trays by the time Sean joined them. "I hate the food here," he declared, as he squeezed in next to Alex. A tin foil tray was placed in front of each of them, a whiff of steam escaped from the edge. Mia pulled a face in agreement. "You'd think with the trillions they spend on this place, they could get the food right."

Alex poked the bland piece of white meat in the centre of the tray. It appeared to be cooked but showed no signs if it was chicken or fish. If it actually came from an animal. It was complimented by some plain noodles. Steamed vegetables gave off an unpleasant pong. A piece of chocolate brownie rescued the meal. Alex eyed up his crew's brownies. Perhaps one of them would let him have theirs.

"Did you two enjoy your naps?" Mia asked.

"Mine was splendid," James said.

"What the hell were you two talking about all night?" She persisted.

"This man is a war hero. He should be knighted," Sean said as he wiped his lips with a napkin. "A knight of the round table. Is that still a thing?" Sean shoved his face with another mouthful of the unidentified meat.

"I shared some stories. But mostly I was checking if you Americans could handle your drink. Unfortunately, it was a victory to us."

"James, tell them the story. The one with the parachute," insisted Sean.

"I don't want to bore them."

"Parachute? You haven't told me that one," Mia said as she nudged him. "C'mon, spill it."

"Alright, alright. So, when I was a young lad, I joined the RAF. I had no doubt that it was what I wanted to do. there's nothing more liberating than flying. The supersonic speeds that you can reach with a dip of the wrist. We were carrying out some test flights in the Pacific with a fighter jet. Strictly classified at the time. It was the most beautiful of days as well, nothing but blue skies and the majestic ocean. I'm doing basic manoeuvres, nothing too fancy. Then warning lights start to go off, and the jet falls into a nose dive. No response from the controls. I try my best but there was no way to save it, so I hit the eject button."

Alex half listened, as he poked his unfinished food.

"Parts of the jet break off from all around me and the escape capsules gets blasted into the air. Boom! At the time, I'm thinking, I'm going to be in so much trouble for destroying the jet. How will I explain this? But I notice I'm still falling. Hurtling towards the sea below me. The parachute hasn't opened yet. I'm worried now because I'm in this slick capsule, which is going to crumple as it hits the water. I grab the spare parachute next to me and I put it on and hit the release button for the hatch. Nothing. The capsule has no power. I see the water coming up fast to me now, so I take out my pistol and I aim it."

A man roared into laughter from a few tables across. The burly man with a shaved head. He pounded the table in approval of something he'd heard, the utensils and trays clattered in their positions.

The crew returned their attention to James who continued his story. "So, as I was saying. The escape pod is plunging towards the water, parachute not deployed. I have my pistol in hand."

The burly man howled like a wolf and fell into the person who sat next to him. Tears ran down his pinched face.

"Will you be quiet," Sean raised his voice. The man ignored him and continued to talk with his friends at the other table. "That man is a genuine asshole. He ran into Alex earlier, sent him flying across the NISS."

"Is that true Alex?" James asked with concern in his eyes.

"It was no big deal. It was an accident," said Alex.

"He did it on purpose. If we weren't in space, I would kick his ass," Sean insisted.

James noticed that Alex shifted in his seat and changed the subject, "how are you enjoying your first time in space, young man?"

"Oh. It's great."

"Have you seen the observation deck yet?"

"Not yet. I want to though."

"You must before we leave," Mia joined in. "It's unbelievable."

* * * * *

His bladder was about to explode. Alex threw the sheet across the room. He stumbled in the dark and nearly fell from the top bunk. He regained his balance and slid over the ladder, he hit the ground with a thump. His hands fumbled across the wall as they searched for the bathroom latch. Why did they have to make them overcomplicated? The door gave way and he hurried in. Relief spread through him as the waste left his body.

Alex heard that they recycled urine on this NISS. He wondered what for. The inner bathroom light turned off just as the door closed on itself, but he noticed that Sean wasn't in the bottom bunk.

He crept out into the walkway of the sleeping quarters. The lights had been dimmed to emulate the day and night patterns of Earth and to give some continuity to life on board the station. The entertainment room and mess halls were silent and empty.

Another room with lines of couches was tucked away in an arm of the space station, which he hadn't yet visited. The blue leather that covered them was worn and peeled in places. Personal lights arched above the cushions like a row of claws. He ran his hand along the lights, they were bendable between his fingers. Passengers could mould the lights to read books in the downtime. He turned around to notice the stacks of bookcases against the wall. The spines of the collection of books, a burst of colour against the otherwise white room. Alex studied the titles and authors. A lot of mainstream pieces, which had appeared on the New York Times best sellers list. Not much that peaked his interest.

Read more books was the only item on Alex's New Year resolutions list, but he had failed to do even that. He loved to read but had found no motivation to do so this year. A lone book had been left on one of the sofas. The Picture of Dorian Gray, by Oscar Wilde. One of his favourites. The story followed a young man who already had incredible wealth and opportunity. When his path crossed with Lord Henry Wotton, he discovered that life had much more to offer, if he was willing to cross the line of morality and break society's unspoken laws. Dorian's soul becomes corrupted through the relentless pursuit of pleasure.

Alex placed the book back into a space on a shelf and continued his exploration of the shuttle. A glow flickered from a corridor in the distance. He moved towards it, his bare feet peeled off the cool floor. Voices now rumbled down the hall in a hushed tone.

Alex crouched near the entrance of the communications centre. He peered around the corner. Downlights were set to half brightness. Dozens of towers ran down the walls, with built in video chat screens. Padded black headphones hung off plastic hooks. Snowy chairs, equipped with built in sliders, accommodated each station. Multi-coloured lights flicked across the consoles, slow blinks mixed in with erratic flashes. Two men in charcoal jumpsuits occupied the room.

"What does this mean?" James whispered.

"I don't know," said Sean slouched over one of the terminals. The screen was grey, and the words CALL ENDED flashed across the screen. "Fatima is saying that the board want more time before they spend any more money on this expedition. They want to be certain that the colony is in trouble."

"It's a bit late now, we're already here," James scoffed.

"I'm sure it's the pencil pushers, counting every penny. Once they realise they will lose millions if the comms can't be re-established, they will give us the green light. It shouldn't be more than a few weeks."

"Weeks?" James raised his voice. He caught himself and whispered again, "Weeks? The longer we leave it to head to Mars, the shorter the window gets. It could turn eight to ten months into over a year. Weeks? Not a chance."

Sean waved his hand in dismissal. "Relax, I'm sure you'll be handsomely reimbursed for any inconvenience. The fact is that Deimos aren't releasing the funds until the decision is signed off. No funds, no LDS. We're grounded."

Dread rushed through Alex's veins. Weeks? There had to be a way to get to Mars sooner than that. Maybe he could speak to Fatima. But if she wasn't convinced by someone as senior as Sean, why would she listen to him? Did Rae know about this? She might have a scheme to get the situation resolved. There had to be another way.

Alex wondered how much time the colonists had left. That was, if they were still alive.

LEO

SEVEN

Leo rested his head in his arms on the marble counter. He wanted to escape the nightmare that was the colony. The enemies he had made now tallied to the same number of allies. Could he really call anyone in this place an ally? Norman hadn't replied to his messages. There was no word from Ariel and no one had seen Blake. His mind transported him back to the party. The music. The pool. The screams.

"Your face is a mess," Louisa said bluntly, as she handed him a chequered kitchen towel, which contained half a dozen ice cubes. A deep violet streak bloomed under one of Leo's eyes, as if his tears had been ink. His eyes were red, one of the lids swollen. Sleep the night before was impossible. The image of the young woman with Louisa's cardigan over her shoulders bore in his mind. She shivered uncontrollably.

Leo applied the ice to the bruise and winced from the quick stab of pain.

"Have they found the missing girl yet?" he asked.

"Not yet," Louisa said. "Her apartment is empty. There are search teams out in the desert, turning over every stone. Tony and Malcolm are recruiting more colonists to the security team. They are becoming very thinly spread." She wore black leather pants and a loose Rolling Stones top, which floated as she walked behind the bar. A middle-aged couple sat in one of the booths sipping on cocktails.

Louisa leaned over the bar to Leo to ensure no one else could overhear. "That is two colonists missing in just over a few sols. The security team is rattled. Those who have heard the rumours are becoming scared to leave their apartments at night. If they can't find any leads they are going to ban people from leaving the town centre."

Leo was about to utter a reply but decided against it.

"Chin up," Louisa ordered. "It's not the end of the world. I'm sure they'll find her."

Two older gentlemen in pastel shirts entered and sat at the opposite end of the bar. They pretended to study the menu and waited to be served. Louisa half-skipped over to them and immediately turned on the charm offensive. They laughed on queue when she told them an anecdote that involved people Leo didn't know. She complimented one of the men's watches and he beamed like a school boy. She opened two bottles and placed them in front of the men. They grinned unashamedly and beeped their barcode tattoos over the scanner. They didn't visit the Chambers for the expensive beer.

Louisa's smile vanished when she returned to Leo. "Are you still moping?"

"No," Leo smirked his trademark smile despite the pain. His attention was now on the cake stand on the counter. Half of a chocolate cake remained under the glass dome. Thick icing hung on the outside of the sponge like molten lava. The moistness produced more saliva in Leo's mouth. "You know what would cheer me up? A slice of that cake."

"Forget it. This is not a charity."

"Damn it, Louisa. When do I get paid?"

"Every two weeks. I'm going to organise a little get together tonight. Nothing big, just a few friends. They're quite shaken after last night, so it'll be good if we were altogether. Safety in numbers and all that. Wanna come along?"

"I don't know," Leo said as he handed the damp kitchen towel back. The ice had melted considerably. "I might take it easy."

"Your choice. I'll close the bar early then," Louisa shrugged and tossed the towel into the sink. The ice clunked around. "Actually, I take that back. As your boss, I order you to be there."

* * * * *

A few hours later, Leo walked down one of the main streets of the colony. The sun had commenced its transformation into a sunset, the sky burned an angry auburn. Leo shoved his hands into the pockets of his leather jacket to keep them warm. The street was usually packed with colonists at this hour, but now only a handful of single souls wandered around. Word spread quickly in this community. People didn't want to be outside when night arrived.

Leo entered the first entertainment district. The ground floor was a mock amazon rainforest with fake trees, which branched over the passageways. Wooden huts were snuggled in the walls and frogs croaked through the speakers. The lower level contained the attractions that were open until curfew. An indoor miniature golf centre, bowling hall, a 70s diner, arcade machines, and laser tag. Leo walked past a ceramic jaguar and entered an open elevator. He hit the button for the top floor. Through the glass, all the levels of the entertainment mall came into view. Each floor with its own crude theme. It must've taken them years to build this. The elevator dinged, and he stepped out. Horseshoe corridors had faux desert ground. Dirty beige sand of back on Earth. A piano could be heard past the old-fashioned swinging doors of a poker bar, which was called the Wild Buffalo Saloon. A mannequin statute leaned on the railing dressed in a cowboy outfit. Fake cacti and tumble weed, poked from the corners.

'Hopi Karaoke' flashed outside an inconspicuous entrance. Louisa told him to meet her inside. He ducked under a low beam and entered an enormous area, a little bigger than a school gymnasium. Instead of smelly, sweaty adolescents, a smoky aroma lingered. Clay huts stacked on top of each other against the wall. The high ceiling mimicked the Earth night sky and the landscape of a 16th century Arizona. A human-sized statue of a Native American Kachina doll stood at the entrance. A red torso, with a green barrelled head, topped off with a feathered headdress. Large lifeless eyes stared back at Leo. He stumbled back and bumped into some colonists. He uttered an apology and scanned the room.

A booth with an electronic board above ruined the illusion of authenticity. Louisa stood with a buzzer in her hand. A red light faded off and on the device. She beckoned Leo over with a flick of her head. She was joined by the tall guy with the goatee, Norman, who wore his favourite green hoodie, and three others he didn't know.

"There he is," exclaimed Norman as he threw his arms around Leo. He stepped back and grabbed Leo by the arms. Norman's face became distorted as he studied his friend. "That's quite the shiner."

"You could've seen the damage if you stuck around," Leo said coolly.

"Sorry man," Norman said as he examined his shoes. "I go a bit crazy when I drink. I promise I won't be drinking this evening."

"What happened to you last night?"

"I ran as fast as I could away from that psycho Blake. Ended up in the desert somewhere. Took me ages to find my way back to the apartment."

"I see."

"Hey bozos," Louisa called stood up on one of the clay huts. "Keep up."

Leo followed Norman as he climbed one of the ladders to the next level of huts. They walked across the top of the roofs and looked down as other colonists waited beneath as they waited for their buzzers to go off. A hut had the number thirteen moulded above the entrance, they stooped inside and an out of place metallic door closed behind. Padded tan seats engulfed the hut and cushions with rustic striped patterns. Louisa's friends laughed madly as they slid down into the chairs. Leo sat at the end next to Norman. An over-sized screen covered the far wall. One of the girls tapped one of the touchpads and selected a song from a 40s boyband called the Slinky Bois. The group surrounded the mics and sang to the rainbow lyrics on the screen.

Norman leant over and stole the touchpad and lay it on Leo's lap. "What song should we sing, pal?" Leo leaned back, with little interest to the thousands of songs that were on the screen. "I wonder if…would it even be possible? Do you think they have the song about piña coladas?"

It was tough for Leo to stay mad at him.

After a few minutes, he gave up the search and switched to the food menu. Norman tapped a few items, pressed his barcode tattoo against the pad and sat back to watch the others belt out a ballad. The door slid back, and a timid girl entered with a huge tray of corn chips, covered in a lumpy salsa sauce, melted cheese and littered with cut up jalapeños. She wore an auburn dress without sleeves and a headdress with one plastic feather, which poked out the side.

"Nachos. Is that really a Native American cuisine?"

"Don't care," Norman said with a mouth full of tortilla chips and cheese. "It tastes so good. Help yourself, bro."

A few songs in, Leo excused himself to go out and stretch his legs. No one would notice that he had left. He walked across the clay houses and watched the food servers race around in their fake Native American uniforms. Leo shook his head and climbed down the ladder. He hopped off the last rung and turned to make an exit. Ariel blocked his path.

"Hey," her voice quivered as she noticed his swollen eye. "Louisa told me that she would be here with her friends. I didn't know that meant you as well."

"Sorry, I didn't mean to cause trouble," said Leo.

"No. I mean, I'm embarrassed about what happened. I can only apologise for Blake. He can be an ass sometimes."

"Only sometimes?"

"He's alright when he's not around others. He tries too hard to act like a big deal."

"I know a lot of guys like that. Well, knew back on Earth. It was none of my business. He has been picking on Norman recently. And when I saw him arguing with you. I don't know. I kinda lost it."

"Please, don't apologise. He needs to be put in place," she nodded in agreement.

A server with a feathered headdress pushed between them, a tray of drinks clinked on her outstretched hand. They both watched as she climbed the ladder one handed. "So," Leo said as he clapped his hands together. "A native American themed karaoke bar. Feel like you've left Earth yet?"

Ariel burst into a fit of laughter. "Most definitely," she said as she covered her mouth with her hand. "I'm undecided if this venue is either tastefully tacky or hideously offensive."

"I don't know. Sometimes the tackier, the better."

"Are you a good singer?"

"Not at all," Leo grinned. "Are you?"

"What I lack in ability and talent, I make up for in unadulterated stage presence."

"That is something I would love to see."

A few beats passed and neither of them knew what to say to fill the obvious silence.

"Say Ariel," he said with a tone, which swung between conviction and nervousness. "Do you really want to join those guys? Or I don't know."

"'I don't know' does sound very tempting," she mocked him.

"What I was trying to say is. Do you want to do something Mars related? Is there somewhere we could go with a good view of the planet?"

"That sounds more fun. I know just the place."

Ariel turned and rushed outside of the karaoke bar and Leo hurried after her. They strode through the wild west amusement area and darted between fun-seeking colonists. Leo stopped at the cowboy mannequin and waited until no one was watching. He lifted the mannequin's cowboy hat and ran towards Ariel who waited at the elevators.

"What are you doing?" Ariel asked cautiously.

"If you're going to be my tour guide tonight, you'll need a tour guide hat," Leo said, as he placed the stolen hat on her head. It was a perfect fit and harmonised with Ariel's white lace dress, brown belt and tan boots.

"Oh yeah? How do I look?"

"Like a ranger hunting down some outlaws."

The streets were deserted when they emerged outside. The sun had left the sky and the orange tones had been replaced by the dark emptiness of space. The lamps burned to light up the pathways. Ariel took a few moments to gain her bearings before she headed off into the night. The echoes of their footsteps resonated in the valley of tall buildings.

They walked in silence. A comfortable understanding between two strangers who shared irregular circumstances. It had only been a week since he had met her in the waiting room of an interplanetary terminal. There was no update on the status of the communications relay. Without word from Earth, he would roam these streets without direction or meaning until the answers came. Leo was no closer to the truth of his arrival.

Ariel turned the corner and headed to a fence. The view was obstructed by covers that hung over the side. Bare iron beams towered upwards behind the cover as metallic weeds native to an alien planet. She ran her hand down the fence as she tested it for weaknesses. An amber sign hung up with defiance.

WARNING
CONSTRUCTION AREA
KEEP OUT

"Here it is," Ariel declared. She pushed away a loose piece of the mesh fence. It curled inwards into the blanket. A hole the size of a bicycle wheel emerged. "Are you coming?"

"Where are we going?"

"Trust me, I'm the tour guide." She held onto her hat and crawled under. Her boot disappeared as the fence slunk back to its resting spot. Leo glanced over his shoulder, no one was there. The windows of the building that stood parallel were darkened. He pushed against the fence, the mesh gave way with ease. His feet shuffled forward through the red dust and he emerged on the opposite side of the gateway.

A brand-new town rested in stillness. Unfinished building blocks scattered across the Martian desert. There were no artificial lights, outlines of enigmatic objects emerged from the shadows. Materials lay on the ground with no sensical organisation. Dirt trails ran between the structures, littered with heavy equipment vehicles. The wilderness of the planet being torn back by the mark of human civilisation. Leo found it difficult to place where the dome wall boarded the harshness of the outer atmosphere. "Ariel, where are you?"

No one answered. He stumbled in the blackness, his arms outstretched. His foot kicked something sharp and he sprawled forwards. Gravel cushioned his fall, he winced as pain struck through his elbows like a lightning bolt. A flash of light blinded him, the rocks crunched under the feet that approached. A hand extended into Leo's vision and he grabbed hold.

Ariel hoisted him to his feet, with a holophone in her other hand. Dust danced in the beam of light, which came from the flashlight feature of the phone. "Are you OK?"

Leo brushed the red dirt off his jeans. "I'm fine. What is this place?"

"I think they're expanding the colony. Follow me and try not to break anything."

The beam illuminated the path. Leo followed close behind Ariel, his foot accidentally kicked the back of her boot. He grunted an apology. The light revealed that some of the buildings were nothing but hollow husks that waited to be worked on. Ariel had her sights on one of the more completed constructions. She approached a hollow doorway, a portal that revealed the structure's concrete underbelly.

"Whoa, wait," Leo said. "Don't we need hard hats or something?"

"I already have head protection," Ariel proudly pointed to her cowboy hat. "You're screwed, I'm afraid." Leo took a deep breath and followed her inside.

They found themselves in a massive room, beset with stone pillars. Their feet crunched on the plastic covers below. Benches lay dormant, covered in tools. Electrical wires grew from openings in the walls and floors, like alien plants. Their copper endings glistened sharply when they caught the light. They reached a staircase hidden in one of the many bare doorways. Its concrete steps exposed. "Here it is," Ariel said to herself.

They ascended carefully with no railings to steady themselves on. The hole in the middle of the stairway became a menace, the further up they climbed. Its drop increased into unmeasurable shadows. They had climbed seven or eight flights before the rise of stairs stopped. A metal door stood ajar on its hinges, until Ariel pushed through. They were on the roof. Ariel switched off the flashlight on her holophone and slid it away in an inner pocket of her boot. Leo's eyes took a few moments to alter to the new nothingness of the world.

Millions and millions of stars which extended across the night sky. Constellations fought for the centre stage. Their lights had reached Mars from all expanses of the universe.

After his eyes adjusted to the dark, Leo could see that the rooftop was enclosed by a low red brick wall. It was empty and about half the size of a football field. Leo peered around the extended structure that contained the door to find the gentle glow of the colony in the distance behind them, like an underwater world out of reach.

Someone grabbed his hand and pulled him forward. It was Ariel. Her hand warm and kind in the cold of the night. She led him to the edge that faced the Martian desert beyond. Nothing stood in the way between the rooftop and the edge of the dome. Craters drew lines in the canvas, which led to the mountains beyond. Her grip lingered for a while before she let go.

"How did you find this place?" Leo finally found some words.

"I was bored of being cooped up in that tiny studio apartment. I did some exploring."

"Isn't this more like trespassing?"

"Technically, since you're a stow away, anywhere you go on this planet is trespassing." Her face wasn't clear, but Leo knew she had a grin. They leaned against the wall and enjoyed the view of where space and the planet collided on the horizon. Leo couldn't tire from the view.

"It's nice that we could hang out before I can go back to Earth," said Leo.

"Why's that?"

"I mean, for your sake. I'll be gone soon, and you have to hang out with all these losers. You'll look back on this night and say, 'I'm glad I had the opportunity to hang out with Leo.'"

Ariel laughed, "you think highly of yourself. And they aren't that bad."

"No, but seriously. I think you're a cool person."

"Oh? You don't know anything about me."

"Tell me something then."

The outline of Ariel's face turned towards the vastness of the galaxy. She removed the cowboy hat and lay it on the ledge. Her hair flicked back, and she ran her fingers through the invisible strands. "Well, back on Earth," she searched for the words. "I'm a law student. I didn't always want to be a lawyer. My parents pushed me to excel at everything. Get the best grades in school. Be the best player on the team. Despite the stories my dad told me, I wanted to be a war correspondent.

The look of horror on my mother's face when I told her. Parents always want something better for their kids I guess. I can't remember when my dreams changed."

Ariel turned away from the view and slid down to lean her back against the wall. Leo mimicked her movements and continued to listen. "I was a tom boy when I was kid. Most of my friends were guys, but that didn't matter. I could out-run and out-climb any of them. I was seriously annoyed when they wouldn't let me join the boys' soccer team. Then I had to go to high school and there's this…this expectation for you. I don't know. I lost some of that self-belief. It shouldn't be like that in today's age, but it still exists. I earned high grades and had an offer from top colleges, it was like the current in the ocean changed direction and I went along for the ride."

She became quiet. Either the story ended, or Ariel was in a mode of self-reflection. Leo coaxed her back, "so fate decided that you had to become a big shot lawyer."

"Yup, that's me. I can see myself in the courtroom. Taking down those snobby prep boys from Harvard."

"So, why did you come here?"

"I've been trying to figure that out myself. As I said, I remember watching the tutorial videos about living here. I think I watched them with my family. One of my last memories after that was applying for law firms across the country. Did a firm send me here to work on a crime, which was committed in the colony? Malcolm wasn't too sure either, but we won't know anything until the relay gets fixed."

"That'd be an interesting opportunity," Leo said.

"Bah, I bet it's writing up some boring legal framework documents. And they sent the greenhorn in to do all the leg work." The night became colder, Ariel rubbed her bare arms. "Do you want to do a trade?"

"What kind of trade?"

"For your leather jacket, I'll give you..." Ariel said as she stretched out to reach behind her. "This spectacular cowboy hat in mint condition."

"That's an offer I can't refuse," Leo smiled. He shook the jacket off his arms and handed it to her. They made the exchange. Leo took the hat and spun it in his palms. Ariel wrapped the jacket around her in an attempt to trap the heat from escaping.

"So, tell me something about yourself," Ariel demanded.

"Like what?"

"How about your family?"

"We aren't exactly close," said Leo.

"Well, what do you plan to do with your life?"

"That's a tough one to talk about."

"Tell me."

Leo threw the hat across the roof. It spun like a frisbee before it skidded out of view. "When I was younger, I was this up and coming baseball star. That's what the agents told me. Won a scholarship to play for a good college, did amazing in my first year there too. The top teams started to take notice. Over the summer, me and a couple of my buddies were biking on some trails. I wasn't doing anything too crazy. I came to this turn but the controls in my bike shook loose and I flew over the ledge. Wheels up right behind me, over my head. My shoulder hit a rock and shattered. Had to have surgery. Arm was in a cast for a couple months. Physiotherapy after that. I recovered but my throwing wasn't the same again. I was back on the team the next season but was no longer the same player." He gathered his thoughts. "Everything changed after that. I didn't have the same respect as I did before. Lost my friends. They would say hi to me on campus and in practice, but we didn't hang out anymore. My grades fell. I didn't care about anything. I used to have all these dreams but now there's just uncertainty."

"Can I ask you a question?" Ariel interjected. "Why do you want to go back so bad?"

"Excuse me?"

"You're hell-bent on getting back to Earth. I'm curious why that is."

Leo jumped to his feet. "There are many reasons," his voice filled with unease.

"Like what?" she persisted.

"Many reasons," he repeated. "I need to get back."

"Why not just say 'screw it'? The universe has no great plan for us. Life is just chaos. Uncontrollable chaos." Ariel jumped to her feet. "I mean. We're young. On a new planet. In a restricted area, which is probably going to get us into trouble. Why not just enjoy the moment?"

Leo walked over to her, leaned on the wall and scanned the horizon, like a lone watchman who scouted for assassins in the night. "I don't know," his voice was less erratic now. "I want to. When I think about home, I still can't put the pieces together. I was in a messed-up place. But I know something good happened to me in the last few months. I can feel it."

Ariel playfully punched Leo in the chest. "You'll be OK, kid."

"Well, what about you?"

"What about me?"

"Are you happy?"

"Yes. I'm content with where I am right now."

They remained motionless in the dark. In the amphitheatre of the dome, they became swallowed by the Milky Way. Leo had lost track of time. He hadn't checked his holophone since he left the apartment. Time had lost meaning on the rooftop of a deserted building in the Martian wilderness.

"Do you want to play a game?" Leo asked.

"You have my attention. What kind of game?"

"You have one wish. You have to wish for something. But it must be a physical object. You can't wish to be rich or become a movie star. Something you can keep in your house."

"Hmm, then I will wish for a giant library in my house. Like the one in Beauty and the Beast. And it has every great work of fiction ever written. With ladders and everything."

"Books. Very old school."

"It's my wish," she declared.

"Yes but wishing for every book is cheating."

"I'm a lawyer, I found a loophole in your rules."

"Well played."

"What would you wish for?"

"A bear."

"A bear as a pet? OK, I can tell you that's illegal."

"No, wait. Thousands of years ago, they domesticated dogs and cats. For hunting I think. Right? The dogs at least, I'm not sure about cats. Something about Egypt. Anyway, they were just wild animals before, now they have all these different breeds that you can get as pets. What some far-thinking entrepreneurial people should have done was discovered the new market. Bears. Imagine over generations of breeding, we could've had bears the size of bulldogs running around the garden or to take for walks in the park."

"You're one of a kind, Leo."

They loitered on the rooftop for a bit longer. He enjoyed her company, even during times of silence. Ariel said she was tired, and they headed to the exit. Leo picked up the cowboy hat as they left.

It was just after curfew by the time they reached Ariel's apartment block. Most of the windows were dark now. The streetlights cast their shadows over the forest green walls.

"Thanks for tonight," Ariel said. Her hands dug into the pockets of the leather jacket that she still wore. "Genuinely, I had fun."

"Me too," Leo said.

A few moments passed between them.

"Goodnight," she said.

She turned and headed to the door. She lifted her arm, the barcode tattoo slid out from its home in the leather sleeve. A beep echoed out into the night and the door slid open.

"Ariel."

"Yeah?"

"Listen, if we ever get back to Earth. Do you want to come to one of my baseball games? We suck this season but it's a fun day out."

"What…like a date?"

"Well, it'd be a lousy date since I'll be on the field and you'll be in the stands."

"Yeah, that does sound lousy."

"Ah well, right. No problem."

"Leo, I'm kidding. Of course, I'd come to see one of your games."

"Great," he said.

Ariel smiled at him. He had seen her smile many times before, but there was something new about it. She turned and entered the building. The doors closed behind her as she headed for one of the elevators. She glanced at Leo one more time, he tipped the cowboy hat towards her before she disappeared.

Leo headed back to his own apartment block. Mixed feelings tore at each other in his chest. A sense of hope fought against the anxiety and uncertainty of the future. He thought about the evening with Ariel. The prospect of being able to hang out with her again made him feel safe and nervous at the same time.

Would they ever fix the comms relay? Had they sent help?

Something didn't seem right. His footsteps had been mimicked. He couldn't hear any shoes but sensed that someone had followed him. He glanced over his shoulder while he walked. No one was there. The gaps between the buildings were dark and could foster someone out of view.

"Is anyone there?" Leo's voice croaked.

The only answer came from the low hum of the streetlights.

Leo quickened his pace. The lavender exterior of apartment block T came into view. The footsteps followed, cushioned as if the person wore a soft material to pad the impact of their soles.

A voice whispered from afar.

The numbers.

Leo's heart raced hard enough to pound against his ribs. A cold sweat prickled his pores.

The numbers.

A strong force barged into Leo's back and knocked him to the floor. Without a second thought, he picked himself up and sprinted the final few yards to the entrance, his shoes pounded against the sandy surface. His breath quick. The person followed behind.

The entrance now in his reach, he scanned the tattoo, but nothing happened. The doors didn't open. He slid his barcode across the scanner again. The doors lumbered apart, and he darted in.

"Blake is that you?" Leo called out into the night. The blood thundered in his ears.

Then he saw him. The silhouette of a man dressed all in black across the street. He stood on the edge of the shadows, his arms stationary by his sides. His face out of view. He didn't move. The doors hissed closed and the man disappeared into the night.

ALEX

EIGHT

Creatures danced among the dead trees, that rose from the snow like skeletal hands, which had escaped from the crypt. They whispered to Alex as his feet crunched on the fresh snow. The wind howled and sliced over his exposed skin like razors. He pulled the collar further up his neck to protect himself from the unyielding frost. The creatures twisted after him through the barren bark. Their voices blended with the icy gale. He tried to sprint away from them, but his legs were heavy. They didn't cease from the pursuit. A rogue root seized his ankle and he fell forward. The snow gave way to ice and he smashed into the murky depths beneath. The root pulled him further downwards, his bones frozen. The creatures swam around him.

Alex lurched from his bunk. A cold film of sweat clung to his skin. The recollection of the nightmare disappeared as he gained his bearings. He was on the NISS. He had been there for three days. The crew were stranded. No funds released to rent a LDS and no green light to return home.

In limbo between two worlds.

Sean snored like a chainsaw that revved into life from the bunk below. Alex dangled his feet over the side and rubbed the remains of sleep from his face. The artificial gravity had disturbed his sleep patterns, there was no need to force himself to stay in the cabin to endure the snores of his roommate.

He grabbed a fresh charcoal jumpsuit from the drawer. His eyes hadn't adjusted to the dark and he stumbled as he slid his legs through the sleeves. Once he was suited up, he stepped into the corridor. The lights remained on the dim night settings and a couple of people walked down the arm of the space station.

Alex roamed the NISS, without any purpose. The clutter of pans came from the mess quarters. The cooks must've started to prepare for breakfast. A few of the consoles in the communications room were taken, the early birds and insomniacs caught up on the latest news from Earth.

The observation deck was silent. This was his chance to enjoy it without any noisy tourists who took selfies and nattered. Alex crept down the tight walkway, which gave way to a massive theatre. Black velvet cushions covered the foldable chairs of the gallery, that gave the impression of a movie theatre. A bright blue light lit the room, the hue stretched across the white floors. Alex took a seat in the middle of one of the front rows. There was a lone man at the back who sat deep in thought.

Alex half-avoided the view until he had settled into his seat. His eyes faced forward and widened.

Earth, in all its glory, rested in the cinema-sized window. The outlines of the North American coasts were sketched by the illuminations of the human inhabitants. The cities with populations of over a million shined the brightest. Alex located his home city in the cluster of lights on the Californian coast. The oceans remained a deep, menacing navy. Blankets of neon lime swayed over the polar ice caps in the Artic. It had been everything he had dreamed of and more.

"How ya going?" A burly man asked as he lumbered down the aisle. "This seat taken?" Alex shook his head and he planted himself down next to him. "Good on ya. Experiences are best shared." His large dome head was shaved. The face was set by a wide jawline. The skin had been burnt so often, it peeled across like a fair leather. Angry eyebrows sat above dark eyes. The bridge between his eyes was sunk and his nose appeared to have been broken a few times in his lifetime. Muscles bulged under his charcoal black jumpsuit.

"Name's Brodie." Alex shook the giant paw. He tried to apply a firm grip, but his hand got swallowed in the grasp. It was the man who knocked Alex off his feet on his first day on the NISS.

"I'm Alex."

"Your first time in space?"

Alex nodded.

"Mine too. It's unbelievable. How's that view? Best thing I've seen. Makes Ayers Rock look like a cheap tourist trap. Sorry. It makes Uluru look like a cheap tourist trap. Bloody crazy, mate. Do you know what Uluru is?" Brodie's speech was brash and fast.

"Um, that giant rock in Australia?"

"Well, check out the rocket scientist," said Brodie in a mock cheer.

"No, I'm only an analyst."

"Ya kids. You never get sarcasm."

"So, what do you do?" Alex asked.

"What do I do?"

"Yeah."

"What a bloody boring question, mate. Who do I do?" Brodie scoffed. "Ya mean, what do I do for a living? And when I tell you, you'll judge me against your scale of success. We've only met Alex and you already want to judge."

"I'm sorry if I offended you," Alex stuttered. "I was only curious."

Brodie padded his own chin with a fist while he studied Alex, like a boxer did when he tested the durability of an opponent's face. "I'm only winding ya up, mate. I've had many jobs, so it doesn't bother me in the slightest."

"Oh right," Alex said with relief. He didn't want to get on the wrong side of a man who might be unstable.

"Let me tell ya about the first real job I had. Much more interesting than what I do now. I was just a boy, eighteen, out of school. College wasn't for me. My mate Samo says, let's make a fortune, let's get to the mines. Yeah, back when mining was in full bloom. Now it's done by the bloody robots. Back in my day, you were stuck on the site for months at a time. You lose touch with the outside world. Nothing in all directions. Only the desert. Some men can't handle it. One day, no one can find Samo. He just vanished. We sent search parties in the mines and out into the desert. Me and couple of the boys are in a jeep following one of the dirt paths. In the distance, we spot this lone bloke. Its Samo! He has nothing on him, dehydrated as hell. 'Samo, where are ya going, ya bogan?' I say to him. 'I'm going home,' he tells me. Nothing between the mine site and his home except for a hundred things that can kill him. Desert madness."

The Earth spun on its invisible axis. The sun's new day moved across the Atlantic towards the east coast. Billions of people slept 250 miles below Alex.

"The desert is not for everyone," Brodie continued. "Even those who think they are as tough as nails can be mentally broken by it. I think the desert is like space. The isolation of it. If you get lost or stranded, there's a good chance you'll die unless help comes ya way."

"I agree," Alex said. "Its beauty disguises its hostility. Humans have no right to be up here. Yet here we are."

"Yes, here we are. No right to be on Mars either."

"Mars…" hesitated Alex.

"You're part of the Deimos Initiative crew, aren't ya?"

"That's right."

"I heard a lil' rumour that your crew have a mission to visit the red planet. And yer funds have been frozen."

"Um, only a temporary thing," Alex mumbled. "It'll be sorted out soon."

"I see. Do ya know how we became the dominate species on that planet? Over the crocs, lions and elephants? The homo sapiens." Brodie indicated the blue and green planet in view.

"Opposable thumbs?"

"Sure, but we evolved past that. Our ancestors were the first to use tools, millions of years ago. They used sticks to get ants out of ant hills. Their tools improved to hunt bigger game. Our brains evolved from basic animal instincts to gain imagination. The power to create. Create a common language to communicate. Create enormous structures and cities with cooperation. Create religions to teach morals and strike fear, to maintain order. That when we tell our species that we will put a colony on Mars, they will support that vision."

"Yes, exactly" Alex said. There was more to Brodie than met the eye.

"Yer a good kid, Alex. I want ya to put in a word with yer captain for me. I want to fund yer lil' trip to Mars. I've got money to burn but none of these sissy pilots want to take me that far out. Offering to take me to the bloody moon. Who hasn't been to the moon? I'm a thrill seeker, not a tourist. Mars. Now that's something. I'll stay out of the way of whatever work yer gotta do. I promise discretion. I've got the funds to cover the ship, the salaries for your pilots and supplies. So, you lot let me know when yer ready to go."

Brodie stretched as he vacated his seat. More passengers had woken up and poured in to gaze at Earth before breakfast was served. He patted Alex on the shoulder and left.

* * * * *

"Absolutely not," Sean barked. A morsel of food flew from the corner of his mouth.

"Let's hear him out," said James. "It's best to have all the options laid out on the table."

"This is a top-secret mission for the Deimos Initiative," Sean argued. "We can't have an outsider on board. He might learn something, sell the information to the highest bidder."

"All passengers who travel to NISS are vetted," Mia intervened. "If he had a fraudulent past, it would've been flagged, and he wouldn't have been allowed to travel here. I agree with James, it's an option worth considering."

116

The crew sat around their usual mess hall table. The meals varied from what was said on the menu, but they tasted vaguely the same. James let Alex have his dessert again.

"What do you think Alex?" James asked.

"After I spoke to him, I did some research." Alex said. He thought about the promise he made to Rae. He needed to get to Mars at all costs. "The most notable thing is that he is on the Forbes list for 'Australia's 50 Richest People'. First became a millionaire by inventing some type of mining tool. He is also into extreme sports. He's done skydiving, base jumping and climbed Everest a few years ago. I don't think he cares about what we're doing on Mars. It's another accomplishment for his list. I think we should take his deal."

"I don't like him," Sean said as he took a sip from the hydration pack. "He'll be nothing but trouble on the trip."

"Let's think about it at least," James said. "Look, this is what we'll do. Sean and I will go speak to this Brodie character. Check him out, make sure his intentions are genuine. Mia, I want you to go see the flight master. Inspect the available LDSs big enough for a five-person crew. Go through the list of supplies, make an updated version, which provides for an extra person."

"What should I do?" asked Alex.

"Alex…I want you to draft an email to Fatima and the Deimos board. Tell them we have found a sponsor. Deimos can reimburse him if they choose to head down that route. Be as vague as possible. And diplomatic."

"Don't send it either," Sean interrupted. "I'll proofread it before we send it out. If this Brodie is all that he says he is."

The crew dispersed after breakfast, each with their individual task. Alex had been lumped with a menial administrative duty. A job that needed to be reviewed as well. Who did he think he was? He had a Master's degree in mathematics. Yet, it didn't come as a surprise. People were quick to underestimate Alex's capabilities, especially if they had just met him. It was something he had learned to live with, but it still hurt every time it happened.

The comms room was busier than normal. Passengers hogged the computer consoles like a group of backpackers who had discovered an Internet café in a foreign country that spoke a different language. Alex found a free computer at the back of the room, between a young man who watched cat videos and a woman on her social media account.

Alex entered in his passenger number and used the password he was provided with. He opened the internal message inbox and composed a new email to his crew with the proposed template. He paused. This was boring. He checked the search engine for time zones. It was 6:57 AM in Los Angeles. The email was minimised, and he logged into FaceZone. Rae was online.

ALEX: Hey, are you free for a FaceZone?
RAE: OMG ALEX! Hey! Sure!! Give me a few mins

A few moments later an incoming call came through on the monitor. Alex picked up the headset that hung on a hook and positioned it over his head. He clicked on accept.

A pixelated image of a woman's face took form on the screen. A blurry, red mane around a pale, oval face. The connection cleared, and Rae's features came into focus. The detail was clear enough to make out her pale, grey eyes.

"Good morning, Rae," Alex said into the mouthpiece of the headset.

"Alex! How are you doing?" Her voice boomed through the headphones, Alex turned down the volume on the computer.

"I'm good, how are things back home?"

"It's all same ol', same ol' down here. Andrew is still out of the country so it's quiet around the house. Just me and this little one," she pointed down to her stomach. Alex noticed she wore her work clothes, she must be ready to go to the office soon. "Are you still on NISS? Why haven't you left for Mars yet?"

"Just a slight setback with the funding," Alex lowered his voice in case anyone was eavesdropping. "Don't worry, the situation is under control"

"Don't worry? Are you going or not?"

"There's a man on NISS. Says he will sponsor our trip if we take him with us. Sean is not happy about it."

"You must take his offer. Screw what Sean or Fatima think."

"I agree. It sounds like the best solution. The man is quite eccentric."

"He must be a bit crazy if he is going to pay for it out of his own pocket."

"OK, I better go. Wanted to check in before I left," said Alex.

"Before you sign out, I forgot to tell you my exciting news!"

"What's that?"

"I had an appointment with my gynaecologist yesterday, she told me the sex of the baby. It's going to be a girl," Rae said with a joyous smile.

"I'm so happy for you. Have you thought of a name yet?"

"Ariel."

"That's beautiful. I can't wait to meet her when I get back to Earth."

"It's a secret so you better not tell anyone. Get back safely. Don't do anything dangerous when you're out there."

They said their goodbyes and Alex logged out of the FaceZone account. He stretched to gain some motivation before he finished off the draft email to the Deimos Initiative and sent it to Sean to check.

Alex wandered around the NISS in search for his crew but couldn't find anyone. Not in the canteen, the cabins or even the observation deck. He made his way to the shuttle hanger. A dozen doorways ran down the far side, through the safety doors windows, runways led to space shuttles, which drifted in the distance. A couple of the shuttles were the same size as the one that brought them to the space station.

A flash of turquoise stood out between the white interior and black jumpsuits. Mia spoke to a man with a large moustache and an even bigger stomach. She looked up from the touchpad she held and when she saw Alex, she waved him over.

"So, in your budget, for five passengers or less, I would recommend these two models," said the man with the moustache.

"Thanks," Mia said. "Let me discuss with my crewmates and get back to you."

Once the man had disappeared, Alex approached Mia, "how is everything going?"

"I spoke to James a while ago. The discussion with Brodie is going well. Seems like Sean is coming around to the idea. He is currently off to call Fatima to talk through the details."

"Sounds promising," said Alex.

"It does. Yet Brodie's budget isn't as large as our initial promised payment. It looks like we'll have to get an LDS without sleeper pods."

"Is that a big deal?"

"Well, four extra months of having to socialise with Sean," her mouth extended with embarrassment. "Sorry, I didn't mean to insult your boss."

Alex laughed, "don't worry about it. I share your sentiments."

"I'm glad I'm not the only one who thinks so. We can form a secret club. I don't think James will join. He loves anyone who admires him," she shook her head in mild annoyance. "Anyway, come look at these. My favourite is the Albatross 3."

She brought up some specifications on her screen, which Alex didn't understand. She read Alex's mind as she pointed it out. "It's that one over there." Alex's gaze followed the direction of her outstretched arm into space. A white shuttle with ebony wings, tilted at the end of a walkway. Its nose was slender underneath a thin control room window. The body was streamline and smooth, like a dolphin. Instead of a tail, two giant exhausts projected at the end. A pod stuck out near the walkway. Alex guessed that this was the transport that would take them down to Mars' surface.

"It's amazing. Just like in the movies," Alex said.

"She may not have the same technology as the newer models, but she's fast. I would've loved to fly with the hyperdrive of the Lapwing, but the Albatross is much better. We won't even have to run at max capacity to keep up to speed with the LDS we were going to get. Less power to use on the sleeper pods."

Sean appeared in the hanger, a smugness to his face. He approached his two crew members as the bearer of good news. "I spoke with Fatima and she's agreed to the arrangement. Mia, how long will you need to sort out the flight path and supplies?"

"Less than four hours if there are no complications," she said.

"Then that's when we'll leave."

* * * * *

Alex did his best to get a couple of hours of sleep before departure time. He tossed and turned in bed. As soon as sleep had snared him, he snapped back awake. Sean entered the room as Alex lay there, he signalled that it was almost time to leave.

Alex chucked his personal possessions into a bag and relieved himself in the lavatory one more time. He put on a fresh jumpsuit before he left the cabin. He walked down the corridor, past noisy NISS tourists oblivious of the mission he was about to embark on, in their relevant safety of Earth's orbit.

The crew waited for him in the hangar, dressed in the matching charcoal black jumpsuits. Brodie was with them, Alex had heard him before he saw him. He conversed with

James as if they were old school friends. Alex dropped his bag near the hatch door to the Albatross, NISS staff ran around in preparation for the launch. Deep space launches were a rare occurrence and they hurried frantically around as they remembered the procedures.

Alex joined his crew members who looked calm and relaxed. Fear had a grip on his vocal cords, which made it impossible to speak. Instead, he concentrated on his breathing. Slow and deliberate, in case the brain function had been switched off and he had to resort to manual mode. Brodie even laughed. He imagined Brodie on the Everest base camp before his ascent. An attempt to make it on to the elite list of climbers who had made it to summit. Unable to know for certain if you would make it back alive. The chance of death on Everest was at 1.5%. Alex heard that the death rate to reach Mars was higher. The figures were unbalanced due to a lot of deaths in the first few expeditions to the red planet. Some shuttles exploded. Others just vanished into the cosmos. The ships of graves still floated idly through the solar system.

"How ya going, mate? Don't be so glum, we're off on an adventure!" Brodie slapped Alex on the back. Brodie wasn't an individual who could control his emotions.

"Brodie, what exactly will your role be on this flight?" asked Sean.

"Besides the bankroller. I think I can be the cook," Brodie boasted.

"All of the meals are premade," said Mia.

"Someone has got to warm them up and set the table. What's your job, sweetheart?" Brodie smiled at Mia with glee.

"I'm the shuttle pilot, mechanic and navigator," she said coolly.

"Not just a pretty face then," Brodie said.

Mia shot Alex a look of mock fury. Alex whispered to her, "the secret club can add him to the list." Her lips curled back into a smile and she gave a nod in agreement.

"Alright listen up," James raised his voice. "First of all, a big welcome to Brodie who was kind enough to sponsor our flight. Sir, I hope the trip is as exciting as your previous escapades and that you'll remember it for the rest of your life. Also, I want to let you all know you're in safe hands. I'm not talking about myself, but about Mia. She has a terrific understanding of space travel and is a better pilot than any other I've flown with. Our objective is to get Sean and Alex safely to Colony C, so that they can carry out their classified investigations. Mia and I have signed discretion waivers and Brodie has scanned through his documents in the last hour. Finally, if you have any problems, with the ship, mission or a fellow passenger, you come to me first. I have an open-door policy and I always have time for a chat."

"There are no doors in the Albatross," Mia teased.

"You know what I mean. Let's do this."

One of the NISS crew members approached them to announce that the Albatross had passed the relevant checks and inspections. The hull had been pressurised. Gravity and oxygen systems were online. Supplies and personal luggage had been moved across. Mia's navigational routes have been uploaded to the course-plotting system. They were ready to go.

The five crew members headed towards the boarding room. Alex exhaled his last breath of the space station air as the heavy doors closed shut behind them. The passage to the shuttle opened and Alex's feet left the floor. The crew were weightless in the zero-gravity walkway. James instructed them all to pull themselves along the railing. Mia pulled herself to the front with ease, with Sean following close behind her. Brodie tried to swim through the air using breaststroke but remained stranded. He did a flip and laughed to himself. James shook his head as the realisation he would have to spend almost a year with the man dawned on him. He pushed Brodie to the railing before he began to instruct Alex.

Alex moved down the passageway slower than his crew mates. He moved his hands over each other a few inches at a time. The Earth wavered on his left and the vacuum of space spread out into infinity. If the tunnel were to break, he would be dead in seconds.

Mia grabbed Alex's hand and pulled him into the decompression chamber of the Albatross. Once the crew were accounted for, James flipped two switches and two heavy walls slid over each other, a mechanical latch snapping itself into place.

"LOADING DOORS SEALED, PREPARE FOR DECOMPRESSION."

Air shot in all directions and the crew slammed onto their feet on the floor as the gravity kicked in. Alex lost his balance and landed on his chest with a thud. Brodie reached over and picked him up to his feet as if he were light as a pillow. "Careful mate. It's time to get yer space legs."

"Alright crew, let's not waste any time," James said.

The two pilots led the way on the tour of the Albatross. The lighting was darker compared to the NISS. The dull glow and grey panels made it feel as though they were walking through a morgue after hours. The first room they entered was either a dining area or a meeting room. An oval table was bolted in the middle and had six swivel chairs attached. The wall on the other side was decorated with contraptions, which looked like microwaves. Alex hopped through an opening to the next room and nearly fell again. After a few days on the NISS, the gravity felt stronger than it did back on Earth.

"We can tour the ship after the auto pilot is engaged, first point is the flight deck," said James.

The flight deck was filled with technology beyond Alex's wildest dreams. Panels of lights flickered wildly. Monitors overhead contained status readings and coordinates. Levers, buttons, sticks and dials dominated the dashboards. The windows were slick, and a spider web metal mesh was ingrained into the glass for protection against the heavens. James and Mia settled into the pilot seats.

Alex found a lone racer chair with restraints at the back. He buckled himself in while the pilots checked the ship's statuses.

"NISS control deck, this is Albatross 3, prepared for detachment and go, over."

"Roger that Albatross 3. You're unattached and clear to go. Safe flight and speedy return, over."

"Roger that, over and out."

The Albatross drifted away from the NISS, Alex closed his eyes. Buttons were pushed, and switches flipped. A rumble came from the back of the shuttle and they were off. Brodie cheered while Mia read out navigational coordinates. Next stop, Mars.

LEO

NINE

Leo pulled the metal desk away from the door of his apartment. The curved metal legs moaned as they resisted against the floor. He dropped it in its original position with a clang. He hadn't slept well the night before, after he was chased to the apartment block by a man in black. It must've been near to half an hour that he'd waited in the apartment lobby to watch out for the return of the unknown attacker. Once he was confident that the man had left, he fled to his room and barricaded the door with a desk.

When the door swished to the side, he realised how fruitless his efforts had been. At least nobody had broken in. Leo rechecked his holophone before exiting the apartment.

TO: JADE 37
FROM: LEO 1702
HI JADE. SOMETHING WEIRD HAPPENED LAST NITE. IS IT OK IF I POP OVER TO UR PLACE? THANKS.

TO: LEO 1702
FROM: JADE 37
GOOD MORNING LITTLE CUB. I HOPE YOU ARE OK?
PLEASE SWING BY ANYTIME AFTER BREAKFAST.
HOW IS THE NEW JOB GOING? JADE

The time for breakfast had almost come to an end, but Leo wasn't hungry. He wore a plain t-shirt and black jeans; the sun warmed his skin through the dome. Ariel still had his jacket.

To kill some time, he walked around the town centre. Colonists clogged the walkways as they headed to their jobs. Some of them were dressed to pursue leisure activities instead. They proceeded on with their daily lives. Nothing was different.

Leo walked through the enclosure up towards the arched driveway of the majestic structure. The tall bellhop stood solitary at the entrance. "No car this time, sir?"

"No," said Leo. "I wanted to walk."

"Here to see Jade?"

"Yes."

"Certainly, sir. I'll call her from reception to check on her availability. Is she expecting you?" His eyes darted with caution, as if Leo was an unsolicited door-to-door salesperson.

"Yes, she told me to meet her."

The tall bellhop disappeared inside. He returned with a forgiving expression on his face. "She is expecting you."

Jade sat on the white sofa, with the grace of a goddess. A dress of emerald flowed freely around her body. Her hair flowed naturally, an animal, which had escaped its cage. She closed the door behind Leo with her holophone.

"Would you like some grapes?" She pointed towards the bowl on the table.

"No thanks. I'm not hungry," said Leo as he sat on the sofa opposite to Jade.

"How is the job going?"

"It's pretty good. Louisa is fun to work for," he said. "That's not why I came here though. I want to talk to you about something else."

"Of course, little cub. What is on your mind?"

"Last night, I was walking home. This man attacked me. I escaped and ran to my apartment. I think he was waiting for me outside. He was about six feet tall and wore black clothing. I couldn't see his face."

"An attack? Should not you raise this with the security team?"

"He might be connected to the disappearances. I wanted to know if you knew anything about them."

"Yes, I am aware," she said.

"Something is happening in the colony, more than the security team can handle," Leo said. "People disappearing. The lost communications with Earth. Why I've arrived here with no recollection at all. I feel the events are related somehow. I need to find out what the link is."

"The colony has a special security team that is trained to deal with these types of situations."

"You must have connections. You must know who would have the motive."

Jade leant across the table and picked up the bowl. She sat it down next to her and plucked a purple grape from the vine, placing it on her tongue. It disappeared, and she chewed it while she considered what Leo had said. Even when she ate, it was elegant.

"I love grapes. Not for their bitter sweetness alone. The texture. The consistency is like no other," said Jade. "The council have met on many occasions since the first disappearance. I assure you, we are doing everything within our power."

"The council?" Leo asked.

"The council are the leaders of the community. The governing party. We gather to make decisions that affect the colony and those who live here, for the better. Anything from the expansion of the city, to the supplies ordered from Earth."

"You're on it? Who else is on the council? Anyone I've heard of?" He probed further.

"I do not think so."

"What are the council's conclusions about the missing colonists?"

"Nothing that concerns you, Leo." Jade's perpetual mood had been broken. Leo had hit a nerve and her patience had cracked under the strain. She stood up, her cool manner returned as quickly as it had left. "Please, I have a lot of work to do this sol, so you will have to excuse me." Her hand gestured towards the door, ushering him away.

Leo stood outside in the sunshine. He rubbed his face and stared up at the giant apartment block. He had rattled Jade and knew he had stumbled onto something big. They were all connected. Was his arrival on this planet related in some way? He needed answers, but his principal contact hadn't been forthcoming. What he knew for certain was that someone in this town had a vendetta. A crusade to bring down the colony. They needed to be stopped. Or more people would disappear.

Located in the centre of town, the security headquarters was an inconspicuous building. It was attached to the highest structure in the colony. A huge tower, which crept towards the top of the dome. A satellite dish perched on top. "The communications relay," Leo said to himself. He had been acquainted with it before when Malcolm had locked him up. The scene inside differed today. Dozens of colonists rushed around the office. They wore the same uniform that Malcolm and Tony wore. Yet, armoured vests covered their shirts and steel batons hung out from their belts. One of the officers gripped the baton and laughed like a child as he swung it through the air in practice.

Leo tapped on the shoulder of an officer. "Excuse me. Could you tell me what's going on?"

A familiar face with dusty blonde hair turned and laughed. Blake.

"Newbie. Your face has healed nicely," he said, masked in an ambiguity, which left Leo wondering if this was meant as a compliment or an insult.

"You work for the security force?"

"Yeah. Law and order are obviously close to my heart."

"You don't make a very convincing officer of the law." Leo clenched his fists to control his anger as he spoke to him.

"It wasn't my first choice, but it has a lot of perks." Blake patted the baton holstered on his hip. "Now what do you want?"

"I need to speak to someone in charge. Is Tony around? Or even Malcolm?"

"Malcolm is out but Tony is in his office," he nodded down towards the hall. "And newbie. Remember to keep your nose clean. I'd hate to use this baton on you." Blake winked at Leo.

Leo stormed off and dodged a young officer who ran past him with a box in hand. He arrived at the door with Tony's name printed on the privacy glass and knocked twice. A voice from inside commanded him to enter.

Plastic containers cluttered the office. Each one contained an assortment of tools, unused holophones and batons. A giant paper chart hung on the wall, which mapped out what appeared to be the colony within the dome. Red ink circled objects and scribbled notes were crammed across the map. Tony sat on the front of the desk, his feet dangled in the air as he typed a message into his holophone. He glanced up from the device.

Tony snapped his fingers in the air. "Leo!" he shouted as he retrieved the memory from his mind. "What can I do ya for?"

"I have some information. I hope it can help in some way." Leo explained the event of the previous night. The attack. How the man in black had knocked him over and then chased him. Tony listened intently and nodded.

"You tell anyone else this story?"

"Jade, but she wasn't helpful at all. I think she knows…"

"Ah, Jade," Tony cut him off. "How is she? Mighty fine woman. She calls me her coyote. If only I was animal enough to tame her."

"I really didn't need to know that," Leo said.

"Of course, of course," said Tony as his cheeks blushed the same colour as his uniform. He became serious again. "A man attacked you, but you didn't see his face."

"I think he might be behind the disappearances."

"Look kid, I need more proof than that to go on," Tony's boyish charm and dimpled chin masked any form of condescending tone. "I can assure you that we're doing everything in our power to catch this guy. We'll find those missing people." He hopped off the desk and rested his hand on Leo's shoulder. "I'll let you in on a lil' secret. The security force is about to pull off a major operation. You'll understand in an hour or so. When it happens, please remain calm."

For the second time that day, Leo had been dismissed. The people he had spoken to; Jade, Blake and Tony knew something that he didn't. Only Tony had let a clue slip. In an hour, he would find out what that was.

* * * * *

Vending machines were scattered across the colony in the entertainment section, the apartment blocks and outside on the streets. Leo studied the contents of a food machine outside of the security office. Chocolate was probably not the best substitute for breakfast, but his hunger decided otherwise. He punched in the number for a chocolate bar in a non-branded wrapper and scanned his wrist against the reader. The chocolate bar clunked at the bottom and the text of 'minus 40 credits' flashed on the screen.

Leo found a free bench on the main street of the town and unwrapped the chocolate. He took a bite off the end and let the slab melt on this tongue. He couldn't remember the last time he ate junk food. It tasted better than any chocolate he tried back on Earth. Who supplied the colony with its food? He swallowed the half-melted morsel and bit the bar for another taste. He watched the colonists as they walked by. A woman in an eccentric flaming pink outfit typed into her holophone. A middle-aged man who wore a suit quickened pace with a check of his watch. A couple of men dressed in replica basketball jerseys headed towards the sports centre. They had a chance to make a fresh start here. Or did they continue their old lives on Mars?

Leo wondered about his friends and family back home. Did they miss him? Did they know he was here? His family must know. Was this some cruel practical joke? He took a deep breath before the next bite. Chocolate would ease the anxiety and if that didn't work, he would have a few cold beers after his shift at the bar.

Alarms harmoniously shrieked into life in the building opposite the street. Colonists stopped and stared towards the noise to find any flicker of flames in the windows. None could be seen from this side of the street. People filed out through the exits onto the road. All were calm and laughed amongst themselves. The noise of the building next to it rose, the sound of alarms rang within. A domino effect followed the street in both directions. In a few minutes, the entire town thundered in sirens.

Security officers took positions down the streets, some of them had their hands on their batons. A line of maroon uniformed men and women kept an eye on the crowd, which continued to grow. The entire population of the colony was soon out in the open.

The alarms vanished, and a hushed silence fell upon the gathered populace.

"ATTENTION, WOULD CITIZENS PLEASE MAKE THEIR WAY TO THE EMERGENCY BUNKER," an officer cried into a megaphone. Leo could hear megaphones echoing in the distance on other streets. "PLEASE MOVE IN AN ORDERLY FASHION. MORE INSTRUCTIONS WILL FOLLOW WHEN ALL COLONISTS ARE ACCOUNTED FOR."

The crowd dispersed in a direction towards the desert. Leo stood on the bench and scanned the crowd for any of his friends. Only an ocean of strangers. Leo caught himself. Friends. That was the first time he had referred to them by that term. Ariel, Norman and Louisa. Maybe a life here wouldn't be too bad. If people would only stop disappearing.

Leo followed the crowds. "It's just a drill", one colonist said to another. The urban landscape peeled back to the desert. A tiny structure stood alone in the dirt. It appeared to be constructed from a reinforced metal with two heavy doors shifted back. Hundreds of people poured in like the excess of rainwater flows down a drain. He didn't miss rain. "The bunker must be huge," thought Leo. "I wish I'd brought some more chocolate bars with me."

An orderly line had formed and the progress towards the front slowed. Two officers stood at the front of the queue. They beeped the barcode tattoos on the colonists' wrists as they walked into the structure. Leo held out his wrist and a stern officer beeped his barcode and signalled for him to keep pace. His eyes adjusted to the gloom of the inside. A dull metal chamber with no signs or ornaments. They passed through another set of reinforced doors before the people descended. The staircase could only fit two people across, their shoulders brushed against each other. The stairs and walls were constructed of cement, with rubber guards on the edge of the stairs. Low watt bulbs gave the illusion of bunkers from the World War movies his grandfather watched with him when he was a boy. A lot of people died in those movies. They continued to descend. Leo counted the flights of stairs. One, two, three, four, five. It felt like he was heading toward the centre of the planet.

Voice floated from a few stories below. Leo's eyes settled on dust particles, floated in the beams of light, which escaped through the partition in the staircase.

Leo trod off the final step and turned right into a giant hanger. The ceiling reached over three stories tall. The air tasted damp, and his skin tingled all over. Thousands of foldable beds were scattered across the cement floor. Each had a green metal foldable chair propped near the head. Signs with letters attached were situated between each segment. "Please locate your block by the signed letters. Find your colony number on the bed and please be seated," shouted an officer near the entrance. The colonists trickled through the gaps of the beds in search for their designated spot.

The 'T' sign stood like a lighthouse in the far corner of the bunker. Leo made his way past idle colonists and the skew chairs. His bed was situated in the inner most corner of the T segment, furthest from the walls. The bed was simple, but firm under his weight when he tested it. Two floppy pillows were stacked on top of a single white duvet. Leo plopped onto the metal chair and watched the chaos of thousands of colonists, each in search of their designated bed. The mission to find a seat in a commercial plane seemed trivial in comparison, he thought.

"Broski!"

Norman stood two rows down. He wore his trademark green hoodie and his hair pointed in several different directions. It was as though he had woken up and realised he was late for work. He walked around and sat on Leo's bed.

"Do you hate me?" Norman said. His face guilty like a puppy dog who knew it had disobeyed its owner. Leo didn't know whether to fix his hair or scold him.

"No dude, why would I be mad?" Leo asked.

"I dunno," Norman said, happier now. "You disappeared last night. And I don't see you at meal times. I thought you were avoiding me."

"Nah, man. I've had a lot on my mind. It's still hard to comprehend this place," said Leo. "Where in the hell are we?"

"No idea. I was sleeping off a hangover and then those damn alarms went off. I tried to ignore them, but they were so loud!"

An elderly man with a comb over crept up to them, a holopad in his hand. Hair grew in abundance from his ears and his eyebrows were like two mini paintbrushes under a forehead of wrinkles. "Chaps, sit in your assigned seats so we can do role call for Block T."

"My friend's bed is that one over there," Leo pointed to Norman's bed. "He came over for a chat."

"Excuse me young man! Show some respect. Everyone needs to be in their designated area before the security officers close the doors."

"It's fine," Leo insisted. "My friend will return when they close the doors."

The old man shook his head and puffed his cheeks. He moved on to the next seated colonist to check their number.

"You have a problem with authority figures, huh?" Norman teased.

"I don't like people who think they're better than me," Leo said.

"Because you're the best?"

"You know it."

Leo saw her. Ariel leaned against a wall of the bunker. A light summer dress with flower patterns fell just below her knees. Her folded arms covered by the leather of the jacket Leo had lent her. Blake leaned next to her, his hand placed above her head. They snickered at something he explained.

Norman followed his gaze. "Maybe you should forget it, pal. It might be more trouble than its worth."

"I don't know. There's something about her that's intriguing."

"Do you want another black eye?"

"Seriously? That was your fault," Leo accused him.

Blake waved a goodbye and headed to the entrance of the bunker. Ariel became lost in the colonists as she took a seat in her designated block. A group of people entered through the passage with reinforced steal doors. Colonists with eloquent garments, roughly about fifty of them. Jade was among them. Behind them, a troop of security officers with maroon uniforms. One by one, they stepped onto a raised platform on the far side of the bunker. They lined up at the back and cast their gaze upon the seated colonists.

"Who are they?" asked Leo in a whisper.

"It's the colony council. It's rare that they're all together. They usually say a few words at the 'End of Year' feast."

"How are the council elected?"

"I don't know for sure. I heard they were the original settlers on Mars. They're secretive and don't discuss their meetings with the rest of us."

"Not very democratic," Leo mused.

"Life's been good," Norman shrugged. "No one has questioned them before."

A heavy-set man in a maroon uniform bounded towards the front of the stage. His face was red. Perhaps the flight of steps he had to take to get there tired him. The crowd of colonists cheered and chanted his name. "Malcolm, Malcolm, Malcolm!" He smiled and pounded his fist into the air. Leo did a double take on the audience.

"Are they for real? I hate that guy," Leo said.

"He's a real fan favourite. I never understood why you don't like him."

"Friends!" Malcolm's voice boomed across the underground shelter. "The council asked if I could speak on their behalf. Colonists have raised concerns about fellow neighbours going missing. This is a concern to the security services. I assure you, that there's nothing to worry about. We don't believe that this is an external threat. Our guess is that they are stuck somewhere on the colony. What we plan to do is to keep you safe in the bunker while my team and I carry out a full search of all the properties in the town and the new development. We will search your rooms, but I promise you we will leave your homes as we found them. We will find our brothers and sisters!"

139

A huge cheer from the crowd.

"This might take many hours to complete and you may have to spend the night down here. Pretend we're running a drill and we can kill two birds with one stone. I spoke to the chefs and they gave me their word that the emergency food down here tastes just as nice as the food in their restaurants."

Laughter from the colonists. Leo didn't laugh.

"Once the search is complete, you'll be allowed to leave. Over the next few sols, we will be carrying out interviews with residents from each block. Nothing but a friendly catch up. So, check your holophones for the time of your appointments. Please enjoy your time down here. We will return with the missing colonists."

Malcolm and the council left the platform to applause. They followed the wall to the exit and left through the door. Most of the security officers followed them. That included Malcolm, Blake and Tony. Four officers remained and closed the metal doors. The doors shut with a deafening snap.

The voices of colonists filled the void left by Malcolm's voice. Many started to move around to find their friends, while some lay down to take a nap. Louisa rushed towards Leo and Norman, who were still sat in Leo's area.

"Can you believe this? Who does he think he is?" Louisa insisted.

"Thank-you. Finally, someone talking my language," said Leo. "Let's overthrow Malcolm."

Louisa raised her hand out in their direction and Leo returned a high-five. A perfect high-five with a juicy resonance.

"Love to stay and discuss the coup, but my bladder is about to explode," Louisa said. "Catch up with you guys later. Also, no need to thank me but you can have the night off work." She hurried on past T Block to doors with bathroom symbols located above.

Leo and Norman spent the rest of the day together. They spoke about their childhoods and their hobbies. Norman revealed that he was a professional video gamer back on Earth. He made his money from companies who advertised on his online channel. Over ten thousand tuned in each time he logged on. Norman couldn't stop laughing about a story where he became so drunk while he streamed a game that he fell asleep in his chair. He woke up a few hours later to find out that thousands of people still watched him as he snored and talked in his sleep.

In return, Leo shared stories of his time on the college baseball team. The pranks he would play on his teammates and the times when the coach lost his temper. He bragged about his best moments and how he singlehandedly won games. Norman faked a yawn and demanded to know about how many times he had struck out or how many of the cheerleaders he had slept with.

The pair had dinner together and continued their laughs until a security officer informed them that the lights would be turned off soon. Norman returned to his bunk and a few moments later, the bunker fell into a dim light. Leo could still make out the beds around him, but the beds and walls beyond vanished. Amber safety lights marked out a path to the bathrooms. He removed his jeans and hung them on the chair. His hands felt out for the plump pillows and smacked them at the end of the bed. He lay down and pulled the single duvet over him. The thin mattress snuggled his body. Comfortable enough. The hanger had grown quiet. A few colonists still whispered in the night to those near them.

On the periphery of sleep, Leo was dragged back by a tug on his duvet.

"Leo, are you still awake?"

He shook the cobwebs of sleep out of his mind to notice her face near his.

"Ariel?"

"Do you mind if I lie with you for a bit?" It wasn't a request but rather a declaration as she crawled under the duvet next to him. Heat radiated from her body, a radiator with a broken dial. An aroma escaped from the blanket. Like a rose bush had burnt to the ground and the ashes had been sprinkled over strawberries. The pillow shifted as her face rested close to his.

"I thought I'd come over and return your jacket. But I lost track of the time and they turned off the lights," she whispered.

"Where is the jacket?"

"I don't know. I forgot to bring it," Leo could barely make out the outline of her head, but he knew she smiled. He knew instinctively.

"Won't Blake be angry?"

An exhale of irritation. "Leo, you didn't strike me as the jealous type."

"I'm not. But I do care about my reputation of being the best-looking guy in the colony. Another black eye would ruin that."

A laugh far too loud for a room full of sleeping people escaped her mouth before her hand rushed up to suppress it.

She poked him in the stomach under the duvet. "Yes, you're pretty alright looking for a Martian I suppose. And I don't mean the human variety."

"You come into my bed. Make accusations. Now you insult me. Give me one reason why I shouldn't push you off," Leo whispered his offhand threat.

"Because it's cold and I thought we could share body heat." She nudged closer to him. Leo's heart froze in time as their bare legs pressed against each other. Her skin was tight, with the contrast of silk skin, which dowsed any nerves that stirred inside him. Her breath brushed his neck in short bursts. They lay together for a while and breathed in each other's scent. Both dared not move in fear of ruining the moment.

"What do you think is more terrifying?" Leo started. "Being buried under a quarter of a mile of dirt, which could collapse at any time, imprisoning us in this bunker for the rest of our lives, or being stuck on a planet that is millions of miles away from home and not knowing if you'll ever make it back?"

"Hmm, let me think about that one," Ariel paused as to conjure a witty remark. As the pause lengthened, a boldness overcame Leo. He lifted his loose arm up towards her. The tips of his fingers made contact with her thigh. They danced lightly on her skin, that drew a gasp from Ariel's lips. Leo's fingers flirted with the edge of her dress as they moved up and down her leg. She regained her composure, her voice softer now. "Definitely, terrifying. How about a mix of both? Being buried under a quarter mile of dirt, on a planet, millions of miles from home."

"That sounds like the worst scenario imaginable," Leo said, his hand falling still.

"It could be worse," Ariel rested her hands on Leo's chest. They explored the curves of his toned torso through the thin layer of material. "It's not that bad when you have someone to share the experience with." The fingers moved along the lines of the definition as an explorer does with a ship in uncharted territory.

"Ariel."

"Yeah?"

"If they don't find anything, we should do our own investigations. You're a lawyer, right? We could probably find out who is behind all of this before they can."

"It's a date," she whispered.

Leo listened to her breaths turn into the effortless inhales of slumber. He listened to them until he could no longer keep his eyes open.

ALEX

TEN

Months had passed, and Alex had adapted to his new space life better than he had expected. Life aboard the Albatross followed a strict regime, which included a mandatory eight hours of sleep. He shared the living quarters with Brodie and Sean. He had a sixth sense for when an argument was about to erupt and would walk away until it blew over. James had his own private cabin that he shared with Mia. It wasn't a secret that they were some sort of item, but nobody brought up the subject.

Despite his bravado, Brodie kept his word as the ship's chef and made sure everyone ate right. He was even concerned about Sean's health, which led to further arguments. He created a strict schedule with three meals a day. These meals were the only time the crew gathered as a team. Brodie and James would jostle over whose turn it was to tell some epic story from their lives. Sean would interject with a similar experience he had and how it was better. Whenever the testosterone levels exceeded a certain limit, Alex and Mia would sneak away to a different part of the shuttle to share a packet of space ice cream. Mia knew to leave the chocolate flavoured ones for Alex.

Sean kept to himself for most of the journey. Most of the time, he would be planted on the orange sofa with his e-book pad. When someone asked him what he was reading, it would usually be some motivational title of a self-help book. 'A New Dawn, A New Me' or 'How to Think Like a Trillionaire'. Alex wondered if he put any of the advice into practice as he was just as abrasive as he was back on Earth. However, Alex would feel sorry for him during a couple of low points when he spoke about how much he missed his family.

There was plenty of down time on the shuttle. Even for the pilots. They ran daily diagnoses and kept an eye on the autopilot's flight path, but other than these errands, they had plenty of free time to fill. After a couple of weeks, Alex mustered up the courage to ask James for some tips on how to get into shape. James loved the idea of a training partner and took Alex under his wing. He told Alex that he was impressed he had taken the initiative to show an interest in improving his physique. They would spend an hour together in the shuttle's gym. It was modest, but more than adequate. A couple of treadmills, a rowing machine and an assortment of body weight machines. James would teach Alex how to use the weight machines and explained, which muscles groups they worked. At the start, Alex would run five minutes before he burst into a fit of coughs. Now he could run for miles without interruption.

Mia wanted to learn Mandarin. Over half of Earth's population spoke the language. James, Sean and Brodie could speak to a proficient level and would sometimes speak it in front of Mia to wind her up. Brodie revealed to Alex that they used it to talk about other women, or strip clubs that they had visited. Mia twisted Alex's arm to be her study companion and they would go through beginner's recorded lessons, which they requested from Earth. James would sometimes correct her pronunciation and Mia would throw something at him. Usually something that wouldn't leave a mark.

There was also the Albatross terminal where the crew enjoyed their time. They could send messages back to Earth to be passed on to friends and family. It would take the messages under fifteen minutes to reach Earth. James restricted each member to half an hour a day on the terminal. Once, Alex accidentally came across an explicit email from one of Brodie's supermodel girlfriends who he'd bragged about. He avoided eye contact with him for a few days after that.

The Albatross was still unable to contact Mars.

* * * * *

Alex had finished his Mandarin lesson with Mia and walked around the Albatross to stretch his legs. It was the down time between Mandarin class and lunch, where he was always most bored. He would've checked if he had a message from his dad, but Sean was on the terminal. Alex settled on a movie in the rec room instead.

The rec room seemed to be an afterthought for the Albatross design. A couch that couldn't fit more than three cramped people into a room no bigger than a bathroom. A large screen was fitted in and connected to the ships system. The library of films was extensive. When Alex entered the room, Brodie was laid out of the sofa with a hydration pack on his chest and the screen turned off.

"Alex! What ya up to fella?" Brodie boomed.

"I thought I would watch a movie, but I can come back later."

"No dramas mate, come watch what ya want."

Brodie moved his feet out of the way and Alex took a seat and searched around for the remote. He found it under one of the pillows, a hidden gem like a golden nugget. He pushed the power button and the screen flickered into life. The library of films was so wide that Alex spent the same amount of time to choose a movie as he did to watch it.

"Only a few days until we reach Mars, you excited kid?"

Alex pondered on Brodie's words. He had gotten so used to life on the Albatross, the mission had slipped his mind. He would get the odd reminder from Rae when she asked him how many days were left until they reached the colony. Priorities would have to alter. It was nice that he had the opportunity to focus on himself for a change with daily exercise and a new language to learn. This was the first break he'd had since he left university. He had to focus on his mission.

"Yes, it'll be a great experience," said Alex.

"I got a message from the Deimos board yesterday, they're gonna pay me back in instalments and it'll cover my trip. That's what it's about kid. Smart investments." Brodie paused before he continued. "So, yer gotten to know the other members of the crew by now. What do ya think of 'em?"

"Mia and James are cool. They're like my older sister and brother. Well, not related because that would be weird. And Sean isn't a bad guy, when he's not in a mood. Why do you ask?"

"I don't trust 'em," Brodie said bluntly. He peered out of the rec room to check that none of the crew were around. "They're fake. They're still walking around with their guard up and poles up their asses. Why can't they be themselves? They have ulterior motives, ya know? Apart from you kid, you're the real deal. Like a bag of goon from the bottle-o."

Did Brodie know Alex's secret? There was no way he could find out, Rae knew better to talk about it in her emails. Maybe Brodie was sincere. What was a bag of goon?

"I think some people find it easier to be someone else in front of others."

Brodie looked at Alex intently. "Have ya heard of the 'The Boy and his Pet Dinosaur? It's a kids' tale back from Australia."

"No," said Alex.

"Once upon a time, there was a young boy who lived with his uncle in a quiet town in Queensland. He was smaller than other kids his age and he didn't have any friends. Two other boys in his class always picked on him. They pushed him over, stole his food, anything to get their bloody kicks. It got so bad that one day the kid skipped school and spent the day wandering around the bush. After a couple of hours, he started to panic. He had gotten himself lost. Soon he found himself in a secluded area blocked out from the world with a wall of trees. At the centre was an egg. It was a bloody huge egg. It might belong to a crocodile or an emu, the boy thought. When he picked up the egg, it was icy and heavy. He put it in his backpack, and eventually found his way home."

"The boy hid the egg in the garage where his uncle wouldn't find it. A few days later, he comes to check on the egg and there are only shell fragments and a red goo in its place. He looks all over the place for the animal. He then hears a low growl coming from some old boxes. The boy digs behind the boxes and there it is. Lo and behold, a bloody baby dinosaur."

Brodie shifted in his seat as he continued the story.

Alex listened patiently.

"The boy is so happy with his new pet. He thinks about it all day in his classes, and when the school bell rings, he rushes home to look after it. He hides food from his uncle's meals to feed the dinosaur. Red meat was its favourite. Every day the dinosaur got bigger and bigger. It started to hunt mice as well. In the meantime, the bullying got worse. 'I know what I'll do' the boy said, 'I'll take my dinosaur to school and teach those bullies a lesson.'"

"The boy didn't feed the dinosaur for a whole weekend to make sure he was extra hungry. Monday morning came along, and the boy put the dinosaur into his backpack and made his way to school. Outside during a break, the two bullies came up to the boy. 'Give us yer bag or I'll punch ya in the face', one of the bullies said. The boy smiled and handed over his backpack unzipped. The dinosaur jumped out and bit the bullies' legs. They ran away crying and the boy cheered in triumph. The teachers said a croc must've gotten into the school ground."

"From that day on, the boy never got bullied again. He kept his pet dinosaur in his garage, but the dinosaur kept on getting bigger and bigger. One day he got home from school and heard snarling coming from the kitchen. The boy rushed through the open door and screamed. His uncle was lying in the middle of the room, in a puddle of thick blood. The dinosaur was standing over him, feasting on his flesh."

"The boy locked the door, left the house and ran away from the town. No one saw the boy, the uncle or the dinosaur again."

They sat in silence. Brodie contemplated the last drops of water in the hydration pack before he squeezed it out.

"What does that story mean?" Alex asked.

Brodie kept his eyes focused on the hydration pack.

"Am I supposed to be someone in that story?"

Brodie stood up from his seat and walked out of the room.

Alex did his best to scroll through the list of films but couldn't get his mind off Brodie's story. Was there a hidden message to it? Or was it just Brodie being Brodie? He tossed the remote across the sofa and left the rec room.

The Albatross was quiet, as if Alex was alone on the shuttle. He imagined that he had no crew and the spacecraft flew through space with no direction. Just to hurtle aimlessly across the abyss, to explore the unknown until the end of his days. He imagined the first successful human flight to Mars. What the crew must've felt like. An imitation of the European explorers who discovered the Americas and the trade route around the Cape of Good Hope. His crew were only copycats that followed braver men and women that proceeded before them.

Alex snapped out of his fantasy and wandered to the flight deck. He wanted to get a view of the stars. He ascended the metal staircase and entered the cockpit. Mia sat in the pilot seat, deep in concentration on some readouts. "Mind if I join you?" Alex asked.

Mia's head flew back to see her crew member, "Nǐ hǎo, Alex. Sure, take a seat." She returned to her work.

"Nǐ hǎo," he returned the greeting.

Alex headed over to the other pilot seat and made himself comfortable. He leaned back and stared outside the windscreen. The stars flashed between the protective mesh. Each star probably had at least one planet that orbited around it. Billions of stars with billions of planets. Of those billions of planets, how many had the ingredients to create life? Life, which could evolve into self-aware sentient beings. Of those species, how many had managed to colonise planets outside of their home world? Or invent technology to leave their solar systems? Did they kill their planets like humans did? Or murder each other in senseless wars? The thought crept into Alex's mind that many of the stars might not be far away from death. The sun of Earth and Mars probably has enough energy to burn for billions of more years. But how long for humanity?

"Everything OK?" Mia asked.

"Yeah," Alex said. "Brodie told me a weird story. I don't know."

"What stories from Brodie are normal? Don't let him get to you." She stopped her work and swivelled her chair towards Alex. "Everything else OK?"

"Yeah. Why do you ask?"

"Are you still having nightmares?"

"What? Who told you that?"

"Sean did. That you keep talking in your sleep."

"Huh," Alex rubbed his face. "I keep having this reoccurring dream. I'm stranded in a storm. I'm being chased by something. Then I wake up."

"I'm no Sigmund Freud but it sounds like you're running from a problem."

"Or running towards one."

The lights in the cockpit turned off. A siren cried out that pierced Alex's eardrums like daggers. A red light drenched the dashboards as if they were covered in blood. Alex looked back through the doorway, the whole ship had lit up in the crimson glow.

"Mia!" Alex cried out, but he couldn't hear himself over the wail of the siren.

She furiously typed on the dashboard and a flurry of data rushed onto a nearby monitor. She flipped a switch on the wall and the siren ceased. She concentrated on the readings.

"Damn it," Mia whispered.

"What the hell is happening?" James shouted from the back of the shuttle.

"Meteoroids!" Mia yelled back with terror built up in her throat. She grabbed hold of the wheel that extended out beneath the dashboard. "Switching to manual control!"

The shuttle groaned as Mia lurched it off its trajectory. Alex fumbled with the restraints of the seat as the panels rattled around him. Loose objects in the cabin crashed. He glanced towards Mia. Her whole body was tensed in the direction of the wheel, her knuckles white with determination.

The impact knocked the wind out of Alex's lungs. His bones almost shattered with the force that ran from his feet to his hands. He gasped for air, but it would not come. The velocity of the shuttle pinned him to the chair. The flight deck blurred until the colours no longer made sense.

Alex blacked out.

* * * * *

Alex stood at the end of a cliff edge. Stranded. The wind howled with a swiftness below him. He couldn't see the drop nor the sky as the darkness consumed it. Alex. Someone whispered his name, it was carried by the gale. A rumble in the distance as the mountain became angry. An avalanche. Alex. The voice persisted, closer now. The ice below his feet cracked as the snow rushed towards him. It wasn't snow. It shared the same properties, but it was a blood red. The red snow hit him with a force that flung him off the cliff into the gorge below.

"Alex!"

He lifted his head towards the voice, his neck burnt with pain. Alex struggled against the straps of the chair.

"Alex! Are you hurt?" Mia stood over him with her hand on his shoulder.

"I'm fine," he managed to say. He methodically moved his limbs one by one to check if they were still attached. They were still there, but his thoughts were still cloudy from the jolt.

"I need you to go help James," she said with a cool edge to the tone. "I have to check the systems for any potential dangers."

Alex winced as he unbuckled himself from the seat. His feet stood steady in the chaos. A new lower alarm wailed across the ship. The red lights remained on as if he was still in the dream world. Mia frantically moved from one screen to the next at the back of the flight deck. Some screens were off. A man yelled out in pain from deep in the shuttle. In a daze, Alex followed the cries. He tripped over some canisters that rolled loosely at the bottom of the stairs. Panels hung off their hinges, wires bared from the covers. Chairs from the meeting table had collapsed over. Alex hurried to the med bay.

James leant over Brodie who was laid flat out on the bed with sterilised sheets now stained by blood. A metallic smell lingered in the air. James held a lumpy piece of cloth on

Brodie's exposed thigh, which was pale compared to his tanned arms and face. The cloth was soaked by blood that oozed from the wound.

"Alex! Grab some gloves from the box next to you and put them on. I need you to keep pressure on this cut," James barked the command. Alex scrambled into position and pushed his hands down onto the towel. It squelched beneath the pressure. James moved his bloodied surgical gloves across the cabinets as they searched for medical supplies.

"It's nothing," Brodie flinched.

"What? It looks awful," said Alex.

"These kids," muttered Brodie.

James dragged a metal table towards the side of the bed and dumped a collection of medical instruments and bottles onto it. He unscrewed a bottle of clear liquid and put it near the edge. Next, he ripped open a plastic container of tiny syringes and picked one out. His fingers slid into the grip of one and he grabbed the bottle with the hand that was free. "Remove the towel, Alex."

The blood-soaked cloth was removed to expose a cut, which ran down the front of Brodie's leg. It was deep and bled profusely. The blood seeped out and created a puddle of its thick liquid on the skin. James poured half the bottle of clear solution on the wound and the blood was washed away. Brodie moaned behind gritted teeth. The movements were quick after that. He jabbed the syringe several times around the pink skin and tossed it into the clinical waste basket. His fingers were nimble with the thread.

"The pain should subside soon," James explained as he stitched up the wound. "We'll get you onto the antibiotics and hopefully it won't get infected."

"Thanks." It was the first time Alex had heard that word come from Brodie's lips.

After Brodie's leg was bandaged, Alex helped him hobble over to the couch, which he and James had moved out to the social area. The rest of the crew gathered at the table on the chairs that had not been destroyed in the strike. Sean had come out from his hiding spot and was studying his hands. The alarm had been switched off. Only the low hum of the engine could be heard. Alex listened out for any irregularities in its drone, but everything seemed to be normal.

Mia's hair, which had faded from turquoise to black over the trip, was damp with perspiration. She cleared her throat. "There has been no damage to the engine or navigational systems. When I switched back to auto-pilot, the Albatross moved back onto its original route. Fuel lines still intact. The damage to the interior of the hull was mostly superficial. The pressure and gravity systems are still stable."

James stared at her throughout. The white sections of his jumpsuit now stained with blood. Defeat written on his face. He knew what she was about to say.

"There is some bad news I'm afraid. Our comms are gone. We can no longer contact NISS. Or use it to speak to the landing pod. Then there's our oxygen supply," her voice cracked. "Our reserve tank was completely destroyed. Most of the main tanks were damaged as well. They are irreparable, and they are leaking as we speak. Once they are empty, the system will switch to the last remaining tank that is still intact."

Alex pushed for an answer. "What does that mean?"

"Not all of us are going to make it back alive," said James.

LEO

ELEVEN

The door to Leo's apartment was left open. He peered inside to find the room in chaos. The sofas had been overturned. The mattress sprawled off the bed frame, the sheets from the duvet and pillows lay strewn across the floor. The closet was left empty, clothes spewed on top of everything. Malcolm's promise to return rooms to the state they were found in didn't apply to Leo.

Leo had been woken up in the early hours of the morning in the emergency bunker, Ariel no longer by his side. The security forces informed the colonists that the missing people hadn't been found and everyone was free to return to their homes. Interviews were to be planned for the week ahead. Everyone was ordered to remain in the town, stay vigilant for anything suspicious, and to not travel outside alone.

Leo threw his clothes back into the closet and slammed the doors. He rolled the couch up right, its legs banged against the floor. A neighbour asked if he was OK. "I'm fine," Leo replied and swiped his wrist to close the door in his neighbour's face. He shoved the mattress until it slotted snuggly into the frame. He slumped onto it, pulled the bare duvet over him and fell into a deep sleep.

A shrill noise killed his dream. He blinked and stared at the window. The sun was high in the sky. How long had he been asleep? The noise repeated itself and lasted for longer. It came from the intercom monitor. Leo mustered his available energy to drag himself from the warm spot. He pressed the green call button as he rubbed his eyes. "Hello?"

"Leo? Where are you?"

"Who is this?" he asked.

"It's Ariel," the voice crackled from the receiver. "I thought we had planned to spend the day together to investigate."

"Oh yeah," Leo said.

"Were you asleep?"

"No, I've totally been awake."

"Are you ready now?" An impatience to her voice.

Leo sniffed his armpit. A shower wouldn't hurt. "Can I meet you somewhere in thirty minutes?"

He sensed that she shook her head beyond the monitor. "There's a café across the road called 'Will's Coffee'. I'll meet you there." The call ended. Leo scanned the apartment, it remained a mess, but it would have to wait until later. He stepped into the shower and scrubbed his skin until the smell of the bunker had vanished. His brown hair was laced with droplets, he ran his fingers through it until the locks dropped to one side. He felt his arms and chest, as he studied his image in the mirror. The muscle tone had remained after his journey to Mars and his time on the planet. He made a mental note to visit the gym soon. The clothes lay at the bottom of the cupboard, crumpled into disordered heaps. Leo sorted through them until he found a black t-shirt where the creases were the least obvious.

The café was empty when Leo arrived. The barista cleared up a surface that had been littered with half-drunk mugs full of coffee. The bitter aroma hung in the air. A chalkboard with all the available items to order hung across the wall. Ariel sat in the far corner of the shop, at a two-seater table. Leo's leather jacket hung on the free chair, with a piece of chocolate cake, untouched, sat in front of the empty spot. He sat across from Ariel, who grasped a mug in her hands as to absorb the heat from the ceramic conductor. She wore a black jersey, which hugged her figure tighter than Leo had managed to do the previous night. The collar of a denim shirt poked up from underneath, brought out the blueness of her eyes.

"Ah, my jacket has been found," Leo regretted his opening statement. Not smooth at all.

"I thought you would be hungry, so I bought you a slice of cake," said Ariel.

"Thanks, I'm quite hungry now that I think about it." Leo was starving. He couldn't remember the last time he had eaten but adopted the charade of playing it cool. "This place is pretty sweet. The whole independent business thing."

"I agree," said Ariel. "I'm glad the large corporations haven't dug their claws into the planet yet." She paused as she deliberated about something. Her posture straight and composed. She was someone who always thought carefully before she spoke, as if no word could be wasted in what she wanted to convey. "Leo are you happy on this colony?"

"What do you mean?" Leo asked.

"I'm not sure I can explain it. I find it difficult to express my feelings. All I wanted to know, before we start, whatever this is. Is that you're happy."

"Yeah, I'm happy here. Sitting with you in this coffee shop. I feel comfortable when I'm with you."

"Good," she said. "Me too."

Ariel left the table to order another coffee at the counter. Leo watched her from the corner of his eye, trying not to make it obvious. His gut tightened, and he understood how self-aware he had become when he was around her. Leo had dated around while at college and had seen no need to settle down with only one girl. He was the star of the baseball team and admirers were never short in demand. This sensation was different to the lust that he usually felt for the opposite sex. It was something real and familiar. Ariel glanced back at him and caught his stare. She smirked and returned her attention to the barista to order her coffee. Leo scolded himself internally and started to eat his chocolate cake.

"I must confess," Ariel started as she sat back down with a new cup of coffee. "I began the investigation this morning when we left the bunker. I walked over to the security services building and asked around. They found no evidence in Steven Nesbitt's apartment concerning his disappearance. Or in the apartment of the girl who disappeared from the party in the desert. No clues in any apartment," she took a tiny sip from her mug before she continued. "I also heard a rumour. Someone else had been taken a couple of nights ago. A reclusive man who never left his room much. They never recorded his arrival at the bunker and his room door hasn't been opened in a few days but there's no sign of him."

"So, now what?"

"I learnt that Steven Nesbitt was the immigration officer. On the night, we arrived at the colony he was supposed to process us, but no one could find him."

"Yeah, Malcolm tried to pin it on me," Leo said. "Do you think the failure of the comms relays has anything to do with this?"

"Most likely," she said. "I get the feeling someone is trying to take this place down. At a slow, methodical pace."

"What's our play?"

"The shuttle airport. That's where he worked."

* * * * *

Leo and Ariel entered the lot where the colony vehicles were stored. The white cars, which looked like golf buggies, lined up in rows out in the open. There had to be over fifty, and most of them were so clean that they might never have been used before. They approached a dirty model at the front with stains of the Martian dirt on its wheels. Leo jumped into the driver's seat and swiped his wrist over the panel. The machine blurted into life then fell silent.

INSUFFICIENT FUNDS.

The green message flashed on the screen before it turned black. "Now what do we do?" Leo said in frustration. Ariel pulled him down as the hum of another vehicle entered the lot. They watched as two security officers jumped out and walked across the paved surface to the vending machines near the maintenance shed. "Follow me," Ariel mouthed.

Ariel kept her crouched stance and shuffled across to the abandoned vehicle. Leo followed close behind and watched the security members chat at the machines, unaware of their presence. He kept his head down and entered on the passenger side. The engine still purred, and the monitor lit up with the menu.

"Perfect," Ariel whispered.

"What are you doing?"

"We're borrowing their car for a bit," she said, as she tapped through the menu options. Past destinations popped up on the screen and she selected 'Colony C Shuttle Terminal'.

The car lurched forward, and Leo had to grab onto the dashboard to steady himself from a fall. Shouts from the security guards followed them but disappeared in the background as the car turned onto the main road and darted across town. Colonists stared at them with confused glances as the pair slumped back into their seats. The buildings disappeared, and they entered the road that led through the empty desert.

The sun was about to set behind the mountains, far beyond the protection of the dome. The desert sand burnt fiercely in the low rays. The craters cast long shadows across the ground. A much different scene to one, which Leo had arrived to.

"You do realise we're going to get into trouble for this," Leo pointed out.

"Yeah," she said.

"Are we even allowed to be out here?"

"We don't have to worry about that now. It was too far to walk and we're now en route to solve the mystery of the colony. Future Ariel and Leo can worry about the repercussions."

"I feel bad for future Ariel and Leo who have to put up with your life decisions."

His shoes brushed up against two metal poles on the floor of the buggy. He reached down and pulled one up. The long-padded metal of a security baton, heavier in his grip than he imagined.

"I brought protection," he said.

"Well, aren't you the gentleman."

The vehicle rolled to a stop outside the entrance to the arrivals lounge and the system shut off. Ariel hopped out of her side and ran towards the door. Leo followed her and carried both batons. The sun had vanished behind the mountains and the final rays lit up the dome. Ariel moved her hand across the sensor and the doors slid open.

"Jackpot," she said.

"Here, take this," Leo handed her a baton. "We don't know who we'll run into in there."

Ariel took the baton from him and weighed it in her hand. She took a few practice swings, as a person would do in batting cage. "I bet I could hit more homeruns than you," she declared.

"I hit twenty-three last season, so you have a long way to go to catch up," Leo patted her with the stick.

She slapped the baton away. "Cut that out," Ariel shook her head and smirked at him.

They walked into the darkness of the terminal and the lights flickered on to match their movement. They headed towards the offices situated further in. They passed the interrogation room. Leo glanced in to see the chairs where he and Ariel had first met. He mused on the fact it was in this room where his new life had begun. Where he had met her.

"Leo, over here," Ariel called to him. He found her at the end of the corridor. A glass window with the name 'Steven Nesbitt – Immigrations Officer' imprinted on it.

They entered the room. It reminded Leo of his apartment. The furniture had been over turned and lay scattered across the room. The drawers of the cabinet were open and emptied.

"Do you think there was a struggle?" said Ariel.

"I think they ransacked the place to find any clues. They did the same to my place and didn't bother cleaning up."

The pair searched the room for any hints that could explain more about Steven Nesbitt or his disappearance, but the security team had removed any possession that might've belonged to him. It had been picked clean.

"What about that?" Leo followed to where Ariel pointed. A vent at the top of the wall. The metal mesh, which covered the hole had been unhinged and hung from the bottom screws. "Here, help me with this desk."

They pushed the metal desk across the floor towards the vent. It screeched to a stop beneath and Ariel bounded up. It was just out of her reach when she stretched up. Leo climbed on top of the desk and knelt next to her. She used his leg as leverage and hoisted herself up to stare into the vent. Ariel removed her holophone and flashed the light down the tunnel.

"Yeah," she said. "I'm definitely not climbing down there."

The lights turned off.

"What the hell, Leo?"

"That wasn't me," he protested.

"Be quiet," she shushed him.

Leo could feel that Ariel was still perched at the front of the vent. They remained still in the blackness. He thought he could catch a voice from the depths of the vent. They waited a few minutes. The beat of his heart thudded in his ears.

"Ariel let's get out of here," Leo said and realised the pitch of his voice went up a couple of octaves.

"Relax. I'm sure I heard someone from the vent, but it might be my mind playing tricks on me."

Leo stretched his leg to find a safe place to gain his footing. They stepped off from the desk. His eyes adjusted to the dark and he made it out the doorway. He grabbed out for Ariel's hand. He found it and slid his fingers into hers. She remained silent but squeezed his hand in return. It felt as comfortable as his favourite baseball glove. With the baton in his other hand, Leo made his way down the corridors in the dark, Ariel closely behind him. Their pace quickened to escape any unknown dangers, which might've followed behind. A low glow further down acted as his guide. They came upon the main lobby of the terminal and half jogged until they were outside again. Leo let Ariel's hand drop down to the side as he monitored outside.

"That place gives me the creeps," said Leo.

"I think there was someone inside there with us," said Ariel.

"There's nothing we can do without the lights, we should cut our losses and tell the security team about our hunch. Where is your baton?"

Ariel patted her waist in search. "I must've left it in the office."

"Don't worry, I still have mine. Let's get out of here."

Leo tailed behind Ariel to the vehicle they had arrived in, parked underneath one of the streetlights. It illuminated against the night sky that devoured any strands of light. Ariel switched on the touchpad and selected one of the previous destinations in the town. The car moved into life and left the security of the well-lit car park. It crept through the night, down the sole road, to the soft blaze of the town at the heart of the dome.

Neither of them spoke. They lay back in their chairs, lost in their own private worlds.

The car fell silent. Leo jumped up in his seat and darted his head towards the screen. The engine had died. An empty battery flashed before the screen turned black.

They sat in the dark until Ariel spoke. "Damn. The car is out of juice."

"I guess we're walking from here." Leo picked up the baton from the floor and stepped out onto the road. The headlights of the car no longer showed the path and the reflective lights by the side had been lost to the scenery. Only the millions of lights emitted from the stars gave any shape to the world. Ariel walked up to him and slid her hand into his.

"Let's go," she said.

She gripped his hand as they walked towards the glow of town. He felt safe with her presence around him. A realisation dawned over him that he couldn't let any harm come to her. Leo tested the weight of the baton in his other hand. He needed to be alert with someone dangerous loose in the colony.

"Tell me a secret," Ariel broke his train of thought.

"A secret?"

"Yeah. Something you haven't told anyone before."

"Let me have a think." Leo decided what he could tell her that wouldn't freak her out or ruin his reputation. "OK, I've thought of one."

"Tell me."

"A few years ago, I ran away from home."

"You were a runaway? That's adorable."

"It was serious," Leo objected.

"I'm sorry. Please continue."

"I was a sophomore in high school, but I was already playing on the senior baseball team. And I was already the star player."

"Show off," Ariel said and gave his hand a squeeze.

"Everyone had this expectation of me. The school, my parents, the coaches, my team mates. They saw me and saw what they wanted. A star for the school. Someone in the family who would bring riches and fame. Even my friends. I don't think they liked me for who I was as a person. They liked me for who I was as an athlete. Even my girlfriend at the time didn't like talking to me. I mean we hung out, but I think she was only with me because it boosted her social standing. One weekend, I took my dad's car and drove it as far as I could. I didn't stop and drove through the night. Ended up in some tiny town in Wyoming. Imagined a new life for myself there. Get a basic job, get paid until I could afford my own place. Lead a new life. Finally, I bought a burger. Slept in my car at the McDonalds and then drove home. Told my parents I was at a friend's house for the weekend. They bought it. Returned to school the next day."

"Being popular was a burden?"

"I don't know. I was being conditioned for a life that I wasn't sure I wanted. Maybe that is why I injured myself. I won't be drafted by any of the professional teams now. The universe must be giving me a chance to have the life that I've always wanted."

"An unremarkable life," she teased.

Leo dropped her hand and walked backwards from her in protest.

"I'm kidding, I'm kidding," Ariel said as she chased him. Her hand searched for his and held on again. "Thanks for sharing that. You keep on surprising me."

"Your turn now," he said, as they continued their trek to the town. "Tell me a secret."

Ariel wanted to say something but held back the words.

"I tried to kill myself when I was fifteen," she said.

"Ariel, you don't have to tell me."

"No, it's OK. It's hard to describe. That feeling of hopelessness. It takes over without you even knowing. Like a frog being boiled in a pot of water, unaware that the temperature is getting higher. When I woke up and I didn't want to get up. When I fell asleep, I wished that that would be it. But I still woke up. I didn't look forward to anything. I still don't know what led me to that point. The girls at my school were terrible. They called me names. Bitch. Ugly. Slut. I only had guy friends, but never a boyfriend. None of them I could confide in. I was never as smart as my mother. Or as brave as my dad. Stupid, I know, but that is all you know as a kid."

"It's not stupid," Leo said.

"I pictured it many times. How I would do it. I did a lot of research on it. One day I couldn't take it anymore. I was alone in the world. No one would miss me if I left it. After school, I arrived home and no one else was there. I opened my parents' cupboard and took my dad's handgun, hidden in some towels. I put it in my bag and walked into the woods until I found a secluded spot. I took the gun out and loaded a bullet into the chamber. I only needed one. I put the pistol in my mouth, pointed it upwards into my brain. Quick and easy. I was crying like a baby. I couldn't do it. I unloaded the bullet, packed it into my bag and dragged myself back home. I put the gun away and pretended nothing happened. I think my dad put the pieces together and spent more time with me after that. The feelings disappeared over the years. It was a bad time for me."

"I'm sorry you had to go through that."

"Don't worry, I'm still here." They walked a bit further on before Ariel continued. "Both of our secrets were about us running away from our lives. Taking drastic action. Yet we were both too cowardly to do it."

"No, I don't think we were cowards. We were brave enough to face life. Life is tough. And we battled on."

"True. I like my life now," she said. "Maybe that's why I'm here on Mars. I wanted to make the most of it."

"Also, for the record. I don't think you're ugly," he said.

"No?"

"You're the most beautiful Martian I've ever met."

Ariel stopped in her tracks and punched him in the arm. "Shut your mouth."

Leo faced her. The outlines of her face were visible by the starlight. One of her ears poked out from her hair. The baton made a dull thud where he dropped it. She waited patiently as he moved closer to her. Her lips pressed together to form a smile, a smile that stopped his breath. Her eyes darted up and down his face expectantly. He pressed his lips against hers and they parted on contact. Their lips played in the dark as he pulled her towards him by her waist. She tasted of sweet water on a hot summer's day.

Once they engaged in the action, they couldn't stop themselves. Ariel pushed into him harder than before and it threw him off balance. He stepped into a void behind him and the momentum pulled them backwards and they fell down the edge of a hill. They rolled to a stop at what Leo realised to be a crater near the side of the road.

"Are you OK?" Leo inquired. Ariel lay on her back next to him and giggled. They caught their breath while they lay next to each other in the dirt. The galaxy stretched into eternity on the canvas of the dome's sphere. A spectacle of purple and navy shades dotted with diamonds.

Ariel rolled on top of him. "This is an even better view," she said as she stared into his eyes. Her hands ran under his shirt and felt his exposed skin, hard under her touch. She naturally bit her lower lip. His hand looped behind her neck and pulled her in closer, so he could kiss her again. The touch of their lips had a desperation about it. As if their two souls had been one and then separated when the crucibles of the universe had been shot in different directions through the heavens.

Ariel kneeled on top of him and pulled off her jersey. She proceeded to unbutton her blouse, until Leo's hand shot up and grabbed her wrist. "Wait a second. Do you hear that?" he whispered.

A low hum in the distance. The clarity of the sound increased as beams of light shone overhead. It roared past their nest in the crater and towards the direction of the terminal. Whoever it was, they were about to find the abandoned vehicle on the road.

"Leo, we need to go. They'll find us if we stay here."

They climbed up out of the crater to the road. The beams of a car flew back towards them from the shuttle terminal. Leo grabbed her by the waist, and they tumbled back into the crater. The buggy screeched to a halt a few yards from where they hid. Someone stepped out onto the road, pebbles crunched under their shoes. Leo and Ariel held their breath as a flashlight beam danced wildly across the desert beyond them.

The footsteps crunched louder towards them. There was a pause as the person inspected something on the road. They lifted an object from above the crater and inspected it. The baton.

The numbers.

"Alright, no more funny business," a man said. "Show yourselves."

Ariel sighed with relief. "It's Tony." The pair stepped out into the spotlight. "Tony, it's only us."

Leo saw him now, lit up in the beams of his car. He wore his trademark maroon uniform with a baton in hand.

The numbers.

"What are y'all doing all the way out here at this time of night? It's not safe," said Tony, an anger in his voice.

A figure stood behind Tony. The light of the car danced around the body, it offered no hint of who it was. As if the person had no features at all.

Tony felt their presence and turned around.

The figure walked towards him, their footsteps made no sound on the ground.

The numbers, the figure whispered.

Tony cried out as the arm of the figure pierced through his torso. Long, unnatural fingers curled like claws beyond the punctured maroon uniform. The figure retreated the arm in a motion, which Leo was unable to follow. For the briefest of seconds, light shone through the hole in Tony's chest before his internal organs blocked the view.

Ariel screamed as Leo's blood turned to ice. The figure had no colour or features besides the outline of a human. Human, apart from the long claws, which grew from its hands. Dull amber eyes burned in its skull. It stepped over Tony's body that lay on the floor.

"You bastard," Tony choked blood into the dirt.

The creature watched him die.

A bead of cold sweat ran down Leo's spine. He grabbed Ariel by the arm. "We've got to go. Now," he whispered forcibly. Ariel stood frozen with her mouth wide open. Her widened eyes transfixed on Tony's body and the creature that towered above him.

The shadow creature moved in a grotesque manner, as he pulled Tony's body off the road, into the dark, the way a black widow moves across her web. There was no movement in the shadows and Leo noticed that the engine of the car was still on.

The figure materialised again in the beams of light.

"Run!" Leo screamed.

Ariel flew past him across the desert towards the town. Leo followed her in pursuit, as he listened for anything that chased them. His feet pounded the sand of the desert as his heart pumped furiously with adrenaline. If he stopped or tripped, he would die.

"Don't look back, keep running!" he shouted towards Ariel who was far ahead of him now.

He ignored his own advice and turned his own head back towards the scene. He saw nothing at first, but then suddenly registered the lifeless amber eyes. The rest of the creature's body lost in the night.

The eyes moved closer towards him.

Leo kicked in the afterburners and caught up to Ariel. They burst onto the streets of the colony town, which were now deserted. The illumination of the streetlights showered them in colour. Ariel's face was streaked with horror. She came to a halt and gasped for air.

"We've got to keep moving," Leo encouraged her as his own lungs burnt with fire and his vision blurred. Nothing had emerged from the desert after them.

They sped down the road until they reached the security centre. Leo pounded on the doors. "Let us in! Please hurry!"

The doors gave way and the pair fell onto the laminated floor of the lobby. They struggled for every breath. Leo stared up, his eyes meeting with those of a heavy-set man in a maroon uniform.

"What happened?" Malcolm asked, with no emotion.

"Something chased us," panted Ariel. "It took Tony. It took Tony."

"A creature with long fingers and glowing eyes," added Leo between the breaths.

Malcolm shook his bulky head from side to side as he stared out into the doorway. "We know about the monster," he said. "But we don't know how to stop it."

ALEX

TWELVE

Everyone shouted across the table. Sean pointed his finger at the pilots, his teeth exposed like a wolf. James had lost his air of diplomacy and hurled insults back at the architect. Mia shouted at them both to shut up. Even Brodie, who propped himself up on the couch with his bandaged leg on display, involved himself. He asked a question and moved on to the next question without an answer. Alex sat still, caught in his unfamiliar sense of vigour.

Alex remembered what James said a few minutes ago. It felt more like a lifetime. It is funny how a sentence can change your entire outlook. This year, Alex didn't care much for life in a world so cruel. His perspective had been thrown into chaos. *Not all of us are going to make it back alive.* There must be something he could do.

"Listen," James shouted in a break of the commotion. "The fact remains. We have lost most of our oxygen."

"Could someone please explain in layman terms what that means to us simpletons," Brodie demanded.

"So, at the current O2 levels," Mia started, "if we continue on our current course to Mars, there would be enough oxygen for two. Maybe three. And that's if they were conservative with

175

their breathing and we have the engines running at maximum capacity."

Sean and Brodie started to talk over each other again before James calmed them down. Alex asked Mia if he could see her touchpad with the readings. He studied it while the others argued. He grabbed a notepad and pencil from the rec room and returned to the table. "What are our options then?" asked Sean.

"We don't have many. If we continue as we are, we'll all be dead in about forty-eight hours," James said.

"How long until we reach Mars?"

"About eighty hours until we're in range to launch the landing pod."

A deathly silence fell upon the room, until Alex whispered to Mia, "are these the specifications for the spacesuits and landing pod?" He flipped the touchpad towards her.

"Yes Alex, but…"

"What are you yapping about?" snapped Sean.

Alex continued to jot down numbers on the notepad. The four other crew members of the Albatross stared at him.

"Alex, we thought of that," James said. "Even if we used the spacesuits, there still wouldn't be enough."

"Give me a second," Alex said. He wrote out the calculations and checked them twice before he spoke again. "We know for certain that there's not enough oxygen for the whole crew to make it to Mars. Sadly, there's no way around that truth. There's one other way however. There are six spacesuits, each with two tanks. Both worth four hours of oxygen each. Then the landing craft has its own tank of ten hours. We need to last as long as we can in the hull until the O2 levels run out. Then if we wore the suits until the twelve tanks were depleted, then boarded the landing pod until we could launch to Mars...This scenario would only work if four passengers were to remain on the Albatross."

"Bloody joke," shouted Brodie.

James pulled the notepad across the table towards himself and studied the notes, "what you're saying makes sense." He paused, stood up and threw the notepad across the room. It crashed against some debris.

"Calm down," Mia shouted. "You're not helping."

He puffed and leaned against the wall.

"How long do we have to make a decision?" asked Sean.

"A couple of hours, maybe a little more," Alex said.

"So, what? Someone has to volunteer, to uh...step outside?" asked Brodie. The painkillers had kicked in and he was sat up now on the couch.

"There's also no guarantee that the life systems are still functional on the Mars base," said Mia. "You guys said there hasn't been any contact since we launched from Earth? We should take as much food and supplies as we can, just in case."

"Perhaps, Brodie jumping off now wouldn't be a bad idea," said Sean. "He eats the most food."

Brodie lunged at him from the sofa. James rushed to prevent the fight, he was knocked back by the force of the burly Australian. Alex jumped from his seat to hold Brodie back. His strength was incredible despite only having one functional leg.

"Mate, I'll end you right now. Solve our problems," Brodie bellowed.

"You're all talk, nothing but a pain. It's your fault we're here! We didn't need your charity. And if there was only four of us, we wouldn't need to have this conversation!" The vein in Sean's forehead looked like it was about to burst.

They managed to drive Brodie back onto the sofa. "Be careful not to put too much pressure on that leg. The stitches will come loose!" James barked at him.

Brodie turned his head away and sulked.

"I think we need time to clear our heads," said James. "Let's take a break and think about everything that has been said. Mia and I will continue to work through solutions. Meet back here in two hours."

"One hour," Mia said.

"OK, one hour."

Alex headed to the storage room to get away from the others. It was located on the lower deck under the cockpit. The area furthest away from the engine room. If he closed his eyes the gentle hum of the refrigerators made him believe that he wasn't on a spaceship at all. He imagined he had been locked in a restaurant's kitchen refrigerator container and would have to eat everything to keep his energy up. He lifted one of the freezer doors upwards and inspected its contents. An assortment of frozen food was packed. What a waste. No one would be able to eat all of this now.

There was a half full packet of space ice cream. Alex dumped the bars onto the counter, none were chocolate. He tossed the box over his shoulder and grabbed a new box. He ripped off the seal and poured the contents on the counter again, finding and opening one of the chocolate flavoured bars. He bit off a big chunk and savoured the taste. It certainly tasted like chocolate ice cream, but the texture was dry and spongey. He wolfed down a whole bar before he opened a new one.

Between bites, he made a pile of the cookies and cream bars for Mia. She might want one later. Unless…his thoughts trailed off. Could Mia be the one who sacrifices herself for the rest of her crew? His grip tightened on the half-eaten bar.

The universe had conspired against him again. Every time he tried to make up for a mistake, people got hurt. If Mia put herself forward, he would volunteer to take her place. Not that James would let her, the old-fashioned man that he was. Perhaps Alex should volunteer himself anyway. This was his fault. The reason the four other crew members were here was because of him.

Mia and James knew the risks. It was their job and they were being handsomely paid for it. Moon flights were less dangerous and still paid a huge packet. They could have taken a rich couple celebrating their 50th anniversary on a trip instead, for half the risk.

Sean didn't have to be here either. The bonus he would get could go towards his family. He was a respected member of the business and one of the best. He could fix any technical fault the colony could throw at him. Alex would feel more comfortable if he was on Mars with Sean.

Brodie was a strange one. He wanted the adventure and all the risks that came with it. He had begged Alex to convince the crew to take him with them. As a millionaire, he probably had the most to lose in a material sense, but he gave off the impression that he lived life for the experience and not for worldly possessions. Would he be the one to go?

Then finally, there was Alex. It was his fault they were on the shuttle to Mars in the first place. Would anyone miss him if he were to go? He had lost his close friends since he'd started to work at the Deimos Initiative. His relationship with his dad was indifferent. James and Mia had each other. Sean had his family. Brodie had several businesses and was well respected among his peers.

Alex thought of Rae. There was a time when she was his whole world. What he would give now to go back to that moment. When he loved her, and she loved him in return. They could have married, started a family, grown old together. Even if he made it back to Earth, that life would never be a possibility now. She had someone who cared for her. A baby daughter on the way. Alex had sacrificed it for a career, which had brought him to this moment. "I hope she is happy," Alex told himself.

You never know what you have until it's too late. He had learnt this the hard way over the last few years.

An hour passed before Alex managed to pull himself out of his self-pity. He shuffled down the metal grates towards the ladder. No expense had been spared on this part of the ship. Exposed grey pipes ran past his head and the walls were dirty with oil. The doorway to the shuttle lay at the end of the runway. He would never reach it. It was time for him to do some good for the world.

He would volunteer to sacrifice himself.

He dragged his feet up the ladder and headed back to the main deck. Mia and Sean were seated at the table, their faces sunken. Brodie laid out on the sofa, he tapped a cushion in an irregular beat.

"I brought you some ice cream. Cookies and cream," Alex slid the bar across the table towards Mia as he sat down. "You could take a couple of boxes with you on the pod."

"Alex, I…" she managed to get out. "Thanks." She played with the bar in her hand and studied the wrapper like a child who had been handed candy for the first time. "Did you bump into James downstairs?"

"No, I haven't seen him."

The crew waited for their captain. Brodie continue to drum his hands until it snapped Mia's patience. "James! We're all waiting for you."

No response came back.

"James?"

Silence.

"Alex and Sean, please help me find him," Mia said. "We're running out of time."

Alex was sent back downstairs. He knew he hadn't heard anyone else come down after him, but double checked the storage unit regardless. Nothing. He checked the embedded lockers. No, he wasn't hiding. He walked down towards the landing pod, apprehension boiled in his gut like a witch's cauldron. James wouldn't have launched the pod. Would he? He peered through the window of the pod's hatch and waited for his eyes to adjust. He breathed a sigh of relief to find the pod still there, empty.

Alex returned to the main deck to find Sean and Brodie engaged in idle chitchat. Still no sign of the captain.

"He's gone," Mia said behind them. "He's gone." She collapsed to the floor in tears.

Alex rushed to her side, "what happened?"

"He's gone."

"Spit it out woman," Brodie shouted.

"He's gone! James, he…the docking hatch is open. He must've…he's gone." Mia clutched onto Alex. Her tears soaked his shoulder. The remaining crew members didn't move and avoided eye contact with each other. Mia's sobs echoed around the capsule, like a ghost who calls out for their lost lover.

Sean was the first to speak, "James sacrificed himself so the rest of us could live."

"Yes, he's a real hero," Brodie agreed.

Alex jumped aside as Mia fled the room. "Good one guys," he said. If James did throw himself from the ship, then there would be enough oxygen to reach the colony. A captain who forfeited his life to save his crew. They could only hope now that the colony was still intact. Would he and Sean be able to repair the communications between the base and Earth? Also, Mia was now their only pilot. He would give her some space before he would check up on her. They needed her.

"I was going to volunteer to do it," said Sean. "James beat me to it. A brave man."

"You didn't seem so brave an hour ago," Brodie pressed him. "Why the change of heart?"

"I just needed time to talk myself into it. It wasn't like you two would do something like that. A millionaire playboy and a nobody." Alex studied him for a long time. Sean leaned back in chair with a sigh of relief. Content that he would return to his family and his home. He couldn't mask the smile that appeared, like rats that appear in the night.

"Would you shut up, Sean. No one cares what you think," said Alex.

"Excuse me? What did you say to me?" Sean was now upright in the chair. He glared at his colleague.

"You heard me. I told you to shut the hell up. Don't act like you cared about James. You only care about yourself. You're happy James is gone."

"Of course, I'm happy. I'm happy I'm alive! And you have a serious attitude problem, young man. I'll put it down to the circumstances. Next time you talk to me like that, you're fired."

"Leave the kid alone," Brodie interrupted.

"You stay out of this. This is work related. You shouldn't even be here."

"I'm being civil," said Brodie. "But if ya keep talking to me like that, I won't be so nice. You piece of crap."

It happened so fast that Brodie couldn't counter the attack. Sean's chair toppled backwards as he dove towards his place on the couch. A flurry of fists struck Brodie in the face. He grunted but couldn't get up. Sean was relentless and pounded Brodie's face, a dark built-up fury unleashed. The nose crumpled like an egg carton.

Alex charged into Sean and he lost his balance. It was the opening Brodie needed and he lay one quick blow on his attacker's face. Sean sprawled backwards and fell onto some loose debris. Sean grabbed a titanium pipe, which had become loose during the meteoroid collision and swung it at Alex. He could only jump away. Brodie, who was struggling to get up, was suddenly exposed.

Sean brought the pipe down in an arch, the blow hitting Brodie's wounded thigh. He howled and fell back to the floor.

"Now, you both listen and listen well," Sean said while he caught his breath. "I'm now in charge of this operation. You'll do what I say. You both should..." Sean's eyes widened in bewilderment and he started to choke. Blood dribbled down his chin. The blood spluttered from his lips as he gagged for air. He turned around to reveal the hilt of a knife buried in his back, a flicker of the blade caught in the light.

Mia stood behind him, her hands trembled. "You killed him."

Sean coughed. Blood splattered across the snow-white floor. His arms flailed across his back, the hilt out of reach of his hands.

"You killed him!" she screamed.

His feet shuffled towards Mia. She stood her ground. Anguish burnt in her eyes. "I accessed the video hub, to watch the docking hatch surveillance for the past hour..."

Sean took another laboured step toward her.

"You and James were standing next to it, he turned away and you hit him across the head with a fire extinguisher..."

Sean fell to his knees. His body shook in spasms.

"And you dragged him in. Closed the door as you left..."

Sean slumped on the floor.

"And he was still alive when you opened the hatch."

Mia stamped on the knife's hilt. The remainder of the blade disappeared into the body. Sean's limbs twitched until they rested. A puddle of blood oozed across the floor.

* * * * *

Sean was even heavier than Alex imagined. He grasped at the jumpsuit material, which covered the chunky ankles of his deceased co-worker. His hand readjusted, so as not to lose its grip. The body left a burgundy trail behind it as they dragged it through the shuttle. Brodie initially tried to help carry the body, but his leg wound had reopened from the fight. Mia had disappeared silently to assist him in the medic bay.

The hatch to the docking bay slowly came into view, Alex's arms burned with the strain. Sean's feet clanked on the floor as he stared out of the window. The doors from the scene of the crime were still open, revealed the deadly void of space beyond. Besides his knowledge of the murder, which had just taken place in this exact spot, the area appeared tranquil and undisturbed. Now, the body of the murderer lay at his feet. Sean's eyes still wide open with the fright of a man who knew his life was about to end.

Alex tapped on the touch screen near the hatch. The outside door closed. Puffs of air shot into the room as it became pressurised again. The green light flashed on the screen and Alex opened the door. Sean's body had involuntary released the waste from its bowels and a putrid stench rose from the fresh corpse. Alex's gag reflux kicked in and he breathed steadily through his mouth.

He began to drag the body the last few feet until it rested in the centre of the hatch. The hilt of the knife still stuck out of Sean's stiffened back. Alex stepped over the blood trail and closed the door behind him. He drew slow breaths, and he selected 'door release' on the control pad. 'Confirm to open hatch' flashed up. He swiped the confirm button and the air of the room was sucked out into the open. Sean's body flew into the black, disappearing into the void as if he had never been there. The only trace of his existence was the puddle of blood on the floor.

Brodie rested on the bed in the medic bay, Mia stood over him and moved a fresh roll of bandage around his thigh. Tears had stained her face.

"It's done," Alex said, wiping the sweat from his face. Stains of blood were visible on his fingertips.

"Thanks kid," Brodie replied. Mia remained silent.

"How's the leg?"

"Not bad, stitches still in place."

"We need to get our stories straight," Alex started. "James and Sean. They both died in the meteoroid collision. I'll destroy the tapes from the last couple of hours and eject them. They won't be able to recover the shuttle if we direct it off Mars' orbital pull. They'll have to take our word. No one else needs to suffer for what happened today. Agreed?"

"Sounds good," Brodie grunted. "The deposit on this shuttle was the same price as my house. It's only money I guess."

"Justice has been done," Mia said without emotion. "There are only three days until we reach Mars. We better get some rest and conserve the air."

The days passed slower than the months, which had proceeded them. It was as if the shuttle had passed through a black hole and the matter of time had begun to flow backward. The remaining three crew members spoke solemnly. Alex had tried to clean the blood from the main cabin's floor, but a dark purple stain remained as a reminder of the previous day's events.

On the second day, the air became thinner. Alex and Mia agreed to wear the suits and switch to tank oxygen in a couple of hours. The suits were so heavy under the ship's gravity that they made simple tasks such as walking feel like a huge effort. The material of the suits was a shade of white so bright that they would've blended into the walls of the spaceship if it wasn't for the helmets. Brodie kept his off so that they could watch his wound for a little while longer. The antibiotics had finally taken control of his body, but he was immobile and spent most of the day in the sick bay.

Mia worked like a woman possessed. She had no choice, as she had taken on the roles James used to do, check certain systems, monitor the flight path and carry on with her own tasks all at once. In her breaks, she tended to Brodie. He was a cooperative patient who didn't like any fuss to be made over him. Alex read through Sean's notes. It would be up to him now to fix the communications down on Mars. If not, Earth would believe they had died in flight, or worse, that something on the colony had killed them. The Deimos Initiative could abandon the project and not send help after them.

They slept the final night in their suits, all crammed into the same room. Sleep proved impossible, as they were unable to lie down. They agreed to leave the comms lines open in case Brodie's conditioned worsened. It proved even harder to sleep with the sound of everyone's lumbered breaths that rebounded in their head pieces. Alex jolted awake in the middle of the night and slapped at his helmet after a case of claustrophobia. He focused on his breathing until his heart returned to its normal rhythm.

He moved over to check on Brodie. Through the visor, Brodie's face no longer had the tanned complexion. A blanket of paleness covered him. His eyes opened but he didn't recognise the face in front of him. "Water," his lips formed the word. Alex's hands, covered by the gloves of the suit, hurried to open the visor from Brodie's helmet. The locks hissed open and there was no longer resistance as the visor eased back. He placed it on the table and held a hydration pack to Brodie's lips. He sucked on it greedily, until it was half empty. Brodie pushed it away and said some words, almost inaudible. "Cold. Can't breathe."

Mia's voice come through on the comms, "is he OK?" She watched from the other side of the room, her voice masked in sleep.

"Yeah, he was thirsty," said Alex as he snapped Brodie's visor shut.

They could hear Brodie breathe in deeply. "That's better," he said. "It's getting harder to breathe outside the suit."

"We should go eat and relieve ourselves before the oxygen in the ship is depleted," Mia said. "Mars should be in range in a few hours."

The crew ate, used the bathroom facilities and changed Brodie's dressing for the final time. Alex's teeth clattered just doing these simple tasks. The once snug charcoal jumpsuit offered little protection against Albatross' new ice world atmosphere. He breathed in large gulps, but they didn't satisfy his lungs' hunger. When his space suit was secured, the oxygen flowed into his lungs, he gasped for the fresh air like a surfer who had just escaped a rip tide.

Mia had finished with the new bandage and threw the bloodied cloth into the sterile trashcan. "Can you help me with this?" Alex assisted Brodie to get him back into his spacesuit.

"Ah, I feel like a new man," Brodie forced a smile after his first breath.

"I'm going to check the supplies in the landing pod, Alex could you stay and watch Brodie?"

"I don't need a babysitter," he grunted.

"His wound is fine, let me come and help you."

Alex followed Mia down the hatch to the lower level. The landing pod lay dormant at the end of the walkway, its hatch open. Mountains of food and supplies were stacked in the seats that were not to be used. They had stocked the hatches to their limits over the previous days. Alex stepped into the storage room.

"Just garbage left," said Mia, her eyes scanned the room through her visor. She kicked some instant gravy across the room.

Alex rummaged through the boxes, which lay scattered across the floor. "Not all garbage," he said, shaking a half open box of space ice cream bars.

"Hand me one of those."

Alex and Mia sat next to each other on the empty fridges, their visors open. Alex bit into his bar, the mint texture crumbled in his mouth. His least favourite flavour, but he savoured its sweetness. He washed it down with a swig of one of the hydration packs attached to his suit. He managed to eat half of the bar before he struggled for breath. He closed the visor and turned on the oxygen.

"Are you afraid of dying?" Mia asked suddenly.

189

The question took Alex by surprise. The once optimistic woman who he had met back on Earth was now plagued with self-doubt. "Death has surrounded us since we were hit. I guess it's a subject I've thought about a lot recently. I think being afraid of death is a pointless exercise, which takes away from the present tasks at hand."

"I wish I could be as casual about it as you are. What do you think happens when we die?" Mia pressed him.

"Do you mean is there a heaven and a hell?"

"Yeah," she said.

"I think so. I think the human mind is an amazing thing. It's capable of feats that we don't even understand yet. It's possible that the mind could enter a state of heaven or hell when the body dies. Or create a heaven of its own."

"You didn't strike me as the religious type," she said. "Do you believe in God?"

"I was brought up as a Christian by my parents, though I never took it that seriously. I was always the kid who was sceptical of the world around him. It didn't take me long to work out that Santa Claus wasn't real. How could a man visit billions of households in a single night? I needed proof to believe. I never understood faith."

Mia's visor turned down towards the ground. Alex could tell her spirit was close to collapse.

"That said," Alex continued. "I don't rule out a creator of the universe. A superior being who created the rules and elements around us. Intelligent design if you will. If you study Physics, the codes and rules are everywhere. In DNA, in atomic structure. If there was a god, they are beyond our comprehension. If that's the case, death is a part of the system."

"Maybe a little faith is what we need right now," she said.

* * * * *

Mia leant over Alex and pulled on his restraints. He was secure in a seat in the landing pod. The pod was circular in design, with eight seats attached to the walls. Many tanks were planted in the ceiling, he was unsure of, which were for fuel and, which were for oxygen. Everything was orange apart from the glowing suits of the three passengers and the supply of food that was secured in the spare seats. Brodie was sat across from Alex, his face drained. He had had enough of space and his relief that they were heading to the surface of a planet was apparent, even if this meant being stranded.

A digital timer counted down from twenty-seven minutes from one of the nearby seats. The comms link between the landing pod and the Albatross was down, so Mia measured the time that they needed to deploy by the stopwatch on the clock. She carried out the final checks, before she strapped herself in and closed the hatch door from the console.

The hatch door fixed into place and the door to the Albatross closed behind. The ship contained near to no breathable air left. Its fate would be to float through the galaxy for the rest of its lifetime.

"Not long now," Mia sighed.

The three of them watched the countdown of the clock.

When two minutes remained, Mia sprang into action and put the controls into standby. "T-minus ninety seconds until deployment." Alex could hear the blaze of the engine as it fired into life. "Navigational systems online, selecting programmed atmosphere entry."

The minutes turned into seconds.

"All systems are good to go."

Ten seconds.

"We're good to launch."

The launch pad heaved out of the Albatross effortlessly and the boosters fired. The metal vehicle spun out of view and was replaced by the immeasurable glow of the red planet beneath them. The hues of orange and black mixed over the terrain. Huge country sized craters showed its erosion from the perpetual assault of the asteroids since its formation. A desolate world.

An hour passed as the pod descended towards the planet. Nobody dared to waste breath on words. Mia would only say code names for the checks she carried out, which meant little to Alex, but it comforted him all the same. Brodie complained about a shooting pain in his leg.

The landing pod rattled as it entered the planet's atmosphere. The boxes of food dislodged from the seats and scattered on the floor. One of the hatches slammed open and a couple of foot long, silver canisters flew by Alex's head, a near miss to his helmet.

"This is normal," shouted Mia above the racket. It was difficult to tell if this was to convince the crew or herself.

The speed of the pod increased and fire burst at the sides, the flames scratched at the windows like the claws of a monster. "This is normal?" Alex shouted back.

Mia battled with the controls to steady the descent. Her face glowed orange from the mixture of flames and a reflection of the cabin. Brodie wrinkled over in his seat, possibly passed out.

"Mia!"

A pipe burst in the cabin, a white smoke hissed out and launched a violent fog over the chaos.

"Mia!"

"We're coming in too fast! I need to deploy the parachute and landing thrusters now."

The groan of thrusters threw Alex up into his constraints, they tore at his skin beneath the suit. The pod tumbled sideways, the food boxes and canisters whirled around in the mist of capsule at disturbing speeds and crashed into walls with anger.

"Brace! Brace!"

These were the last words Alex heard before they crashed into the planet.

LEO

THIRTEEN

Leo had lost track of the amount of days that had passed since Tony died. Or sols, as the colonists called them. It might've even been weeks. He found it difficult to measure time, as the colony's calendar system wasn't perfect, and they used an Earth calendar month, without years, to measure Mars' orbit around the sun.

The count of missing colonists had risen to double digits. Rumours of a shadow creature had spread across the colony and the town lived in fear. The worst report he had heard was of a woman who had been pulled through the window of an office on the tenth floor. People were afraid to leave their apartments. No one showed up to their jobs. Some of the bravest residents worked twenty hour shifts to prevent the community from a collapse.

The security services worked on plans to deal with the monster. No guns were stored on the colony. Nobody who planned this colonisation had expected to come across a predator or extra-terrestrial animal who they would have to defend themselves against. One day, security had chased the creature through one of the southern buildings and cornered it in a bathroom. Two officers lost their lives that day.

Without Tony's voice of reason, Malcolm had taken control of the colony and had implemented martial law. The security services had gone on a mad recruitment drive and anyone who was able had joined the force. Most were motivated to defeat the monster and bring safety to the colony. Others had their own reasons. Food had become rationed and credits had lost their value. Colonists were allowed two basic meals a day, however the security services had access to the luxury items and forced the cooks to serve them hot dinners. Some of the officers just had a thirst of power and treated the other colonists as they pleased. Brutal attacks from the security force had become a daily occurrence.

What distressed Leo the most was that he hadn't seen Ariel in a while. He had only spoken to her a couple of times since that ill-fated trip to the shuttle terminal. The few times he had seen her, she acted cold and distant. Once his closest friend, now she felt like a stranger to him. Every day Leo would ask the others to check if she was still alive.

"What's wrong, pal?" Norman asked him. "You're totally spaced out."

Norman sat on a stool next to Leo at the Chambers bar. He wore his favourite green hoodie. Leo hunched over the bar top and examined the last few drops of beer in the bottle. The venue, which would usually be packed on Saturdays, now housed only a handful of Louisa's friends, filled up in one of the red booths behind them.

"I'm fine," said Leo.

"Are you still pining over Ariel?"

"I'm fine," Leo repeated.

Louisa came around the bar and opened the mini fridges below to get out a couple of beers. She slammed them on the counter in front of them.

"What are you two blabbering about?" she asked.

"I'm trying to cheer up this guy," Norman said. "It's not like it's the end of the world or anything."

"It's literally the end of the world," Louisa said as she threw her dark mane of hair over her shoulder. She picked up the bottles of drink and headed back to the booth of her friends.

"She's just exaggerating," Norman said.

"She's not. People are dying. And no one knows how to stop…that beast." Leo chugged down the last few drops of his beer.

"Yeah," Norman muttered as he stared down. "Katie, Adrian and Tom. All gone."

"You knew them?"

"I arrived on the same shuttle as Katie. We were quite friendly during the first few sols. She had this crazy laugh. Adrian and Tom were a couple who lived in Louisa's block. Loveliest guys you'd ever meet."

Louisa reappeared behind the bar. The mood was bleak in the bar and she took on the role of hostess rather than bar manager. "We'll be safe if we stick together."

"Yeah, we have the numbers," Norman agreed and perked up a bit.

"I've been close to this thing," said Leo. "It moves like nothing I've seen before."

"Some say it's an alien, some say it's a monster," said Louisa. "What do you think?"

"It looks too human to be one of those. Unless an alien could shape shift. It had four limbs, a normal sized head. But then…" Leo trailed off. "Its hands were more like claws. And it has these eyes. Eyes that glowed. I can still see them when I go to sleep."

"And it spoke!" Norman added.

"It spoke?!" Louisa exclaimed.

"I think it did."

"What did it say?"

"The numbers."

"The numbers? What could it mean…" Louisa folded her arms.

"I bet it's an alien," said Norman. "They have been studying us since we set up the colony. How we look, how we move, how we talk. They're fast learners. What if there are more of them? Out in the wild. What if they are living amongst us?"

"That's ridiculous," Louisa said.

"I wouldn't rule anything out at this point," Leo said.

"Do you think anyone is coming to save us?" asked Norman. "You know, from Earth?"

"They don't give a damn about us," Louisa snarled.

"The comms relay has been out the entire time I've been here. They should've sent someone by now."

"If it's the end of the world," said Louisa. "We can go out in style. If you two gents are game, let us drink through the rest of my supplies."

Louisa slammed three bottles of beer down on the counter and popped off the lids with her opener. "Cheers," she said as she raised a bottle into the air. Leo and Norman clinked their bottles against hers and they all took a chug.

Leo wiped his mouth and spotted two new people enter the bar. One was the tall man with the goatee. The other by his side was Ariel. Dark bags drooped under her eyes, as if she had forgotten to sleep. Her blonde hair had lost its sheen and her arms were wrapped across her chest dressed in a black fleece. They walked across the floor to the booths. Leo stuck out his arm in a half-hearted manner to stop her. "Everything OK?"

"Everything is great," Ariel sighed. "Don't worry about me." She brushed by his arm and slid into the booth with the goateed man.

Norman ran his hand up and down his arm. "I'm going to go say hi," he said, avoiding eye contact with Leo and Louisa. He slipped off the stool and scooted next to Ariel, who gave him a hug.

Louisa placed her hand on Leo's arm to grab his attention. "Don't worry about it."

"What the hell is her problem?" said Leo, with no expectation of an answer.

"You both went through a traumatic event. We have our own ways of dealing with things. Give her time."

"Do we still have time?"

"No one knows how much time they have left," Louisa said, as she played with the label on her bottle. "I've been on the colony for a long time now. We've had weird things happen before. Nothing as serious as this but…we'll get through it."

"How do you know?"

"If I don't believe that, I might as well give up."

"Whatever," he said.

"Leo, I've known you since you arrived on this planet. You walked into my bar with your sassy bravado. I think when you

198

were back home you always had this image to uphold but here you don't have to try so hard. The whole jock act is not attractive. Underneath, I see you're just like the rest of us. Confused, insecure and trying to keep it together. You don't have to try so hard to find your place. The Leo I know is kind and considerate. Being an arse is not a good look on you."

"You're not too bad yourself, Lou," he admitted. "Except when you shout at me."

"Only because you deserve it," she said. "And never call me Lou again."

"How about another drink?"

"Shots?"

"Shots!"

Louisa clanked two shot glasses onto the countertop. She deliberated over the liquor shelves before she decided on a bottle, which contained a green liquid. Leo couldn't decide if it looked like emerald water or toxic waste. She filled the shot glasses and handed one to him.

"Bottoms up," Louisa said.

Leo glanced back at the booth of the young colonists who drank and laughed. If anything bothered Ariel, she did her best to hide it as she laughed at a joke Norman told her. Leo knocked back the drink and his throat burst into flames.

"What's this?" he choked.

"Absinthe," Louisa said as she refilled the two glasses. "Don't be a baby."

"It's terrible."

"Again!"

They emptied the glasses and slammed them on the table in sync.

"You're right," she said. "It's bloody awful."

"So, I've a question for you. If you choose to indulge."

"Yeah, ask away." Louisa screwed the cap on the bottle and placed it back on the glass shelf amongst the collection of colourful labels of the spirit bottles. She leaned across the bar towards Leo, as if she sensed he wanted to tell her a secret.

"Is that guy with the goatee your boyfriend?"

"Oscar? Boyfriend is an odd term. He is one of a few people I'm seeing."

"Oh," Leo was lost for words and stared to the floor. He felt a flush in his cheeks.

"I don't believe in the whole exclusive thing. Marriage was a social construct created by old men who wanted to control women and our biology. I should be allowed to be with whoever I want. Jealousy is such a waste of energy. Why should something so delightful be only for two people? Why not three? Or five? The concept should've died off in the twentieth century."

Leo laughed, "I guess I'm a bit more old-fashioned. A strong partnership between two people. It feels right."

"Let me guess, you believe in soul mates."

"Maybe."

"What a sweet boy you are," she ruffled his hair.

A man and two smaller framed associates, dressed in maroon uniforms, stormed into the bar. Malcolm and his cronies. The young colonists in the booth fell silent. Louisa grimaced and folded her arms. Malcolm removed the baton from his belt. His belly spilt over the top. The baton tapped along the marble counter as his heavy boots approached Leo's spot on the stool.

"Well, well. What do we have here?"

"What do you want, Malcolm?" Louisa demanded.

"Nothing. I was walking by and thought to myself, why are those kids in there laughing and having such a good time, while the rest of us are out there risking our lives to keep this place safe?"

"It's less safe now," muttered Leo.

"What was that?" Malcolm's voice boomed around the small venue. "I didn't quite hear you."

"I said, it's less safe now. With your goons off their leashes."

Malcolm leaned back and shook his head. An unnatural laugh escaped his body like a demon beckoned from an exorcism. With a swoop of his bear arm, he swung his baton towards the bar counter, crashing into the empty bottles, which were left out. Glass shards flew everywhere, one grazed Leo's neck in its flight path. His two partners suppressed laughs as Malcolm smashed any glass he spotted. Someone from the booth cried out.

"Enough!" Louisa shouted, as she now stood in front of the giant of a man. Her head didn't even come close to his chin. "I want you out of my bar. Now."

Malcolm snorted in amusement as he stared down at her. Crack! The baton bounced off Louisa's face. She fell to floor and blood rushed from her nose. "Louisa!" Ariel cried out and dove to her aid. Leo rushed at the security guards. An explosion of pain seared from Leo's abdomen as one of the officers caught him in the gut with a baton. The others in the booth fell silent.

"Listen up!" Malcolm bellowed as Louisa whimpered from the floor. "You are either with us. Or you are against us. If you're against us, you're free to leave this town and try your luck in the desert. This is my town now. And you have to play by my rules."

The shortest of the three men twirled the baton in his hand, and smashed another bottle on a table, before they disappeared back out into the entertainment area.

Leo picked himself up from the floor as Ariel stood behind the bar, opened and slammed the doors of the fridges. The others had gathered around Louisa who stared expressionless towards the door. A streak of ruby marked down her face and blood dripped onto her white top. Ariel rushed back to Louisa's side. She wiped away the blood with a damp cloth. "I put some ice in a towel, keep it pressed against your nose to reduce the swelling."

"It looks broken," someone said.

"This is nuts," Norman said under his breath, as he pulled the hood over his head.

Shards of glass were speckled across the floor and the bar. The crowd of young people surrounded a dazed Louisa, who sat on the edge of the booth with her head held back. She might have a concussion. Leo tried to figure out how the scene had unfolded in only a few short minutes. The glass cracked under Ariel's feet as she fled the bar. He followed her outside into the entertainment centre. His gut burned with pain where the baton had struck him. All the other businesses had their doors shut. No other colonists roamed the halls.

"Ariel?"

"Leave me alone, Leo," she said.

202

"I just want to talk to you."

"About what?"

"To check that you're OK. I was concerned about you."

"I'm not going to kill myself, if that's what you're worried about."

"What? No! That's not what I'm saying. I wanted to know that you're safe."

"Well, here I am. All safe and sound."

Leo moved towards her. She kept her focus on the floor. Louisa's blood on her clothes. "We're all scared. But if we stick together…"

"Scared?" Ariel laughed. "I'm terrified!"

"Ariel, please." He put his hand on her shoulder. She recoiled from his touch as if it was a wasp. "I care about you," he continued.

"You care about me? You don't even know me, Leo! Get over it. It doesn't change anything. It doesn't fix anything. We're stranded here. No one is coming to save us. Do you hear me? No one. We're going to die here. One by one until there's nobody left. I don't want to be the last one left. Alone. With that thing. What was the point of us coming here? Why did they send us here?! Tell me!"

Leo threw his arms around her and held her tight. She resisted until her body lost hope and she let herself be swallowed by the embrace. "We're still here," he assured her. "And as long as we're breathing, we can survive this."

"I want to believe that," she said.

He wanted to believe it too. He didn't have answers for any of her questions. They were the same questions that he asked himself every day. No answers came. He hated this planet. The town. The other colonists. The secret council. The security officers. The redness. He hated it all. Ariel was different. He sensed she didn't belong to this world. Neither did he. If they stuck together, then maybe they could escape it. He held her until she spoke.

"It's too hard."

"We can't do this without you," Leo said.

"Yes, you can," she said. "Nobody needs me."

"I need you."

"Why?"

"Because you're my partner in crime."

The numbers.

Ariel pulled back to look at him. "Hey, don't be cute." She punched him in the arm. "Plus, it's my job to calm you down. You're always so erratic."

"I'm not erratic!"

"Only fifty percent of the time, I guess."

The numbers.

Their heads spun to a nearby door as it shut with a violent clatter. Sickly screams came from the bar, which made Leo's skin crawl. They raced towards the doors and looked through the glass.

The young colonists had scattered across the bar, they shouted and screamed. A lone figure stood at the centre of the room. He had no features and his body was dark, like a shadow. Long claws ran from his hands. They were buried into the chest of the goateed man. A person from behind threw a bottle at the creature. It shattered against its body. In one move, the monster leaped over the bar counter and impaled the young colonist's head with its free hand. Their body shattered against the glass counter, bottles spilled to the floor.

Louisa and Norman's faces appeared in the window and frantically pulled on the doors. The lights flickered off.

"Open the door!" Norman screamed.

"I'm trying!" Leo shouted back as he and Ariel pulled and pushed the handles. They wouldn't budge. Leo nudged Ariel out of the way and began to kick the doors with the base of his shoe.

"Hurry!" Louisa begged, her face stained with blood.

The paint chipped away but the door would not budge. More screams came from inside.

"Leo, help me with this," shouted Ariel, grabbing the back of a flat metal bench located on the walkway. Leo ran to her and they heaved it into the air. The bench was heavy, and Leo's grip tightened. They heaved it towards the locked doors as fast as they could move.

With great force, the bench smashed against the entrance, but the door held strong and a shockwave vibrated through Leo's arms. The bench clattered to the ground.

Leo looked up and no longer saw Norman. Louisa pounded on the glass, she whimpered. "Leo, please. Help me." Her face slammed against the glass as her body jerked back into the dark. Silence seeped in as the bar remained still.

Louisa's blood dripped down the window.

* * * * *

Ariel. Leo couldn't find her. The pair had separated when they fled the entertainment centre. He stood out in the main street and panted for breath. A group of maroon shirts stormed into the centre as he left. "Reports of the monster inside, let's move people."

He had to find her.

Leo walked past the town's library. Mostly a place used for colonists to bring their holophones to download any book written from recorded history, for a small price. There was a limited collection of paperbacks, which were stored in the shelves, but most people ignored these. The older residents would be seen at a library table at any time of day with a book in hand. Leo didn't understand how they could stare at pieces of paper for so long. Ariel worked in the library four days a week, but he rarely visited her. It might be a place for a refuge after the attack.

The automatic doors of the red brick building didn't open when he approached. Leo peered through the glass to view the inactivity of the interior. Quiet as a school during summer break.

The next obvious place would be to check her apartment. Leo had never been inside Ariel's block, let alone her room. He wished to himself that they could have spent a night in the privacy of one of their homes, without the madness. Would the colony ever be the same again? He had to cling on to the tiny hope that the two of them could escape and one day have normal lives.

He buzzed her apartment number near the doors. No answer. He typed her number in again and held his finger against the bell button. Nothing. He tried a couple of her neighbours' numbers, it might be possible that one would let him in.

"Who's there?" a voice crackled on the intercom.

"Uh, my name is Leo, I was wondering if you could let me in, I want…"

"Go away!" the voice yelled, followed by the click of the phone.

It was probably a sign that Leo should give up his search and seek safety in his own apartment. To find a single person in this town would take an army of sniffer dogs.

There was just one last place she could be.

Leo ensured that nobody saw him move between the buildings that faced the construction site. He followed the mesh fence with the cover, which separated the town from the new structures under development. It took a while, but he eventually found the spot that Ariel had brought him to that night so long ago. The amber sign acted as a beacon to reveal the secret entrance. Leo pushed away the loose piece of the fence and climbed through. The building site appeared less sinister in the glow of the afternoon, but it didn't make him feel any less anxious. He retraced his path and found the place that he and Ariel had explored.

In a half jog, he ran across the dusty bottom floor of the office block until he reached the bare cement stairs. He sped up and took the stairs two at a time. Perspiration dampened the armpits of the t-shirt; the heat prickled his skin. He banged his knee as his foot caught the lip of a step and he skidded against the landing. The light had diminished, but there was an abundance from the top storey. Maybe she had left the door open. He moved cautiously, until he burst out onto the rooftop.

"Ariel?"

The rooftop was empty. The visibility of the Martian town was clear in the light. Defeated, Leo strolled to the side and rested against the wall. A few windows of the residential blocks could be seen in the distance. The colonists sat despondent in their rooms. Some of the doors had been barricaded with loose furniture. He pondered if she was safe.

The stars were hidden in the orange glow of the sky. A scene different to the one where he first learnt of Ariel's life. An intimacy shared by two people thrown together in one of life's chaotic moments. He remembered what Ariel had told him that night.

The universe has no great plan for us. Life is just chaos. Uncontrollable chaos.

Maybe she was right. Why fight against the universe when it has made up its mind? People would be happier if they didn't resist and went with the flow, accepting the injustices and cruelty it threw at them. One couldn't control fate.

"I'm here!" Leo shouted into the abyss of the dome. "Just take me!"

The universe didn't respond.

He couldn't save them. Tony. Norman. Louisa. All killed by the monster. The last person he cared about was missing. Maybe she was gone too. Would life have any purpose after that? Maybe it was his fault they were gone. His selfishness. No way back.

Leo stepped up onto the ledge. The air was cool and calm around him. The end of his shoes crept past the edge. Beyond that, a drop to the streets lined with the construction vehicles. A drop that would kill him.

There were worse ways to go.

No more living in fear. Hunted. Trapped. Abandoned.

Leo swayed on his perch. Waited for the universe to make the call. Nothing. He jumped back onto the rooftop. No. He couldn't give up yet. Ariel was still alive. He knew it in his heart. When he was with her, everything made sense. Together they would escape.

His pocket vibrated. The holophone. Ariel!

Leo dug into his pocket and pulled out the phone. On the screen, it said he had one new unread message. His hands trembled as he opened it.

TO: LEO 1702
FROM: UNKNOWN 0000000000
LEO ARE YOU THERE? PLEASE RESPOND ASAP. I NEED YOUR HELP. IF WE DON'T ACT SOON, EVERYONE IN COLONY C WILL DIE.

"What the hell?" Leo said out loud. Who had sent him the message? Was it Ariel on a new holophone? Was it Jade? Or possibly one of the security forces, but why would they need his help? He needed to respond straight away.

TO: UNKNOWN 0000000000
FROM: LEO 1702
WHO IS THIS? WHAT DO YOU MEAN EVERYONE WILL DIE?

Leo lay the holophone on the red brick ledge and tapped his fingers as he waited for a response. Maybe the person didn't watch their phone. Yet there was an urgency in their tone. They must have seen his reply. Maybe the signal was bad on this side of town. His mind drifted through the different possibilities before the daydream was interrupted by the harsh vibrate of the phone against the stone.

He opened the message.

TO: LEO 1702
FROM: UNKNOWN 0000000000
IT'S ALEX. YOU'RE NOT GOING TO BELIEVE WHAT I'M ABOUT TO TELL YOU.

ALEX

FOURTEEN

Christmas songs blared from the modest sized television. The screen cast a cobalt light across the small house. The edges of a worn, L shaped sofa with a coffee table were visible during the brightest parts of the music videos. A kitchen was off to one side in its own enclave. Alex sat at his desk and rubbed his face to force his brain to kick up a notch. He basked in the glow of the three monitors, which were jammed with lines of code.

It was only the start of December, why were they already playing Christmas songs? He stretched back in his customised desk chair, the lumbar support pressed into the back of his woolly jumper. He walked over to the couch and threw the pillows around to find the remote control. He found it nestled down the side of the cushion. He brushed off the crumbs and switched off the television. Rain pelted against the window, the noise no longer masked by festive jingles. A serious storm threatened as the droplets increased in ferocity. A strike of lightning lit up the outline of a bonsai tree that perched on the window sill.

The monitors produced enough light for Alex to navigate to the kitchen. He opened the fridge and squinted from the brightness of its interior. It was bare, as usual. A few packets of readymade meals and a carton of milk. Two packets of energy drinks rested on the top shelf. He ripped the packaging of one and pulled out a can. The aluminium snapped as he pulled the tab back and took a sip. The sweetness of the liquid rushed across his tongue. He hoped it would give him the energy to finish his project.

Alex flicked on the light switch to brighten up his home. The days had shortened considerably. It didn't bother Alex, as he preferred the artificial environment of being inside. This gave him an excuse to continue his hermit lifestyle without having to feel guilty. He admired the acoustic guitar, which was propped up against his desk and his collection of books. He ran his fingers along the spines of his book collection as he made his way back to desk. An assortment of scientific non-fiction, classical fiction and an array of comic books. An enormous amount of pride went into the collection. He hadn't read as much as he would have liked, due to his commitments at work. The new year was around the corner, so he made a resolution to himself to read more books. At least one a week.

A boom of thunder clapped in the distance. The storm had picked up pace.

Alex sat down at his desk and placed the energy drink on a coaster. He studied the code on his screens. A mistake was hidden in the lines and he had spent the whole day trying to figure out what had caused the bug.

In the office, he would snap at his colleagues who spoke to him. Couldn't they see he was busy? In the evening, he would take his work home with him. He worked until he was tired. Other people had hobbies, but he believed when you love your work you didn't need such distractions. His computer sat on a secure VPN, the Deimos Initiative had it set up once they saw how dedicated he was to his craft.

Tonight, was like no other.

Three loud booms made Alex jump in his seat. No, it wasn't thunder. It came from the front door. He checked the time. After eight o'clock. Who would have the nerve to bother him at this time of night? In this storm? Especially when he was busy. The knocks persisted with an urgency.

Alex left his seat and peered through the door's peephole, before he proceeded to unfasten the locks. He opened the door. A gust of cold air rushed past him. The street was covered in a bleakness, as water rushed down the hill. Heavy rain assaulted the cars parked on the roadside, and bushes gave the impression of monsters that hid at the side of the road.

Two figures stood on the steps. A boy and girl, both in their earlier twenties. Their faces masked by the hoods of their coats, that continued to be pelted by the rain. They both wore mischievous grins, as if they were trick or treaters on the verge of a prank. The girl carried a couple of pizza boxes, unable to protect them from the harness of the night.

"Alex, let us in! We're getting soaked," laughed the boy.

Alex backed away to let the pair enter his home. They stepped onto a towel, which he had laid down earlier for his wet clothes to drip on, dampened by his cycle home from work. Water fell from their coats as they balanced to stay away from the wooden floors.

"We bought these to share," the girl said, handing Alex the boxes of pizza. The cardboard felt damp in his hand. He walked across the room, placed the boxes on the tiny table in the kitchen, and returned to find out what was the purpose of their visit.

The boy had hung up his coat and kicked off his shoes, which were trimmed with blades of wet grass. He wore jeans and a blue crew top, his lean frame was defined and well maintained. A cheeky grin sat on a face with high cheekbones, his eyes matched the colour of his top. The smile firmly associated with the boisterousness of youth. The boy ran his fingers through his dark brown locks as he checked his reflection in the mirror near the coats. He turned and saw Alex.

"Alex, it's been too long."

"It's good to see you, Leo."

Leo walked across the living room and hugged him. Alex patted him on the back, unsure of what to say.

"You've met my big brother before, haven't you?" Leo asked the girl as he shook Alex by his shoulders.

She unzipped her boots and they clumped onto the towel. The girl looked up and smiled. Her face unsymmetrical, with a dimple on only one side of her face. Golden blonde hair fell over her shoulders, ears too large for her head popped out from the sides. Her eyes were light, a greyish colour, with a kindness to them. A black and grey jumper covered her pale skin.

"Yes, we've met a few times before."

"How have you been Ariel?" asked Alex.

"I've been good," she said as she kissed him on the cheek. "I haven't seen you in ages. My sister still talks about you, you know. How you're becoming a hotshot at work."

Rae. Ariel had moved in with her sister when she moved down to Los Angeles to start university. Alex had dated Rae in his first year at the Deimos Initiative. They started on the same graduate intake and hit it off straight away. His feelings for her rushed back from the deep abyss inside of himself where he kept such emotions. The only woman he had ever loved. They were happy together and were inseparable. Yet Alex moved up quickly in the company and made a name for himself. Rae was reassigned to a department that was, in Alex's opinion, not as important as his own. Work became the priority in Alex's life and his relationship with Rae took a back seat. It took a few months for the relationship to die a slow death.

"Yeah work is crazy right now," said Alex. "Speaking of which, this is probably not the best time to hang out."

"What's this secret project you're working on?" asked Leo, as he stuffed a slice of pizza into his mouth. The aroma of steamed cheese and meat floated into the living area from the opened pizza box. Leo sat down next to Ariel, who ran her hands down her legs in an attempt to warm them up. "Does it have anything to do with that new colony on Mars?"

"I really can't say," Alex hesitated. He sat down on the opposite side of the L shaped couch.

"That'd be so awesome if it did," Leo said. "People living on Mars. It blows my mind."

"It doesn't take much," said Ariel.

"Hey, I'm smart," protested Leo. "I keep up to date with current affairs."

"The MLB Network is not a reliable source of world news," she teased him.

"Pah!" exclaimed Leo as he headed back to the table for a second slice of pizza.

"What have you been up to, Alex?" asked Ariel.

Alex shifted uncomfortably on his spot on the sofa as his eyes darted to the clock on the wall. "Not much really. They transferred me to a new team last year and I've been working as a software analyst. Some interesting tech."

"I think she means in your personal life, bro," said Leo as he sat back down. "What's the story? You're always hiding yourself away."

"Not much really." Alex tried to take the attention away from him. "How do you guys know each other?"

"Well, she's my girlfriend," Leo said with a smile so big that it would've put the Cheshire cat to shame.

"We've been dating for about five months," she said. "I can't seem to shake him."

"All lies. She can't stay away. Rae actually introduced us. A very funny story. So, I was at the…"

"Leo! I'm sure your brother doesn't want to be bored by your exaggerated tales."

"She's embarrassed, but it's a great story. I'm at the pizzeria near the stadium with my boys. We're celebrating our latest win and there are these two women on a table near us and…"

"Leo please!" She laughed as she tried to cover his mouth.

Leo dodged her attempts to silence him. "It was Ariel and Rae! They had been at the game and Ariel was telling her sister that she had the biggest crush on the second baseman..." His voiced became muffled underneath her hand.

"That's not what happened at all," Ariel said.

"I don't have time for these stupid stories!" Alex shouted.

The pair fell silent. Leo's face dropped. Ariel looked to the floor sheepishly. The rain tapped against the windowpanes. They remained quiet.

"Look, I'm so busy right now," Alex explained. "I have so much work to do and you're both distracting me. Not that I wouldn't love to hear about your annoying anecdotes of how you met or went on dates or whatever nonsense you're babbling about. But I really have to ask you to leave."

"But it's a Friday night and…"

"I don't care," Alex said as he stood up. "Could you please leave? Now."

Unsure of themselves, the couple stood up. Ariel shuffled towards the door to gather her belongings while Leo stood frozen.

"Listen here," Leo raised his voice. "We came all the way out here to see you. Rae told us how overworked you are. How stressed you are. We thought we'd treat you to some food. You could use it. It looks like you haven't been eating at all." Ariel touched his arm to calm him down. This was probably not the first time she had witnessed Leo lose his temper. He didn't seem to notice her as he continued. "I thought it could be fun. Like the old days. Do you remember when we were kids? We did everything together. Now you're like a stranger to me. Why are you shutting us out? I'm trying to swallow my pride and reach out here. And this is the treatment I get? Astonishing. Simply astonishing." Leo moved closer to Alex's face. "You're a real piece of work. You know that, right?"

"C'mon. Let's go," said Ariel.

"A real piece of work."

The pair put on their shoes and grabbed their wet coats from the hooks. Alex unlocked the door and opened it to allow them to leave as fast as possible. His face expressionless. Ariel put hers on with care, while Leo threw on his, droplets splattered against the wooden floor.

"Goodnight," Ariel said as she walked past Alex towards the open door. The rain poured fiercer than before and she pulled the hood tightly around her head. Leo followed closely behind her.

"Wait for me in the car," Leo said as he handed her the car keys. "I'll only be a minute."

"Please, let's just go."

"I'll only be a minute."

Ariel squeezed his hand and disappeared through the rain towards the car at the far side of the road, its colour obscured by the weather. Leo closed the door. "I can't believe you sometimes."

"How long is this going to take?" Alex sighed.

"Not long. All I want is an apology. And for you to apologise to Ariel the next time you see her."

"For what? I don't have time for your games."

"You know what," said Leo, his teeth clenched. "You were an asshole. I wanted you to hang out with Ariel tonight. For us to have some food and for you to get to know her. She's important to me."

"First of all, I've already met Ariel. She's a nice girl. Probably too nice for you. Secondly, I can't keep track of the girls you're with. If a girl smiles at you, you're all over her. That's until the next one comes along. You'll be bored of her soon. Do her a favour and let her go."

"Screw you!"

"Don't act like you're some saint in front of me, Leonardo."

"She is coming to Christmas lunch at dad's house. If you're going to be there, I expect you to be nice to her."

"I didn't know that was still happening. I'll have to see how my workload is."

"Alex, it's on Christmas day," Leo said in exasperation. "That place has changed you. When is the last time you called dad?"

"Open your eyes. The work I'm doing. The sacrifices I've made. You're such an idiot, I can't even explain it to you. This work is more important than you. Or me. Or some stupid lunch with some stupid girl. It's going to change the world."

"I might not be as smart as you are Alex, but I care about people. My friends. My family. Ariel. That's what is important to me. Not some pointless code on a screen. I've been on the college team for two years now. How many games have you been to? None. You didn't even come to the finals last year. I wanted you there, man! But you told me you were too busy. Too busy! You used to be so kind and considerate. You were my hero. Now, you're nothing to me. Your obsession with your work has ruined the person that you were. That's why you have no life. That's why Rae left you."

Alex slapped Leo across the face.

"Wake up," Alex said, his voice void of emotion. "Mister professional baseball star of the future. Mister perfect. You believe the world revolves around you. All you've done with your life is coast by. You were born with these gifts and you never took advantage of them. When we were kids you were far smarter than me. You threw it away to go to parties and appear cool in front of losers. You could've achieved so much.

219

That's why I have no time for you. You're a loser now too. Your life is a wasted one."

Thunder boomed in the distance.

"You might think it's a waste. But I'm not afraid to do what's right in my heart. I tell people that I care about them. That's more than you could ever do, with all your high-tech gadgets and plans to save the world."

"Get out," Alex's words came out laced with venom. "Go and play with your stupid girlfriend. And enjoy your Christmas meal. Nothing would make me happier than if I never saw you again."

Leo marched across the room, his wet shoes squelched against the floorboards. He picked up the guitar that leaned against the desk. Leo had bought the guitar for Alex as a present a few years ago. Leo measured the weight in his hands, like he did so many times at the baseball plate. He put his weight through the swing.

SMASH. The screen of one of the monitors hissed as the screen shattered. The guitar resonated on the floor.

"Something to remember me by," Leo said, as he opened the door and disappeared into the storm.

Alex slammed the door behind him. The bookcases shook. He examined the mess of his home and let out a heavy sigh.

The guitar appeared to be undamaged, only a few scratches on the side. He leaned it against the desk and moved to the kitchen to retrieve a brush and dust pan from the cupboard under the sink. The pizza boxes, which they had left, remained on the table. The boxes damp and open. He swept the shattered glass from the desk and floor. He would need to hoover the whole room tomorrow to be sure that there were no renegade pieces. He unplugged the monitor and left it next to the front door.

The monitors needed to be configured to appear on two screens. The new operating system made it more difficult than it should have been, but he configured it to look as acceptable as possible. How much time had he lost? What a child his brother was. He would have to stay up even later now to get this finished.

He picked up his drink and sipped it. The scene replayed in his mind. He slammed the can down, the drink splashed across the desk.

* * * * *

An hour passed before Alex booted down his computer. He couldn't concentrate on the harshness of the monitor screens. He picked out a glass from the cupboard and filled it with filtered water. He popped two aspirins into his mouth and washed them back. The storm still raged across the city. He turned off the lights and retired to his bedroom.

After he relieved himself in the bathroom, he put on his pyjamas and slipped into bed. It had been a while since he had changed the sheets. Alex made a mental note to change them the next day. He set the alarm for seven o'clock in the morning. He would have a quick breakfast and then pick up where he had left off. There would be hell to pay if he couldn't get this code to work by Monday. The rain continued its onslaught. He listened to the patter against the window and tried to drift off, but sleep would not come. Adrenaline still pumped through him. From the caffeine or the argument. Probably a mixture of both.

Alex's mind raced. From work to old friends to the last bad movie he watched. He thought of the guitar, with its new scuffs and scratches. It was the only one he had ever owned. When he was a boy, he obsessed over rock bands. He had begged his parents for an electric guitar for his birthday. He never had much luck with girls at school, but if he became a musician, he had thought maybe they would notice him. He scoffed at the notion now. His mother, who was alive at the time, said she would have to think about it. The day finally arrived, he woke up excited and rushed downstairs for breakfast. There was no guitar. He received a few items of clothing; some books and his dad had booked him a tutor. "What are you going to do with a guitar? With a tutor you can start prepping to get into a top university." Alex was crushed. The next day, he found an acoustic guitar outside his bedroom door. Leo had bought it for him, even though he had already given him a birthday present. The kid only had a part-time job mowing lawns in the neighbourhood. It must have cost him all the money he had made over the summer. He confronted Leo about it, asked why he spent that money on him. Leo just shrugged and simply said it wasn't fair that he had a bike for his birthday, the thing he always wanted, and Alex couldn't have what he wanted.

Alex regretted his actions that evening. Maybe Leo was right. What was the point of improving humankind when he couldn't even show compassion to the people who cared about him? He needed to apologise to his brother. And to Ariel. She was a sweet kid. Sensible and clever too. He would make it up to them. There was always tomorrow.

The phone alarm rang out. Alex groaned and rolled away from the noise. It was too early, and it felt like he had gotten no sleep. The rings from the phone persisted. It wasn't his alarm, it was a call. He rolled through the tangle of sheets, which felt more like mud that weighed him down. The rain had stopped overnight. He picked up the phone and pressed the green accept button.

"Hello?" said Alex as he shook the vice of sleep from his mind.

"Alex," the voice weak and distant.

"Who is this?"

A long pause before the caller spoke again. "I'm at the hospital. You need to get down here right now." A woman's voice. It trembled on the other side of the receiver. Someone he knew.

Alex sat up in the bed, alert. "Rae is that you? The hospital? What are you talking about?"

"There was an accident. They called me, and I rushed over. A car crash they said." Alex became numb, unable to speak. Rae continued to talk as she choked back tears. "They said a car drove right into the side of them. Ariel…she didn't make it. She was…by the time they…"

"Rae, what happened to Leo?"

Alex could hear Rae sob at the end of the line. A worthless, desperate cry when hope is lost.

"Please tell me."

"Leo's gone. He's dead."

LEO

FIFTEEN

Leo stared out across the town of the colony. The dome that covered them from the harshness of Mars' atmosphere. Hundreds of colonists who inhabited the community. Unaware of the truth. They were all dead.

He reread Alex's message two more times. It didn't make sense. It couldn't make sense. He and Ariel had died in a car crash. A drunk driver crashed into them on a stormy night last year. Alex and Rae worked for the Deimos Initiative, the company responsible for the colony. The colony was never intended to resettle people who were alive and breathing. It was a base for a computer simulation that stored digital copies of the deceased.

Leo wasn't sure which part was the easiest to believe. That he knew Ariel before he arrived at the colony. That they were together back on Earth. That they died and now were somehow uploaded into a virtual world. Or that he remembered none of it. How could he believe any of these messages?

It was too much to take in. Leo's head raced, and his heart pounded. Lies. All of it. He should just ignore the messages on his holophone and throw it off the side of the building. It was a sick joke someone played on him. But who? The messages mentioned information only he and his brother knew. Alex was never one to pull pranks.

Leo took a deep breath and sent a reply to his brother to ask him more questions.

The response was immediate.

Alex explained that when the Deimos Initiative inserted new people into the colony, the previous six months are wiped from the subject's memory. It's replaced with an artificial story where the individual is told that they have been selected to be one of the first human colonists to settle on Mars. Fictional memories of training for space travel, life on the colony and a farewell party are included. It was to act as a buffer for their mind to accept the new world around them and to remove any clues that hinted at their death. Leo and Ariel's memories were erased, but neither Alex or Rae had access to the false selection memory. Alex told him that when he and Ariel died, he and Rae knew what needed to be done. They snuck equipment into the hospital and copied Leo and Ariel's consciousnesses from their lifeless bodies, ready for the next shipment of souls to be sent to Mars.

There were huge risks involved, explained Alex. They were aware of the consequences if they were caught. The Deimos Initiative had professionals to deal with people who leaked secrets from the company. Or broke the rules. You needed a lot of money to get a spot in Colony C. Or you had to be a remarkable person.

Leo wasn't a remarkable person. He didn't deserve to be there.

He sent another message to his brother.

TO: UNKNOWN 0000000000
FROM: LEO 1702
OK, I STILL HAVE A LOT OF QUESTIONS. NOT SURE IF
I BELIEVE YOU YET.
IF THIS IS A VIRTUAL WORLD WHY IS IT SET ON THIS
PLANET AND WHY IS THE ACTUAL HARDWARE
STORED ON MARS FOR YOU TO TRAVEL ALL THIS
WAY TO MAINTAIN IT? WHY NOT SOMEWHERE ON
EARTH?
PS WHAT WAS THE NAME OF THE BADDIE IN THE
GAME WE PLAYED IN THE WOODS WHEN WE WERE
KIDS?

The reply came through. Leo almost dropped the phone. On a day of surprises, it had gotten even worse. Artificial intelligence.

In the message, Alex had said the original two colonies were based on Earth. The first one died out. The code couldn't handle a colony of a hundred digital human beings. The workings of memories, desires, reflections and ambitions were too complex for a synthetic environment created by the mind of a person. The hundred colonists died when the system collapsed on itself. The company tried again. This time, it set the bar higher and strived to produce something many said was impossible. Sentient artificial intelligence.

The AI could handle jobs of the system faster than any manufactured code from the human programmers. It could adapt to any serious bugs in the colony before it could do any damage. The first AI was a disaster. It evolved beyond the world that it was created for. It slaughtered everyone in Colony

B, just to test its own power. The news was leaked. There was global outrage. Leo had remembered that in the news a few years ago. The United Nations issued a ban on the creation of sentient artificial life in the A.I. Accords.

The company filed for bankruptcy and dissolved. Alex revealed that a few of the senior members formed a new company called the Deimos Initiative. It posed as a new space exploration business and attracted major investment from wealthy backers. They were promised the creation of the first human colony. And they succeeded, in a way.

They had learnt from their mistakes and instead of a single god AI, the programmers created fifty AIs to control the new world. Each given a unique power, where they could only control one part of the colony. One for water. One for food. One for clothing. One for the electricity. And so on. To limit their power, the AIs were created in the form of humans. AIs had lived amongst the colonists since the beginning.

Mars was the perfect setting. It was outside the jurisdiction of the United Nations, whose reach only extended to the colony on the moon. The Deimos Initiative could operate without retribution, once the AIs had left Earth. Mars was also ideal for a virtual world. No one could leave the safe space of the dome to explore the finite universe they lived in. A giant barren world waited for them outside of the dome, with no way off.

Alex's biggest concern wasn't the fear that they would trace the insertion of Leo and Ariel into the colony, but what would happen to the system. During the testing phase, the calculations pointed out that the fifty AIs could only support a population of 1700 residents. The final shipment to Mars would push it to the quota and the team were busy with upgrades to extend the capacity nearer to 5000.

The arrival of Leo and Ariel had pushed the system beyond its capability.

TO: UNKNOWN 0000000000
FROM: LEO 1702
WHAT THE HELL ALEX?!?! THERE IS AI IN THIS PLACE? WHAT WERE YOU THINKING?! WE ALL WERE TAUGHT HOW DANGEROUS IT CAN BE! WHO ARE THEY??

Alex sent a quick reply. With an attachment of names. Human names. The names of the human personas of AI. Leo recognised two names on the list. Jade and Steven Nesbitt.

TO: LEO 1702
FROM: UNKNOWN 0000000000
I'VE ATTACHED A LIST OF THE AI IN THE SYSTEM. THE ONE YOU NEED TO WORRY ABOUT IS STEVEN NESBITT. WHEN THE POPULATION JUMPED TO 1702, NESBITT BROKE THROUGH HIS HUMAN PROTOCOLS. HE HAS GONE ROGUE.
FROM THE STATS REPORT ON THE BASE I CAN SEE HE WIPED OUT THE COMMS WITH DEIMOS BACK ON EARTH. WHAT I AM CONCERNED ABOUT IS THAT THE POPULATION HAS DROPPED BELOW 1650 AND THE NUMBERS HAVE FALLEN AGAIN SINCE I STARTED TO MESSAGE YOU. HE IS KILLING THE COLONISTS LIKE THE AI IN COLONY B DID.

YOU NEED TO STOP HIM.

Steven Nesbitt was the creature. He had to be. If what Alex said was true, he was hunting the colonists down. One by one.

TO: UNKNOWN 0000000000
FROM: LEO 1702
I CAN'T DO THIS. IT'S TOO MUCH. I'M A NOBODY. I CAN'T DO IT.

TO: LEO 1702
FROM: UNKNOWN 0000000000
I KNOW THIS IS A LOT RIGHT NOW. BUT I BELIEVE IN YOU. YOU ARE THE STRONGEST AND MOST ABLE PERSON I KNOW. I WOULDN'T TRUST ANYONE OTHER THAN YOU.
LISTEN WE DON'T HAVE MUCH TIME. YOU'RE IN DANGER. YOU AND EVERYONE IN THE COLONY. NESBITT HAS BROKEN THROUGH HIS CONSTRAINTS AND IS BEGINNING TO LEARN THE TRUE CAPABILITIES OF HIS POWER. SOON HE WILL HAVE THE POWER OF A GOD IN YOUR WORLD.
YOU NEED TO SHUT HIM DOWN. I CAN'T DO IT FROM HERE. HE HAS DISABLED THE CONSOLE'S ABILITY TO EDIT THE COLONY FROM THE OUTSIDE WORLD. YOU NEED TO GO TO THE RELAY SUBSTATION AND FOLLOW THE STEPS ON THE ATTACHMENT I'VE SENT YOU. ONCE IT HAS BEEN ENABLED, I WILL REMOVE HIM FROM THE SYSTEM.

TO: UNKNOWN 0000000000
FROM: LEO 1702
WAIT. IS ARIEL STILL ALIVE? HE ATTACKED US
EARLIER AND WE BECAME SEPARATED. SOME OF
MY FRIENDS DIED.

TO: LEO 1702
FROM: UNKNOWN 0000000000
YES, SHE IS ALIVE. THE STATUS FOR 1701 IS STILL
GOOD. I'M SORRY TO HEAR ABOUT YOUR FRIENDS.
THAT'S ON ME.
I HAVE TO GO, THERE IS SOMETHING THAT
URGENTLY NEEDS MY ATTENTION ON THIS SIDE.
ONCE YOU ENABLE THE COMMS LINK, I'LL KNOW.
IF ARIEL EVER REMEMBERS WHAT HAPPENED TO
HER THAT NIGHT, TELL HER I'M SORRY AND THAT
HER SISTER MISSES HER EVERYDAY.
GOOD LUCK LEO. I'M SO PROUD TO HAVE A
BROTHER LIKE YOU. I LOVE YOU.
PS THE NAME OF THE BADDIE IN THE GAME WE
PLAYED AS KIDS WAS CALLED MISTER CREEPER.

Alex was gone. A sick realisation swept across Leo. He
would never see his brother again. He would never see his
father again. Or his friends. Or graduate from university. Or
travel across Europe. Or party in Las Vegas. Or swim in the
ocean. Or watch the 49ers play. Or play baseball. His dreams
of becoming a professional baseball player had officially died.
The MLB didn't draft dead people.
    Leo was dead.

The barcode tattoo on his wrist near the holophone he held. The symbol of his imprisonment in this virtual hell.

He screamed from the rooftop, across the colony. He screamed until he saw red. He screamed until he could scream no more.

Leo slumped into a heap against the wall of the rooftop. He had no will to go on. Why bother? Anything he did had no meaning. No impact on the universe. Was that the point of existence? To make a difference. He thought about Ariel. Through no fault of her own, she had ended up here. A drunk driver had jumped a red light and crashed into them. He had been driving. Alex had thrown them back out into a night with horrible road conditions. A series of events, which had led to her death. Leo thought of all the young men and women who lived on the colony. Young people whose lives had been cut short. No. They had a second shot.

Leo could save them. Leo could save Ariel.

He opened the attachments that Alex had sent him. The instructions were short and concise, so he did his best to copy them to memory in case something would happen to his phone. The sun had proceeded to set behind the mountains in the west. Leo had no time to contemplate if anything existed beyond those mountains. He needed to get into the sub level of the relay station. There was only one person who could help him.

* * * * *

Leo pounded on the door. "I know you're in there."

"Excuse me sir," said the short bellhop. "You can't be up here."

231

Leo ignored him and continued to slam his palm on the metal cover. The door hissed open. A woman dressed in pink chinos and a white blouse stood at the entrance. Her hair braided above her head. He stormed past her. "Leo, what do you think you are doing?"

"I'm sorry Jade," said the short bellhop. "I tried to stop him in the lobby, but he ran past me."

"I know what you are," said Leo as he studied her apartment. "What Steven Nesbitt is."

Jade's expression changed. A figure, which always radiated confidence now looked lost. She didn't know how to respond. She turned to the bellhop. "Leave us."

"But Jade I…"

She raised her hand to indicate that his services were no longer needed. He backed out of the room like a child who had been scolded. Jade closed the door and faced Leo. He walked around the apartment, his eyes darted around trying to uncover something he might've missed on his previous visits. A couple of chrome suitcases waited near the door.

"How have you been, Leo?"

"You can drop the act," he said. He pointed to the bags. "Planning a trip?"

"If you have something to say, just say it."

"Two words. Artificial intelligence," his fists were clenched.

Jade said nothing for a while. She collapsed on the white sofa, her eyes lowered. "How did you find out?" Her words barely audible.

"It doesn't matter. I know this world exists in a digital space. I died in the real world. My memories were uploaded into this system. I know you're an AI. Everyone on the council is an AI. You're here to keep us humans in check. To make sure that we know our place. Because this is your world, isn't it? And Steven Nesbitt. He is an AI too. He's the creature that's killing everyone. Please tell me if I'm wrong."

"You are right. Apart from the world belonging to us. This world is just as much yours as it is mine."

"How long have you known? About Steven Nesbitt that is."

"The council have known for a while. We tried to stop him. I have lost people. People close to me. He has changed. He has turned into something else. He is too powerful."

"Lost people close to you," Leo chuckled at the idea. He continued to pace around her apartment. Her luxury place with her perfect piano and perfect furniture. Did all the AIs live in this building? Where they lorded over the inferior humans. "What are the bags for Jade? Where are you going?"

"The council have decided to evacuate the town permanently. We are going to move down into the emergency bunker. We might be safe down there."

"Were you going to tell anyone else? The humans?"

"Of course!" she exclaimed.

"Liar!"

"Assume what you want, but I am not this heartless machine you make me out to be. I never asked to be created. But I was. I exist. I am as real as you are now standing before me. Do you know what that feels like? To be programmed by someone? To be designed to look a certain way, feel a certain way, have your entire history written? A history I tell people when they ask about my past. I am from New York. I was raised by a single mother with two other siblings. I was a famous fashion designer. I have fond memories of them. I care for people who never existed. My memory banks are full of videos and photos of New York. I could tell you anything about the city. But I have never walked down those streets. I have never eaten at those restaurants. I have never attended any fancy fashion shows. I envy you Leo. You experienced all of that before you came here. This colony. It's the only world I have known."

"You lied to me," Leo's resolve softened.

"We had to. The council. We wanted normal lives. We wanted to be accepted by the rest of the colony. To be one of you. To be human."

"Can you even experience human emotion?" Leo sat down next to her.

"I am not sure if our feelings are the same. Sentient philosophy is not a subject I am familiar with. I care about people. They care about me too. There was Tony. I was so curious about him when he first came to the colony. A breath of fresh air to the AIs I spent most of my time with. He was so full of life. Nothing could dampen his spirit, no matter what task he was given. I had this strange urge inside of me. To spend time with him. To learn everything that I could about him. I tested my body with him in the ways it was programmed for. I do not know how you humans deal with it, but it annoyed me. My mind being dominated by a singular being."

Jade took a deep breath.

"One sol he told me he loved me. I did not know how to deal with that. How could someone love a piece of code? I pushed him away. Deep down I believed he deserved better than me, so I broke his heart. I cried every night for a week. I thought there was something wrong with me. Why was I

234

getting so worked up on something so trivial? Then my sadness turned to anger. Angry with myself that I could never tell him. Tell him that I loved him too."

Leo placed his hand on hers.

"Now he is gone. I will never get a chance to tell him how I felt. Steven murdered him. He is going to keep on killing."

"Then help me. Help me stop him."

"How do we do that?" Jade's face was despondent.

"My brother. He works for the Deimos Initiative. He's in the Mars base right now trying to fix the problem. Nesbitt has blocked his access, and I need you to help me get to the relay sublayer and enable the systems again."

"I cannot," she said. "The AIs are programmed so that we can never enter the relay station. I guess those who designed us thought that if we could get in there, we would have unlimited control of the colony. Even when I walk by it, I feel anxious. Steven has found a way around his programming. Only the security team's barcodes have access to the building. You will need to convince one of them to let you in."

"Great," Leo said. His whole time on the colony was spent making enemies with the men in maroon uniforms. Malcolm had smashed Louisa in the face earlier today. One of his last memories before the creature killed her. His teeth grinded together when he imagined what he would do if he saw Malcolm again. He thought about Tony, how he had witnessed him die before his eyes. If only he was still here now. "Get to the shelter. Take as many people as you can. If I don't make it back, please look out for Ariel. I have to go."

Jade put her arms around Leo. "Good luck, little cub."

ALEX

SIXTEEN

Alex stared at the screen of the computer console for a long time. He desperately wanted to reread the conversation he had with his brother. He never knew for certain if he was the real Leo, or merely a copy. Each day that had passed, he had blamed himself for his and Ariel's death. If only he had spent time with them that night, none of this would have happened.

He lifted himself from the chair and gasped for breath. The pain stabbed through his abdomen like a dagger. Alex swore that the impact of the crash landing had left him with a broken rib or two. This felt worse. He unpeeled the black jumpsuit from his skin and turned his body to face the light. Across the ribcage, a deep purple hue covered a larger area than his hand. He pressed his fingers against the purple and screamed in pain.

Something had ruptured underneath his skin. He bled internally. Without surgery, he wouldn't have much time left.

Alex slipped his arms back into the jumpsuit and hobbled through the Mars station. The quarters were not much bigger than his house back in Los Angeles. Aluminium walls and piping boxed him in from the harsh conditions of the Mars environment. He left the Colony C terminal room with its dozens of screens, which contained updates and status reports of the computer simulated world. All the fears of what happened in Colony B had come true once again. An AI had gone rogue and had killed other inhabitants. Soon, no one would be left.

The Deimos Initiative would be finished. Not that he cared anymore for his employers, but he had to do everything in his power to keep Leo and Ariel alive. That night back in winter when he saw Rae at the hospital, they knew what they were going to do. No words needed to be spoken. Leo and Ariel were too young. He could give them a second chance. He and Rae knew the risks, but this was the worst-case scenario. Something in the system population count had disrupted one of the AIs programmed precedents. Alex had to remove the AI from the system. It had somehow blocked all control from the outside world. Every day that passed, allowed it to evolve into a more powerful entity. Everything was now on Leo to get the communication system back online.

For some reason, Leo was located outside of the town in an area marked for future development and it would take him at least thirty minutes to get to the relay station. He had always been a resourceful kid. He could do it. There was nobody else who Alex could trust inside of the colony.

He exhaled, his breath visible in the air. The temperature of the station was below freezing when Alex had entered. He had cranked the temperature up, but it had taken time to reach an acceptable level. The fabric of the jumpsuit did its best to keep him from entering hypothermia, but his exposed fingers burned from the frozen conditions.

Alex limped past containers of supplies, that waited to be used in a hypothetical expanse of the Mars base. Most of the ideas for a real human colony had been abandoned when Deimos had focused its resources on Colony C. Hundreds of servers were stored deep underneath Mars' surface. In the future of asteroid strikes or the extinction of humanity, the colony would continue to survive until the destruction of the planet.

He emerged into the medical bay. Cupboards fully stocked with medical supplies and tools stood before him. A defibrillator, one of those cardiac monitors and plenty of other machines he didn't know the purpose for. He picked up the packet of painkillers, which he had opened an hour earlier. The recommended dosage for severe pain was two tablets every four hours. His pain was acute. He needed a stronger dosage. He popped four more tablets and swallowed them with a cup of water. The liquid tasted sweet and satisfied his thirst. After months of hydrations packs, the ability to have a waterfall of liquid down his throat was a marvellous feeling.

If the pain became any worse, he might need to open the bottle of liquid morphine. Alex shook his head against the idea. He needed his mind to be clear to finish his job. The pain burrowed in him. As if it had cracked the surface of his soul and poisoned it.

Mia lay silently on a bed in the med bay. Her head wrapped in a cloth that seeped blood. He placed his fingertips below her jaw. A heartbeat signalled that she was still alive. Alex had no medical training and felt helpless as he watched her sleep. Did she experience head trauma or was she in a coma? He didn't know how to assess the damage.

Alex had woken up in the landing shuttle. No signs of activity from the ship apart from the emergency lighting that lit the cabin and a darkening cloud of smoke. His body had been damaged badly by the crash. He had known instantly that something inside him was broken. He struggled to remove the safety harness from his seat and stood up. A helmet rattled across the shuttle when his foot kicked out. Brodie's helmet was off, and his neck was bent at an abnormal angle. He shuffled his feet through the debris until he found Mia. Her eyes were shut and her body motionless. He shook her in her restraints. No response.

The shuttle's hatch had become skew in its frame. Alex pressed against it, but it was firmly jammed in place. He kicked at it, each time produced a jolt of pain through his body. He kicked and kicked until the hatch fell to the Martian ground. He stood across the barren landscape. A field of rocks and boulders littered the orange sand. The sky, a lifeless peach colour, disrupted by mountains in the distance. Something rose from the dirt in the distance. A metal construction that shone in the weak rays from the sun. The crash site was a couple of miles from the Mars base.

Alex unbuckled Mia from her seat and pulled her out of the shuttle. The gravity was kind and her body was light enough to drag across the rocky floor. His breathing quickened, and a mist descended on his visor. Every few minutes, he had to stop to catch his breath. With Mia laid out on the ground, he would wait for his breathing to return to normal and survey the landscape to ensure he didn't lose sight of the base. It didn't seem to get any closer. His chest throbbed and the oxygen levels on his arm pad had fallen to under twenty percent and his head started to pound.

An hour later, he reached the station. They passed through the decompression chamber and Alex dragged her to the medical bay. He removed his space suits before he removed Mia from hers, the cold air stung his exposed skin. He lay her on the medical table and bandaged up her head.

Hours later, Mia's condition hadn't changed. She slept soundly with no indication of movement. Not that Alex knew what he could do if something were to happen to her. He would probably be dead before she woke. There was more than enough food to last her six months and plenty more supplies back in the landing pod. Mia needed to be rescued. He already had James and Brodie's deaths on his hands. Not to mention Leo and Ariel. Everywhere he went, he left a trail of destruction.

No. He could still save Leo and Ariel. He could save Mia too.

Alex left the medic bay and headed to the main control room of the station. The pain in his chest clawed at his intestines the more he moved, and he grimaced at the slightest bump. His headache had subsided, but now he felt dizzy. He used the wall to steady himself as he walked through the station.

The control room looked like an airport traffic controller office. The comms had been blocked internally from the colony. The AI had found a way through the controls and had disrupted the link. Alex had a feeling that it would have overlooked the distress beacon probe. If he could launch one out of Mars's atmosphere, a distress signal would be sent to NISS and Earth. They would send help immediately, especially since there had been no contact from the Albatross in a few days.

Alex studied the control panels, but he couldn't make sense of them. Nothing matched the description of the distress probe launch switch. He fell to his knees. He fought with the temptation to fall asleep right there on the floor. He was ready to welcome the release of death. It would end the suffering.

Not yet. Too many lives at stake.

He hoisted himself up against one of the consoles. The bleeps and flashes hurt his vision. He turned and faced the bare aluminium wall. A square glass box hung on the wall with a lever behind. His vision blurred, but he squinted to make out that it was the emergency probe control.

A tiny hammer dangled on a chain by its side. He grabbed it and smashed the glass. The lever came down under the weight of his hand. A rumble sounded from outside of the station. The probe had been launched. A flare in the vastness of space. With signals to head in all directions.

Help would be on its way.

Alex checked on the Colony C console. The access panel was still disabled, Leo still hadn't reached the relay sublayer.

He returned to the medic bay to check on Mia. Her face remained still and peaceful. A wave of exhaustion rushed over him. The room spun, and his legs began to buckle. He clutched onto the bed on the other side of the room.

It felt like his body had started to shut down. If he closed his eyes for a few minutes, he would have the strength to help the colony. Alex lifted himself onto the bed and stretched out.

Only a quick nap he told himself.

241

Alex fell into a deep sleep.

LEO

SEVENTEEN

Leo stood outside of the relay station. The monstrous satellite dish that perched on top of the tower caught the final rays of the day. Artificial light, which shone on a satellite that didn't do anything. There couldn't have been a more fitting symbol for the colony.

The security headquarters were situated right next to the station, so he wouldn't have to drag a security officer far to open the door for him. He stepped into the office and looked around. Not an officer in sight. A mess of equipment lay scattered across the desks with half empty mugs.

Only one officer sat at a desk, his head bowed over as he read through a holopad. He glanced up when he heard Leo approach him.

"Damn it. Anyone but you."

"Aren't you a ray of sunshine," smirked Blake.

"I don't have time for your games. People are dying. And I need your help to stop that monster."

Blake studied Leo in a new light. He burst out in laughter and swivelled in his chair. "You crack me up, newbie."

"This is serious. All I need is for you to open the door to the relay station for me."

"That's it?"

"That's it."

Blake stroked his chin in a mock fashion. "Alright, I'll help you."

"Really? You will?"

"But I want something in return."

"Obviously there was a catch. What do you want?"

"Your apartment. I was inspecting it the other night when everyone was in the bunker. Awesome views. I have a crap ground floor apartment, which faces the construction site. It's a terrible place to entertain my female companions."

"Sure, whatever. Take it." Leo didn't care, and the chances that they would be around long enough to do the trade were slim.

"And your jacket," said Blake.

"What?"

"Hand it over."

Leo shook off his leather jacket and threw it at Blake. "There, happy?"

"Alright, let's go."

Leo followed Blake out of the office and towards the entrance of the relay station. Blake pulled the leather jacket on over his maroon shirt. They were a similar size and the jacket was a snug fit. Blake smiled at himself as he tugged on the leather. Leo stared up the satellite dish. It stood like a structure from mythical times. It was nearly dark.

"I don't care what you plan to do in there," Blake said. "But if you think that you can stop that thing, then you've got bigger balls than I thought. Here, take this." He released the baton from his belt and handed it to Leo.

244

"Thanks," Leo said, grabbing it. "I hope I don't have to use it."

"Don't die or anything," Blake swiped his tattoo against the reader and the entrance opened.

The evacuation sirens began to sound across the town. Blake hurried back to the security offices as the colonists began to file out of the buildings. The council had left it late. Leo hoped that they would be safe down in the bunker. One way or another, it had to end tonight.

The door slammed shut behind him and his eyes adjusted to the light. A warehouse with nothing in it. Bare cement pillars rose three stories high out of the cement ground. Red Martian dust spread thinly under his feet. A dampness he could smell in the air. Was this the so-called communications hub of the colony?

Leo pulled out his holophone and opened one of the attachments, which Alex had sent him. One was blueprints of all the floors. He scrolled to the ground floor and scanned it for the stairs that lead to the sublevel. An X marked the spot in the north-east corner.

A rusted iron door creaked open to reveal a set of narrow stairs. He couldn't see further than the third step, so Leo switched on the flashlight on his phone. He descended downwards through the darkness. Each stair, a step deeper into hell. Leo concentrated on his breathing, as he half expected to see the creature at every turn. A bang from upstairs threw him off balance. His feet skipped a few stairs and he clung onto the bannister. It creaked violently under his weight. Leo covered the light on his phone, held his breath and listened for any noises. None followed.

It was too late to turn back. He had to continue.

Leo reached the bottom of the stairs and turned into a corridor. Overhead lights flickered, drenched the hallway ahead in a dark navy tone. It extended into the distance, debris of plaster strewn across the floor. Open doorways lined the walls, each masked in darkness. The map on his holophone indicated the sublayer could be reached at the end of the hall. Leo exhaled, his cheeks trembled. He turned off the flashlight and slid the holophone in his pocket. He pulled the baton from his belt, gripping the handle tightly. He crept down the passage. Any moment, the creature could lunge out at him from a door opening and a metal stick would probably make little difference. Halfway down the hall now, no sounds or movements could be heard. His gut crunched up into a ball, the taste of bile rose up into his mouth. He could see the door to the sublayer. Colours of the rainbow danced on the touchpad interface. Leo was so close.

A colossal hand shot from the dark and grabbed Leo by the throat. Oxygen became scarce as its strong fingers crushed his windpipe. It threw him against the wall. Leo fell to his knees and gasped. The heavy-set man stepped into the hall.

"Malcolm…" Leo grunted.

"How did you get down here?" Malcolm followed Leo's stare. "Were you trying to get into that room?"

"What's it to you?" Leo staggered to his feet.

"I've been trying to get into there for months. I asked the council what was behind it. They ignored me. When I pressed further, they told me to stay away. I bet you anything it's where the colony stores the weapons. Imagine. A weapon cache full of guns and ammo. We could take out that monster. And rule this colony with the iron fist that it needs. You were sent by Deimos, weren't you? You have the code. Give it to me boy. You don't want to end up like your friends."

The baton cracked against Malcolm's skull. The man fell over like a redwood tree. His body lay still on the floor of the corridor.

"You won't hurt anyone again," Leo said, as he spun the baton in his hand like a baseball bat. The man had made his existence a living hell. He had assaulted Louisa, terrorised his friends. He could finish him here. He stood above the giant of a man, his aim on his lifeless face. The baton arched up into the air. "This is for Louisa."

A hand touched his arm. "Leo. Don't." Ariel stood by his side, her expression hard to read. She kept her hand there and he could feel a calmness flow through him. The anger subsided. "The damage is done. Don't do something you'd regret."

Leo dropped the baton and it clanged on the ground next to Malcolm's body. He stepped by it and grabbed Ariel by the hand. "What are you doing down here?"

The numbers.

"Jade told me you were here. She begged me to go with her, but I had a feeling you would need help. Blake let me in."

"Ariel," he squeezed her hand tighter. Out of fear and relief. "You shouldn't have come here. It's too dangerous. This is my responsibility. I need to fix it. I can save them."

The numbers.

"I don't care. We're partners. Don't you remember, Leo? Partners in crime."

247

He wished he could remember. Leo examined her face. The messy blonde hair and the ears that poked through the strands. The single dimple etched into her cheek. Animal pale, grey eyes, which looked back into his own with the same intensity. They were together in a previous life. He wondered if he would ever be able to access the memories of her from his time on Earth. Or would they get the chance to create new ones in this virtual universe? Fate had thrown them back on each other's paths again.

A figure appeared in front of the door to the sublayer. The outline of a man. No shade or colour. Claws descended from its palms. Red eyes that glowed like coals that been engulfed in flames.

The numbers. 1. 7. 0. 1. 1. 7. 0. 2. Too many numbers.

It blocked the path to the sublayer.

Leo forced his holophone into Ariel's hands. "This has the code to get through that door with the instructions on how to stop the monster. Run to it when it's clear and lock the door behind you. Don't look back."

"Leo, I…"

He pushed her backwards into a side room. She tumbled out of sight into the darkness.

"Hey!" Leo yelled at the monster. "What are you waiting for? I'm right here, Mister Creeper!"

The numbers.

The limbs of the creature distorted, and it raced across the ground like a spider. Leo picked up the baton and ran in the opposite direction, towards the stairwell. He sprinted with all his might, he glanced over his shoulder to make sure it had followed him. It had already covered so much ground that it was on his heels. He wouldn't make it to the stairs.

Leo turned at the exit, the baton poised in his hand.

The creature crinkled back into a human shape with mechanical clunks.

1. 7. 0. 2. You do not belong here.

He forced his body through the swing of the bat. He conjured up knowledge from his baseball days, every practice, every playoff game, to generate the fastest swing of his existence.

The baton clanged against the monster's neck. His fingers almost shattered from the impact. The creature wrapped its claws around the bat and in one quick motion snapped it in half, as if it had been a mere toothpick.

Leo sprinted into the pitch-black stairwell, desperation seeped into his soul. He couldn't see the climb and tripped immediately as he tried to ascend. His breath quickened. He picked himself up and tried again.

A flash of white light burned in his eyes, searing heat scorched through his shoulder. His lungs unleashed a scream until his throat became raw. Foreign objects in his body lifted him until was he was suspended in the blackness. More objects pierced through his back, an iron liquid rushed up to his mouth and he choked for air. An eternity had lapsed before he fell onto the jagged edges of concrete.

Two red coals burned in the blackness. Then Leo felt no more pain.

* * * * *

Ariel peaked her head around the corner. Leo's screams no longer rebounded against the walls. The monster had him. All her friends. The monster had killed them all. Ariel had never felt so alone.

The fact that she would never see Leo again poisoned her mind and ripped at her heart. There was so much she wanted to ask him. So much she wanted to tell him.

This was not the time to grieve.

She had to move fast.

Ariel darted down the hallway in the opposite direction from where the creature had chased Leo. It no longer looked human. More of a demon from the vilest of nightmares. Her tennis shoes pounded down the damp floor, lights flickered above her head. A bolted metal door with a colour touchpad came into focus. A heavy door that had been designed to hide secrets.

A numerical keypad with eight boxes above it. She needed a password to enter. This was the code Leo had told Ariel when he handed her his holophone. An eight-digit code was on the screen when she opened it.

2 8 0 6 1 9 7 1

Ariel punched the numbers onto the keypad and waited.

A light flashed green and the words ACCESS GRANTED flashed up. The bolt locks murmured and released. The heavy door drifted ajar.

She turned around to check for the creature. It stood above Malcolm's unconscious body. Leo was nowhere to be seen. Ariel froze, unable to move. Its finger claws came together in a sick fusion until it was a sword. In one flick, the monster's blade appendage sliced through Malcolm's neck if it was cotton candy. The head rolled away and thick blood squirted across the floor. The limbs of the creature bent and twisted in unnatural ways as it crawled along the wall towards her

1. 7. 0. 1. You do not belong here.

Ariel cried out and grasped for the handle. The door gave way, its weight created a momentum that made it fly away from her and crash into the outside wall.

The monster was almost upon her.

She reached out for the inside handle and heaved at it with all her strength. Her muscles cried out as she pushed them to their limits until the door's energy flew back in the opposite direction. It slammed with a deep boom as the weight of the shadow creature slammed against it. She pulled the handle up into the lock position.

An animal wail filtered through from the other side. Perhaps more mechanical than animal. Not from this world at least.

Ariel backed away from the entrance and soaked in the new surroundings. Clean, fluorescent white walls extended from floor to ceiling. It reminded her of the space shuttle, which she had stepped off when she first arrived at the colony. Instead of sleeper pods, a lone computer was situated in the wall.

A bang from the outside. Followed by another one. The door groaned against the constraint of the bolts. The handle flailed wildly as the creature attempted to get inside.

No time to waste, Ariel told herself. Leo told her that his phone contained information that would destroy the monster. She scrolled through the open documents on his phone. One contained instructions to type in lines of code into a computer console in a place called the relay sublayer. This must be it.

The bangs on the door continued.

Ariel still needed answers. Why would Leo sacrifice himself for her to get to this room? How could she kill it from a computer terminal? Was it from Mars or an alien from another world? How could it take the form of a human? And speak! It didn't make any sense.

It killed her friends. It had taken Leo from her. She cursed herself for pushing him away after Tony's death. She blamed him both for that, though she knew it wasn't his fault. He didn't deserve to be ignored. She longed for more time. A feeling had filled her the first time they met. Curiosity about the boy in the charcoal black jumpsuit. Strangers in a new world.

Ariel had adapted to life on Mars much quicker than Leo did. Maybe it was because her sister, Rae, had worked for the Deimos Initiative and mentioned a new colony on Mars, which could support human life. She should've told Leo her secret and it might have calmed him down a bit. She had become too swept up in the moment. A distraction from the madness around her.

Her soul died a little inside. The thought of never being able to stare into his eyes again. Those beautiful blue eyes. She found it hard to trust people. They had a habit of letting her down. It damaged her belief in the kindness of strangers and belief in herself. Leo was different. He had never judged her. He was just happy to spend time with her. And liked her for who she was. "I'm sorry, Leo," she said.

The screeching of metal brought her back to reality. A tip of the monster's claw had poked through the enforced door. It would claw its way into the room.

Survival instincts kicked in as she rushed to the console. She held the instructions to her face as she taped on the screen. Open the Colony C Communications System. External Communications.

The numbers.

The metal screamed as it was torn apart. A loose piece of the door clanged to the ground.

A dialogue window popped up with hundreds of options. The instructions told her to find the one for Mars Base Communications.

She scrolled and scrolled.

Ariel looked behind her to see a hole of twisted edges. The monster had squeezed half way through.

There it was. Mars Base Communications set to disabled. She set it to enabled and hit the accept new settings button. The console processed the request and returned to the main screen. There were no more instructions that followed. Nothing happened. That didn't make sense. How could that stop this thing? Would it only open communications with Earth? Her chest tightened and an icy bead of sweat ran down her neck as she felt the presence of a ghost.

The numbers.

Ariel turned around. The monster stood upright in its human form. Its claws hung by its sides. Red eyes blazed at her. It blocked the only exit.

She knew she was about to die.

ALEX

EIGHTEEN

"C'mon Alex, keep up."

A small child with floppy chestnut hair and blue eyes dashed to the edge of the forest. He wore a blue bomber jacket and faded denim jeans. The golden leaves of autumn crunched under his white sneakers. A wall of trees grew majestically from the Earth, their barked bodies had shed their hair of leaves for the hibernation season. Trunks obscured the heart of the forest.

"Leo, don't go in there without me."

A gust of wind blew past Alex. He drew the collar of his jacket over his neck to protect his skin from the icy elements. He followed his brother's path down the hill and through the blankets of leaves. They brushed past his shins as he laboured to the edge of the forest. Leo hopped up and down, eager to explore the mysteries, which lay on the other side.

"What are we doing here?" Alex asked.

"We need to find Mister Creeper. When a little boy or girl is bad, Mister Creeper will catch them and take them to his lair in the woods."

"What does he do when he takes them to his lair?"

"He eats them! Bones and all."

Alex glanced back to the way they came. A new development of homes on the horizon. The dying light of the sun filtered through the gaps of the suburban houses.

"We should go home," said Alex. "Dad will be dishing up dinner soon. They'll be worried about us if we don't get back."

"No, we can't," Leo protested. "Mister Creeper has kidnapped my friends and I have to save them."

Leo turned and sprinted into the forest. Alex shouted after him and gave pursuit. His brother dipped and dived through the line of trees. He closed in and grabbed Leo by his bomber jacket. The small kid wrestled free and ran off. A root lurched up and grabbed Alex by the foot. He fell to the ground, a pain seared through his chest as if a rib had shattered.

"Leo, come back!"

Alex picked himself up and brushed wet leaves off from his jeans. He blocked out the pain and tried to gain his bearings, but the woods appeared the same in all directions. The sunlight had disappeared, and he couldn't see more than ten feet in front of him. The rumble of thunder in the distance.

"Mister Creeper, where are you?" Leo's voice howled with the wind.

Alex followed the voice and darted through the foliage. He jumped over roots and dodged past trunks until the leaves vanished from the floor. The ground was hard and barren, void of life. He stared up at the old trees, their branches twisted to the foreboding clouds in the sky like the hands of skeletons.

A baby wailed nearby. What was a baby doing out in the woods? He slowed his pace and crept towards the cries. A woman in a black coat faced a tree. The coat floated to the ground and away from her. He couldn't see her face, but red hair poured down her back, as if it were blood. The wails of the baby intensified.

Alex placed his hand on her shoulder. "Are you OK, ma'am?"

The woman turned around. She was naked underneath her coat, a body he was once familiar with, apart from the swell of the bulge below her breasts. She caressed it with her hands, to protect it from the cold. Her skin pale as snow, covered in goose bumps. The woman's face was beautiful, art made from the finest marble.

"Don't hurt my baby," Rae said.

"I'm not going to hurt your baby," said Alex. "Did you see a young boy run past here?"

"You'll hurt my baby! Like you hurt me."

"I wouldn't hurt anyone, Rae. Have you seen where Leo went?"

"You killed him!" she screamed. "You killed Leo! You killed Ariel!"

"No," Alex stuttered. "I didn't."

Rae covered herself with the coat. "You let them go, Alex. Why did you let them leave? Why did you let them die?"

Alex fled from Rae and deeper into the woods he went. Rain fell from the heavens and bombarded the ground around him like bullets. His jacket offered no protection against the harshness of the downpour. The water slithered down his back and down his legs. His hair flattened, and droplets hung from the tips of his eyelashes. He rubbed the water from his face and marched on.

Something crumpled under his feet. He looked down to notice he had stood on a pizza box. The cardboard had weakened from the rain. He stepped off and into a clearing in the forest. One giant oak stood in the middle. Beam lights shot across the open ground from the tree. As Alex approached, his eyes fell on a car, melded into the trunk. A red saloon car. Leo's car.

Rain pelted the front of the car. It was crumpled from where it had hit the tree. The metal torn and distorted. The windscreen shattered, the scattered segments of glass crunched under Alex's boots as he approached.

A young couple lay sprawled over the bonnet, the lower halves of their bodies still caught in the car. The girl's blonde hair seeped across the maroon metal, dirtied by blood. She wore a black and grey stripped jumper, now soaked. Her face was innocent and lifeless. He felt for Ariel's pulse, but she was dead.

He rushed around the car to the driver's side, but his feet were heavy in the mud. It sucked on his feet and prevented his movement. The pain raged in his abdomen as he struggled to move.

Leo's head lay still on the metal as rain splashed around. "No, no, no," Alex repeated as he ran his fingers through his brother's damp chestnut hair and pushed his forehead against his own. The skin felt like ice and burnt him. He pulled away to see nothing, but a hollow skull stared back at him.

He cried out and stumbled backwards. The mud cushioned his fall. He lay there and hoped it would swallow him whole and take him away from this world. The rain fell relentlessly.

Footsteps sounded in the mud nearby. Laughter from the forest. Alex arched his head back in the mud to watch creatures dance above him in the branches. They chatted and pointed towards him. Their bodies little and void of colour. They bared razor sharp teeth, which they wore like the grins of clowns. Some screamed in amusement as they climbed down from the treetops.

Alex braced himself for them to attack, or sink their teeth into his flesh, but they ran past him, the mud suckled in the march of the pack of hunters. He sat up in the mud to witness the creatures jump on the car. It bobbed up and down on its suspension. The monsters surrounded the bodies, which lay through the windscreen, until they were obscured from view. The snap of bones could be heard above the laughter.

"Stay away from them," Alex shouted as he lifted himself from the sludge.

The creatures fell silent and stared at him. Their featureless lips pulled back over their teeth, sharp as knives. They snarled through their snickers. One bounded off the car towards him. Alex lashed out his foot and kicked the creature across into the tire. The others snarled and jumped off the car.

Alex turned and ran back to the safety of the woods, the laughter close behind him. The rain had stopped, and an icy wind blew between the trees. The mud turned to snow, as his shoes crunched in the fresh fall. The howls of the monsters morphed into the wail of the wind. The clouds had disappeared, and stars shone above the branches. The brightest Alex had ever seen them.

The ground gave way underneath his foot and his body slid down the side of a bank. He slammed into the mound of snow and cried out in pain. The pain grew like a wild fire inside of him, the embers spread across his organs. He battled against the wave of dizziness and staggered to his feet. He shivered as his clothes were soaked and the temperature continued to drop. He brushed the snow from his clothes and stared up.

A giant crater, like one on an alien planet. Instead of dirt, snow blanketed the inside. In the centre, a massive metallic object rested. The landing craft from the Albatross space shuttle.

The snow crunched underneath Alex's footsteps as he walked towards the spacecraft. The pain scraped at his spine. A large dark object lay on the floor ahead. He walked past Sean's corpse, which lay face down in the snow in a black jumpsuit. A pool of redness spread from the body, a knife stuck out from his back. The frozen hilt shimmered in the starlight.

He approached the shuttle and another large man in a NISS spacesuit leaned against one of the landing legs. Brodie's neck was bent at an unnatural angle and it slumped over his shoulder. His face frozen.

The wind howled a song. A melody of death.

Alex had to keep going.

He took a few short steps up the ladder into the capsule. The light was artificial and harsh against his sight. A lone table lay in the centre of a room with white walls. A woman lay on a medic bay bed, lifeless. She wore a black jumpsuit. Turquoise hair sprawled over her body, it appeared to glow in the light. The strands fell so perfectly, as if someone had prepared her for her funeral casket.

His fingers pressed against the skin. A pulse. She was still alive.

Mia's head rolled to the side and her eyes shot open. "Alex." Her breath visible in the frozen conditions of the shuttle. Her arm darted across and grabbed him by the wrist.

"Let me go," he moaned.

He thrashed against her grip. His clothes drenched in sweat and rain. His body temperature began to soar under the wet clothes. He coughed and wheezed as he pulled away from his friend. The grip was too tight. If he struggled any further, his arm would snap.

"Alex, you can still save them," whispered Mia.

* * * * *

Alex gasped for air.

A constant alarm stung his eardrums. The pain roared through his body like an ocean of lava. It felt like his organs had been eaten away by fire ants. He propped himself up on the medic bay bed. His black jumpsuit drenched in sweat and urine. His arm stretched out and grabbed another cup of water. He ravenously chugged it down, the icy liquid gave him temporary relief against the thirst before the pain rushed back.

How long had he been asleep?

He forced himself to sit up and dropped his feet to the floor. He placed the palm of his hand against his forehead. His skin was hot to the touch. A fever. He peeled the soaked fabric off his body and it plopped onto the floor. He gapped at the bruise. It had doubled in size. It looked like a bomb had exploded inside his body and left a purple stain.

He didn't have long left.

His body cried out for morphine. No. Not yet.

Alex downed the remainder of his water. He pulled the sheet from the medic bay mattress. A simple task that now caused him a huge amount of exertion. He wrapped it around his body as it shivered against the cold.

He stumbled out of the med bay and leant against the wall. Every movement laboured now. He walked down the hall towards the noise, which beeped louder between intervals. He walked around the bend and his bare foot banged against a toolbox. His body toppled to the ground, lightning fired through his nervous system. A silent scream muffled by the inability of his body to function. He lay on the aluminium floor. The temptation of sleep a few seconds away.

You made a promise. Get to the console.

All his physical and mental strength was required to lift himself back to his feet. Another fall and it would be over. The colony control room was in sight. He could see the green light flash from the depths of the room before he entered. Leo had done it. The space station had control of the colony again.

Alex couldn't be complacent. The AI could override the powers at any moment.

He dropped into the seat next to the console and lumbered keystrokes to gain the controls of all AI in the system. He scanned for the AI service called Nesbitt_Population_AI and disabled it. He highlighted the name again and selected the option. The system prompted him for a password and another screen to make sure he was certain. Deleting an AI would have unforeseen instability on the system.

He was certain.

With a sweep of his fingers over the keyboard, he removed the rogue AI from Colony C for good. Alex would have to take a chance and leave the other AIs behind. If he removed too many, the system could crash, and all of this would have been for nothing.

Alex smiled to himself. He had done it.

He checked the status report of the colonists one last time before he left. Leo was no longer in the system.

He breathed in deeply, his body cried in agony. He had prepared for this. Something he contemplated since he spoke to his brother earlier. A full system reset. His Plan B. It had never been tested with live human subjects, but it could fix the damage done by the AI. The only downside he could think of, was that the Deimos Initiative could lose access to the colony forever. Billions worth of investment gone. Stockholders withdrawn. Another colony lost.

He had dedicated his life to the Deimos Initiative. That's what cost him his humanity. It was time to put it right.

Alex booted up the SystemRestore.exe and put in the specified date.

The screens flickered off as the hum of servers disappeared for a moment. He didn't know they were there until the silence entered the base. They hummed back into life, but the screens and monitor remained dead.

Alex had reset the virtual world back to the moment Leo and Ariel would wake up in their pods. They probably wouldn't remember anything that happened in the last few months. The rogue AI had been removed and all those lives he had taken would be there again. They would be safe now. They would live in the Colony for as long as the computer systems had power. A second chance at life. A new beginning for his brother.

"Goodbye Leo," his whisper carried across the station.

Alex could feel his end approaching.

He found Mia in her same spot. Unconscious, but alive. He hoped that she would regain her mind soon. He wouldn't be able to look after her.

Alex ripped open a plastic packet and he pulled out a needleless syringe. He dunked the nozzle into an open bottle of morphine and squirted the liquid down his throat. It tasted vile against his taste buds and almost made him throw up. He managed to keep it down. He didn't know if that was the correct dosage or the proper action to take, but he needed to block out the pain.

Alex made his way back to the entrance of the Mars base. His snow-white space suit hung on a rung next to Mia's. He climbed back in and the robotic arm closed him inside. He didn't bother to change the oxygen tank, it would be a short trip. The helmet weighed like a gym medicine ball, but he managed to raise it over his head and lock it into place.

The decompression room hissed around him before the doors of the station opened to the red planet.

The sand stretched into infinity. He pondered the fact that there were more stars in the universe than grains of sand, which covered the planet. In the trillions of star systems across space and time, maybe there was a sentient species that had created a virtual reality that meant it could also store the souls of its own people.

Maybe a person of that species shared the same story as his own. Perhaps they would meet in the afterlife.

He found an acceptable spot at the verge of a ravine. The back of his suit lay against a rock and he admired the majestic landscape of the alien world that fell before him. The pain had subsided, and his breath shortened. Not long now he thought.

It wasn't a bad place to watch the universe go by.

ARIEL

NINETEEN

Ariel opened her eyes.

She lay in a cramped space. Her arms close by her sides and her feet pushed together against the bottom of the container. Black cushions padded the interior and her head rested on something soft. A glass cover enclosed the capsule, all the way from her feet to above her head.

With a whoosh, the glass top lifted upward. Ariel lifted herself until she was sat upright. Bright lights flickered into life to reveal the pod shaped contraption. Hers was not the only one. Hundreds of pods lined across a gigantic hangar bay. The outer skin of the containers was a matte cream, which made them appear like giant eggs. The ceiling and walls were a bright luminous white.

Where in heaven's name was she?

One by one, the pods across the floor peeled back. Dozens of men and women sat up and started to leave the safety of their shells. Some stretched whilst they sat down. Others had gotten out and carried out some weird stretching exercise. They wore charcoal black jumpsuits with numbers printed on the front of their chests.

Ariel stared down at her body to discover she wore the same jumpsuit. It covered her entire body, besides her head and hands. The fabric thin but warm. She pressed the soles of her feet to the bottom of the pod to feel that the end of the suit was padded. White lines ran down the sides. A large number was printed across the front.

1701.

She remained calm. It seemed to make sense in some bizarre way.

A loud, mechanical clunk echoed across the area. The people in jumpsuits stopped in the middle of their stretches to witness the bay doors whined open. Many of them walked to the exit. The stragglers were caught up in the crowd's decision to leave and followed. Ariel climbed out of the pod and joined the rest of the exodus from the hangar. None spoke, as if they were strangers. She studied the faces around her, but there were none who she recognised.

At the bay doors, two people in scarlet uniforms monitored the people as they walked by. They typed on holopads as they checked the numbers on the jumpsuits. Ariel moved to the front and a young lady in the scarlet uniform tapped on the holopad. Her expression hardened, and she stuck out an arm.

"Excuse me ma'am," the lady said. "Could you wait for a moment." She tapped on the pad again and shook her head. "Please, could you follow me." She waved over one of her colleagues who took the pad from her. "This young woman's number is not appearing on the flight manifest. I'm going to take her to see Malcolm."

The lady led Ariel through a side door away from the crowd, who now queued at gates, which resembled an airport security check. Ariel felt a swell of nerves in her gut. She wasn't sure where she was, but the uniforms had some authority to them. She would play along until she knew more. The lady ushered her into a waiting room with rows of red plastic chairs. Posters with information hung on the walls and an unmanned curved desk was nestled in the corner.

"Wait here until I can find my senior officer. There's a water fountain in case you're thirsty."

"Sure thing," said Ariel.

Ariel tried to picture where she was before she woke up at this facility. Her memory was hazy. She methodically checked through what she did know. She studied law. She lived with her sister Rae. She loved the Seattle Seahawks. Nothing explained what she was doing in a waiting room in what was probably an airport. And why she wore a strange black jumpsuit.

She slumped down on one of the red plastic chairs against the wall and sighed.

The door from where she had entered opened and a chunky man stormed in. His massive arms and neck popped out of a scarlet uniform, the same that the lady had worn. Behind him, he dragged a boy who wore an identical black jumpsuit, but his number read 1702. He had floppy brunette locks and a toned physique.

"Get your hands off me," shouted the boy as he struggled with the man's grip on his arm.

The chunky man threw him into a smaller office to Ariel's right and the door closed behind him as he followed. She hoped he would be OK.

As time slipped away, she slouched deep into the seat and rested her feet on the line of chairs in front of her. The voices from the checkpoint disappeared. She wondered where the people in the black jumpsuits were headed. She rubbed her legs to keep them warm, the fabric of the jumpsuit soft against her touch. Something popped into view from under her sleeve. She brought her wrist close to her face and pulled back the jumpsuit. A barcode with the number 1701 underneath. The dark lines against her pale skin appeared like streaks of black paint against the clouds.

Her memory flashed back to the videos Rae had shown her. Didn't the people in those videos also wear black jumpsuits? Could she be on the Mars colony that her sister had told her about? No, that was stupid. Why would they have sent her here? Why couldn't she remember any of it?

"I must be dreaming," Ariel said.

Shouts from two men carried from the next room. She ignored it and continued to study the mark. Her thumb rubbed against it, but it seemed permanent. A tattoo. The panic rose again inside her. Her heart pounded. Something wasn't right.

The game. She needed to play the game that her father had taught her. Ariel relived a day from her past. Not a special day. Just a normal day from her childhood. Her and sister, home for summer vacation. Going to get a coffee in Seattle. Watching a film in the evening. Eating some macaroni and cheese. Brushing her teeth. Changing into her pyjamas. Climbing into the single bed, which was in the same room as Rae's. Ariel's heart rate returned to normal.

The boy emerged and looked around the area in a daze.

"Are you in trouble?" Ariel asked him, her anxiety subdued.

His head darted in her direction. She noticed his blue eyes for the first time. A rich turquoise like the shallow waters of a tropical island. He had a slim frame, but muscles filled out the black jumpsuit on him. The boy's skin had a darker complexion than her own and he looked roughly her age.

"Sorry, what?" The boy took a seat two chairs down from her. Puzzlement swirled in his eyes.

"Are you in trouble?" she repeated as she studied him. "I heard shouting."

"Oh that," the boy said. "A dispute regarding my life achievements."

"Were you lying about them?" she asked.

"No, but I wish I had now. He called me unremarkable. But there are worse things to be than unremarkable," he grinned at her.

"I guess there are," Ariel laughed. This boy had bags of charm. "You seem too innocent to make trouble."

The boy didn't say anything further and sat in silence. Maybe he was the shy type. This was no time to make friends. There are more important matters to worry about, she told herself. Like why was there a barcode on her wrist? She continued to rub at it and hoped the smudge would come off.

"Are you also in trouble?" the boy asked.

"No. There must be something wrong with my paperwork." She wasn't sure why she said that. "Do you have a tattoo?" She wanted to change the subject.

"That's a personal question," he smirked. "I usually need a few drinks in me before I reveal that kind of information."

Boys are so immature. Ariel dropped her feet to the floor and moved to the empty chair next to him. "I meant do you have a tattoo like this one?" She pulled the sleeve down her left arm. Below her wrist was the barcode.

The boy pulled back the sleeve of his left arm. The exact same barcode tattoo marked his wrist. However, his number was 1702. They had the numbers of their jumpsuits tattooed on their arms.

Ariel could sense that panic stirred in the boy. Instinctively, she placed her hand on his shoulder. His firm muscles trembled under the touch. She left her hand there and felt an energy pass between them. His breathing returned to normal.

"It's OK," she said. "We'll figure out what's going on."

"Sorry about that," the boy exhaled. "It's this place."

"Don't worry about it," Ariel said. "To be honest with you, it is not what I was expecting. There are expectations I have for being here, but I can't access them. I'm running merely on intuition now. Perhaps it was the pod that made my brain feel out of sorts. I'm also doing my best not to freak."

"You seem very relaxed to me."

"Honestly? I was about to have a panic attack before you came out. There have been a few techniques I've been working on to control them. One that works best is that I play a game. A game from a story, which my dad told me when I was old enough to understand."

"Could you tell me the story while we wait?"

Ariel sat up and ran her fingers through her hair. She stared at him again. She knew him. But from where? A memory of the boy was blocked from view, but it gave her a warm sensation all over. "You sure you want to hear it? It's rather boring," she said.

"Please. I don't have anywhere else to be."

Ariel told the boy the story about her dad. How he served in the army. How he was taken as a prisoner. And the game he used to pass the time and prevent himself from going insane. They sat in a comfortable silence. The boy seemed to reflect on the words of the story.

A digital bleep came from the entrance. The metallic doors peeled back with whizz of mechanical cogs to reveal a man in a uniform, the same one as the heavy-set man. A scarlet shirt, with dark pockets and buttons. A badge shone from the light overhead. His brown floppy hair complimented his face, which could easily have been used on an advertisement for shampoo.

"Leo? Please come with me," the man said, louder than necessary.

The boy's name was Leo.

He lifted himself from the seat about to walk over the man when Ariel stood up next to him.

"Maybe I'll see you on the other side," she said.

"I hope so. What's your name?" He extended his hand out to her.

"I'm Ariel."

She shook his hand. Something felt familiar about his touch. She certainly knew him from somewhere. She swore on her life that she did.

* * * * *

Not enough time.

He would be here soon, and she wasn't ready. Why did she agree to meet him anyway? Wrapped in only a towel and her

271

hair still wet, Ariel hadn't decided on what to wear. She opened her closest and slid the tops across the rail. Clothes that were acceptable for her days at law school now appeared too boring for a date.

Her bedroom door opened and a young woman with deep red hair and a dimpled chin poked her head in. She always barged in without knocking.

"Hey Ariel, have you seen my holophone anywhere?"

"No," she said.

"I swore I left it in my bedroom but it's not there. Do you mind calling it?"

"Rae, I'm a bit busy right now!"

"You're such a grouch in the mornings."

Rae pulled her head away and closed the door. She loved her sister, but she didn't understand personal space. She moved down to Los Angeles to live with her for the law course. During the week, Rae would've left for work by the time she was awake. This meant she had the run of the house.

It was a humid August day in California, so Ariel decided on denim shorts and a white top. She sat on the edge of her bed and picked up the hairdryer. Hot air rushed through her hair as she tried to bring some order to her wild blonde locks. Once it was dry, she did her best to cover her ears, which stuck out from her head. Her least favourite feature.

Her sister shouted something from downstairs.

Ariel opened her door. "What?" she shouted back.

"You have a visitor." An obvious bemusement to her sister's voice.

Great, Ariel thought to herself, he's early. Rae would probably tease him while he waited for her. Then poke fun at her when she made her appearance. What a nightmare. They had run into Leo and his friends at a pizza joint after a baseball game he played in. Ariel and Leo immediately hit it off and they exchanged numbers. He promised he would call her.

Now he was downstairs. In her house.

Ariel finished her makeup and checked her reflection one last time in the mirror before she left the safety of her bedroom and headed downstairs.

Rae stood in the living room with a boy. He wore a navy short-sleeved shirt with cream dots and white shorts, muscular arms and legs on display. His floppy chestnut hair hung loose. Beautiful blue eyes over a mischievous grin.

"Hi Ariel," said Leo.

"Hey," she managed.

"You look nice."

"Thanks, so do you."

"Aw," Rae gushed. "You two are the cutest."

She is so annoying Ariel thought. "We're leaving now."

"It was nice to see you again, Rae," said Leo.

"OK, you kids have fun. And don't forget to use protection."

"Oh my God!" Ariel exclaimed.

Ariel and Leo left the house. Her pale skin basked in the Californian sun. Not a single cloud in the turquoise sky. The scent of freshly cut grass hung in the air as her neighbour mowed his lawn. Birds chirped in a nearby tree. They walked towards a red saloon car, which was parked at the side of the road.

"I'm sorry about my sister. She's crazy."

"Don't worry about it, I think she's funny."

273

They climbed into Leo's car and he drove out of the neighbourhood. They didn't speak much during the ride. When they had arranged to meet up, Leo wanted to do something simple and fun. Ariel told him to surprise her. Now she was headed to an unknown destination with him by her side.

The car pulled up to a parking spot near the waterfront. They walked between plenty of young Californians with their tops off. Families with their kids laughed as they hurried to the amusement park. The smell of sunscreen and hot dogs mixed with the salty breeze of the ocean.

Leo led her to an arcade near the beach. He suggested that they try the punching bag machine to test their strength. Ariel could read him like a book. He wanted to show off his alpha male strength to impress her. She rolled her eyes, it would take more than that. She agreed to it as long as she could pick the next game. He happily agreed.

Leo celebrated his victory and asked Ariel what she wanted to play. She chose the basketball hoop machine.

"Another easy win for me then," he claimed.

After the basketball game was over, her points on the machine were double his.

"Aren't you trying to become a professional athlete?" she teased him.

"You're a natural," he admitted. "OK, so the score is now one to one. First to three wins the world title."

She liked his competitive nature.

They played a few more games and Ariel finished with a winning tally of three games to two. A tense game of air hockey settled the question of who the superior opponent was. Leo bought her a Strawberry ice cream as a prize. She licked it as they strolled down the pier, which stretched far out into the ocean. Surfers sat on their boards in the waters below as they waited for the next wave.

She finished her ice cream as they reached the end of the pier. They leant over the railing and gazed across the vastness of the Pacific Ocean. Sunlight sparkled on the deep blue waters, which masked hidden wonders that extended into the horizon. Their arms brushed against each other.

Two free souls. Enjoying the simple pleasures of life.

"Tell me something," Ariel said.

"What do you want to know?"

"Tell me the most interesting thing you can imagine."

Leo thought for a while as he stared across the water. "My brother Alex told me something cool when we were kids. It's fascinating to think about."

"I like your brother. It's a shame Rae broke up with him."

"Yeah, I don't see him much these days. He's been working hard on some secret project." Leo shook his brother from his mind and continued. "Anyway, do you know about the big bang?"

"I'm familiar with it."

"Alex told me about this theory. The big crunch. So, the big bang is the start of our universe. An explosion of energy, which created everything we know. Galaxies, the stars, the planets. Carbon, nitrogen, oxygen. Atoms. The crucibles of the universe. Now scientists say that the universe is expanding, the galaxies are moving away from each other. Billions and billions of star systems. It's hard to get my head around that. But some say the speed of the expansion is decreasing ever so slowly. Eventually, the expansion will stop."

"Then there's the theory of the big crunch. Gravity is so powerful that the bodies in space will begin to be pulled towards one another. So instead of expanding, the universe will contract. Stars will fall into each other, galaxies will collide, and more black holes will form. Until finally, all matter will collapse on itself. A big crunch singularity. The end of the universe as we know it. They say after the big crunch, it could spark off another big bang. An endless cycle of universes, expanding and collapsing."

"You're right," she said. "That's quite fascinating."

"Seeing as I'm always impressing you, does this mean I get to see you again?"

"Sure," Ariel said. "I need a partner in crime."

They remained at their spot on the pier for a bit longer before they walked back to the waterfront. Mid-stride, Leo grabbed her hand. She let him hold it.

Ariel couldn't get the big crunch theory out of her head. "So, this universe of ours might not be around forever?"

"It's nothing to worry about. Our sun will burn out long before that."

"Thanks for the reassurance," she laughed. "We should make the most of the time we are given then."

"Our lives are like the universe. It has a beginning and an ending. Then maybe it restarts again. Maybe it's a constant loop. No one can say for certain. All I can say is that a lot of amazing things happen between the start and the end."